Desmond leaned toward her, almost as if he were going to kiss her. "Am I distracting you?"

The question was spoken so quietly that the words were breathed across her neck. Sarah felt that warmth in her cheeks spark and flame. "Something like that."

"You like me but not in a serious sort of way," Desmond said. "And you liked kissing me."

"Are you fishing for compliments?"

"Answer the question."

"Yes," Sarah said, feeling a familiar tension building between them. He needled his way beneath her skin so easily. The problem was she couldn't get him out.

"So, in a strictly hypothetical, nonserious sort of way," he continued, "if my lips were to find their way onto your lips, would you be interested?"

The question, in all its ridiculousness, shot straight to her core, every inch of her skin aching with desire. Sarah suddenly wished they were alone. She'd drag Desmond onto the first horizontal surface she could find.

She took a deep breath. She didn't want this thing between them to end quite yet. If a few more weeks was all the time they had left, then Sarah wanted to make the most of it. "I could be convinced...if the mood was right."

"'The mood,'" Desmond said, smiling with all his teeth. "I can work with that."

Dear Reader,

I'm delighted to say that we're headed back to Hatchet Lake, the idyllic small town in Southern Michigan where romances come alive. This time the story follows Sarah Schaffer as she drops by to visit her best friend, Kate (our lovely protagonist from *Lightning Strikes Twice*). Sarah's only looking for a temporary reprieve in between nursing jobs, but what she finds is something even better.

Hatchet Lake is a place for new beginnings, and as the town rebuilds after a terrible storm, Sarah finds herself building to something more than friendship with a fellow relief worker. Wounded by past rejections and protective of her two-year-old son, Parker, Sarah reminds us that trusting someone with your heart is one of the hardest things to do, but only by letting yourself fall can you land somewhere truly special.

I'm so excited to return to Hatchet Lake in my second Harlequin novel and to share Sarah's story. I hope readers fall in love with this cast of characters, both new and old, as much as I have! If you enjoy this new addition to the Hatchet Lake series, you can find me on Instagram @elizabethhrib swooning over my favorite books and hunting down little free libraries or online at elizabethhrib.com.

Elizabeth Hrib

Flirting with Disaster

ELIZABETH HRIB

HARLEQUIN
SPECIAL
EDITION

HARLEQUIN®
SPECIAL EDITION™

Recycling programs for this product may not exist in your area.

ISBN-13: 978-1-335-59456-3

Flirting with Disaster

Harlequin Enterprises ULC
22 Adelaide St. West, 41st Floor
Toronto, Ontario M5H 4E3, Canada
www.Harlequin.com

Printed in U.S.A.

Elizabeth Hrib was born and raised in London, Ontario, where she spends her nine-to-five as a nurse. She fell in love with the romance genre while bingeing '90s rom-coms. When she's not nursing or writing, she can be found at the piano, swooning over her favorite books on Instagram or buying too many houseplants.

Books by Elizabeth Hrib

Harlequin Special Edition

Hatchet Lake

Lightning Strikes Twice
Flirting with Disaster

Visit the Author Profile page at Harlequin.com.

Chapter One

Nothing would humble a person faster than taking a toddler on an airplane. Of that, Sarah was certain. Controlling said toddler in a confined space for any length of time should've been considered an act of God.

"Share?" Parker said, standing on his seat and shoving a chubby fist full of animal crackers into her face.

"Oh, thank you, baby," Sarah said, taking a cracker. "Let's sit down now, okay?"

Parker flopped down with all the grace of a newborn elephant, jamming the rest of the crackers into his mouth. She'd given him the window seat, hoping to contain his shenanigans. Thankfully, the stranger on the end of their aisle—Pamela—was an older woman who had raised six children and a plethora of grandchildren. She had promptly assured Sarah that the antics of one curly haired two-year-old would be no bother.

Parker picked up the tablet she'd brought along for this exact situation, and she helped him string the kid-sized headphones over his ears again. If anything was going to save her and the rest of the passengers on this plane from a spontaneous toddler meltdown, it was *CoComelon*.

While Sarah was busy untangling the cord of the headphones from between Parker's fingers, a flight attendant rushed past their row. Sarah and Pamela both turned, watching the woman head toward the very back of the plane. Every head in every row snapped around too, morbidly drawn to the sight of panic.

"I wonder what that's all about," Pamela murmured.

"I have no idea." The sight of a flight attendant running was enough to send Sarah's heart racing, but when no overhead announcement was made, she settled back in her seat, trying to ignore the concerned whispers that flitted about.

She turned and watched a familiar yellow school bus scroll across the screen of the tablet, smiling as Parker began imitating the actions to one of his favorite songs. She ran a gentle hand through his hair. Parker had inherited her unruly brown curls. Between those and his bright blue eyes, she could already tell he was going to be a heartbreaker. The hint of mischief so often worn in the turn of his tiny smile didn't bode well for her either. Where that smile went, some sort of destruction usually followed.

"I don't know how you would ever say no to him," Pamela commented, idly flipping through her magazine now that the buzz at the back of the plane had died down. "He is darn cute."

"Oh, I can't," Sarah laughed. "He definitely has me wrapped around each of his little fingers."

"Well, you're certainly braver than I was at your age. I don't think I took any of my kids on a plane until they were about six or seven. Maybe even a little older."

"He's been on a plane before," Sarah said. "But he wasn't quite one yet. I fed him during takeoff, and he slept the entire flight."

"You do a lot of traveling?"

Sarah nodded. "For work."

"Oh," Pamela said with interest. "What do you do?"

"I'm a travel nurse, so every time I pick up a new contract, I have to relocate. Sometimes it's close enough to drive. But usually not." Sarah had spent this last contract in Washington State and the one before that in Texas.

"My, he'll be a well-traveled gentleman before he starts school," Pamela said.

"That's the plan."

Sarah had recently decided to take a break from work in order to spend some quality time with Parker and visit her best friend, Kate. She might've also been using this trip to avoid having to make a decision about where they should go next. The reality was that Parker was getting older. In another couple of years, he would be ready to start school. The next contract she picked up had to be one she was willing to endure long term. It meant settling down, and that was something Sarah was decidedly bad at.

Just the thought of it made her wrinkle her nose.

She enjoyed the *traveling* part of travel nursing. The part that allowed her to pick up and relocate any time she wanted. To start fresh in a new city or a new state. Sometimes even a new country, depending on the kind of contract she accepted. Shortly after finishing nursing school, Sarah had spent nine glorious months working in Australia. Of course, that was long before Parker had been born. In those days she'd been single and mingling all over the place. Now she had to worry about bath time and sleep schedules and stepping on pointy toys in the

dark. With those kinds of priorities, she now kept her
contracts stateside.

The plane shifted, flying through a bout of turbulence, and Parker's eyes widened considerably. Sarah
reached to put his seat belt back on as he looked out the
window. He wasn't all that fascinated by the clouds, still
too young to understand the concept of being thirty-six
thousand feet in the air. He had, however, been completely thrilled by all the work trucks on the tarmac when
they'd boarded the plane.

"Truck?" he asked, looking up at her.

"We'll see the trucks when we land," she said, though
she doubted he could hear her over *CoComelon*. The
flight from Washington to Michigan, where Kate's family lived, was a little over four hours. They'd already
survived about three-quarters of it without any meltdowns. Another hour and a bit and they'd be back on the
ground. Until then, she prayed to whatever gods who
were listening that Parker held it together.

He yawned and slumped his head against her, rubbing his face into her arm. She silently thanked whoever
had just answered her prayer. Now was the perfect time
for a nap. Sarah sat very still, not wanting to do anything to inadvertently excite him. Toddlers were funny
like that. One second they'd be half asleep, their eyelids drooping, and the next they'd be bouncing off the
furniture. Sarah didn't know where the sudden burst of
energy had come from, she just knew this plane was not
big enough to accommodate it. Parker yawned again,
his eyes starting to close.

Sarah had the urge to take his headphones off to
make him more comfortable, but she knew if she tried
to separate the boy and his tablet, there would be hell to

pay. So she let him fall asleep with them on. The idea of being lulled to sleep by *CoComelon* was her idea of hell. But if it kept Parker happy, who was she to interfere?

His head bobbed, almost colliding with the tablet where it was perched on his knees. Sarah gently maneuvered him so that he was leaning on the armrest of the seat instead. After a moment, Parker grew still, and Sarah carefully turned the volume down a couple notches.

She let out a sigh of relief, half expecting someone to congratulate her. No one ever did, though she'd always thought these moments of successful parenting deserved a trophy. Now that Parker was asleep, Sarah pulled a book from her bag and relaxed against her seat. For the first time since the plane had taken off, she no longer felt like a linebacker that had to be ready to stop an escaping toddler.

As she prepared to sink into the romantic entanglements of the very muscled man on the front cover of her book, another flight attendant went rushing past their row toward the back of the plane. A moment later a second flight attendant chased after her.

"Okay, something is definitely going on," Pamela said, putting her magazine aside.

Sarah had always been told not to panic on a plane unless the flight attendants were also panicking. She wasn't sure this qualified as panicking, but something was clearly wrong.

Sarah and Pamela both turned around, as did many of the other passengers. Whatever it was, it was at the very, *very* back of the plane, too far for either of them to see properly. Sarah settled back in her seat, picking up her book, reading the same passage over and over again. There was a distinct murmur of commotion coming from the back of the plane that was hard to ignore.

"You think someone's getting sick?" Pamela wondered. "The last plane I was on, a kid had really bad motion sickness and threw up the whole flight. The entire plane smelled like puke."

Sarah wanted to point out that a full flight-attendant response seemed like overkill for a little motion sickness, but she also didn't want to worry Pamela. "Maybe," she mumbled, turning back to her book.

Then a voice played overhead: "If there is a medical professional on board, please hit your Call button now. We have an in-flight medical emergency."

Sarah perked up at the announcement, her pulse racing the same way it did when she was at work in the middle of a trauma. Despite all her experience, there was a small part of her that hoped someone else hit their Call button. Asking for medical help at this altitude did not bode well.

Pamela glanced around the plane, then back to Sarah. "I think you're up."

"Looks like it." Sarah raised her arm, hitting the button.

A flight attendant hurried down the aisle toward her.

"I'm an ER nurse," Sarah said. "Not sure how much help I'll be, but—"

"Oh, good," the flight attendant said. "Please come with me."

Sarah glanced back at Parker. He was still asleep, and she thanked the headphones for that.

"I'll keep an eye on him," Pamela promised. "You go deal with whatever is happening back there."

"Thanks," Sarah said, sliding past Pamela into the aisle. Dozens of eyes turned her way as she followed the flight attendant. Never in her life had she felt so on display. Toward the back of the plane, the passengers were less interested in her and more interested in what was happening. Some people had stood up, craning their necks to try to get a better view, ignoring repeated requests from the flight attendants to sit down. With everything she'd seen in her line of work, Sarah had learned never to underestimate the power of human curiosity. She was just glad that she hadn't spotted any phones recording yet.

"The pilot is getting in contact with a medical crew on the ground," the flight attendant told her. "But if you could be their eyes and ears…" She trailed off as Sarah nodded.

When they reached the back of the plane, a group of passengers and crew were crowded around a seated middle-aged man. Sarah spotted the two other flight attendants that had rushed by her row earlier. Ignoring the crowd, she immediately started assessing the man with what she liked to think of as her nursing brain. That was the part of herself that automatically started filing away bits and pieces of information, trying to anticipate the diagnosis and what the doctor would order as a result. She'd already determined that the man was in some sort of serious pain based on how he was hunched over and knuckling his chest. A fine film of sweat covered his forehead. Immediate red flags started jumping out at her, and before anyone said anything, she already knew they were likely dealing with some sort of cardiac situation.

Sarah managed not to swear out loud. Instead, she prayed to the god of planes, trains and automobiles that this man was not having a heart attack in the air.

The flight attendants made room for her, and Sarah knelt down beside him. "Hi," she said, taking the man's wrist gently, feeling for his pulse. "My name's Sarah. I'm a nurse. Can you tell me your name?"

"Jack," he gasped, sitting back in his seat and wincing at her.

Sarah finished counting his pulse, noting his short, quick respirations. "Nice to meet you, Jack. Can you tell me what's going on?"

"My chest," he said. "I've got pain in my chest."

"And it just started suddenly?"

He nodded.

"Can you show me where exactly?"

Jack tapped the center of his chest. "Here."

"Does the pain move? Down your arm? Into your shoulders? Anywhere else?"

He shook his head. "No. I don't think so."

There was a first aid kit open on the floor, and Sarah spotted a blood pressure cuff and a stethoscope. She took those out of the kit and wrapped the cuff around Jack's arm. "I'm going to take some vitals, okay?"

Jack nodded as Sarah pumped up the blood pressure cuff and stuck the stethoscope into her ears. She placed the diaphragm over his pulse point, listening for the familiar swish of blood as she watched the pressure gauge on the cuff.

Sarah let the cuff deflate and strung the stethoscope around her neck as she dug around for an oxygen saturation probe. She found one in the kit and clipped it on the end of Jack's finger.

"If you had to rate your pain out of ten, Jack, with ten being the worst amount of pain and one being the least, what number would you give it?"

"Five," he said. "Maybe a six."

Considering his complaints of chest pain, most of his vitals were relatively stable. His respirations were elevated, and he was clearly having some trouble catching his breath, but that could be explained away easily by the pain and anxiety he was likely feeling. Chest pain could mean a lot of things—a heart attack, angina, indigestion. The hard part up here was going to be ruling things out. If this were a hospital, Sarah would be preparing him for an ECG and hooking him up to all sorts of monitors. There were specific protocols to follow when dealing with chest pain. But up in the air, this was going to be a whole different kind of emergency.

"Jack, do you have a history of high blood pressure?" she asked.

"Not usually."

"Cholesterol?"

"My doc said it was a little high last time I was in for a checkup."

"Do you smoke?"

He nodded. "Thirty years."

"Drink alcohol?"

"Socially."

"The pilot has a doctor on the line," one of the flight attendants interrupted. She held the phone they used to speak to the flight deck to her ear.

Perfect, Sarah thought, and she jumped into report mode, rhyming off her preliminary assessment. "Tell the doctor we've got a middle-aged man with sudden onset of acute centralized chest pain. Rated six out of ten. Pain does not radiate. Patient is diaphoretic, clutching his chest and short of breath. Vitals as follows: heart rate 88. Blood pressure 135 over 75. Respirations 22. Oxygen saturation is 95% on room air."

The flight attendant repeated what Sarah said word for word. She looked confused. "They want to know about his history?"

"Patient reports no history of high blood pressure. Discussed high cholesterol with family doctor during last visit," Sarah said. "Patient has a thirty-year history of smoking."

"The doctor wants to know if you've given any medications?"

"No meds given." She looked at Jack. "Do you have medication allergies?"

He shook his head.

"Do you take any blood thinners?"

"No."

Sarah started to rifle through the first aid kit again, looking for familiar drugs. "I've got aspirin and nitro on hand," she said.

"The doctor said give 325 milligrams of aspirin," the flight attendant relayed.

Another flight attendant handed her a bottle of water, but Sarah refused it. She gave Jack the aspirin. "I want you to chew this to get it in your bloodstream faster."

He did, making a disgruntled face.

The flight attendant on the phone was nodding along to the voice on the other end. "The doctor also said to give 0.4 milligrams of nitroglycerin."

Sarah took the other med. "Jack, I want you to put this under your tongue and let it dissolve, okay?"

He nodded, taking the pill. Sarah inflated the blood pressure cuff again and placed the stethoscope back into her ears. As she performed another set of vitals, she noted Jack's breathing ease. If the nitroglycerin was going to help with the chest pain, they would know soon.

"How's your pain?" she asked Jack after another minute.

"Better," he said. "It's getting better. Maybe a three out of ten."

Sarah relayed the improvement and the new set of vitals to the doctor via the flight attendant.

"He said administer another dose of nitroglycerin. And then buckle up."

Sarah raised a brow.

"Well, the captain said that last part," the flight attendant clarified. "We're going to be landing soon. An ambulance will meet us on the ground."

Sarah nodded. She administered one more dose of nitroglycerin, then climbed into the empty seat beside Jack, reaching for the seat belt.

"Not how you figured you'd spend the flight, huh?" he said to her, looking better than he had ten minutes ago.

"No, I actually thought I'd have my toddler hanging off me the entire time, so this is definitely an improvement."

Jack smiled, putting his head back, letting the medications work. There was still the chance that he'd suffered or was currently suffering a heart attack, but hopefully it was just angina and once he was assessed at the hospital they would get him on some regular medication.

He took her hand and squeezed it. "Well," he said, "I certainly appreciate you being here."

One of the flight attendants returned with a form for Sarah to fill out. She documented her assessment, the doctor's orders, the medications given and Jack's vital signs. As the plane prepared to land, she kept a close eye on him, hoping they would touch down before anything else went wrong. The flight attendants scurried back to their seats as the plane began its descent.

And it was at that moment exactly, while Sarah was trapped at the back of the plane, that Parker woke up and started to scream.

Chapter Two

The nice thing about helping with an in-flight medical emergency was that Sarah got to disembark the plane first, along with Jack, in order to relay her report to the paramedics.

The bad thing was that she now had a traumatized two-year-old latched onto her like a tiny squid as she made her way to the baggage terminal. Waking up to find Pamela sitting beside him instead of his mom had put Parker in a foul mood.

"You're okay," Sarah said, bouncing him in her arms. He continued to wail into her ear. "I know, I know. You woke up with a strange lady, and that was scary. You want to go find Auntie Kate?"

"Yah," he cried.

"Okay." As she made her way through the terminal, Parker's wails turned to sniffles, much to the relief of her ear drums and all the other travelers. He rubbed his face into her shoulder. "Oh, thank you for the boogers."

Parker giggled but refused to lift his head. When they reached the baggage carousel, he was mildly interested in watching the luggage spin around the baggage belt.

"Here, Mommy will put you down for a second."

"No," he whined, using that impossible toddler strength to cling to her.

"Okay," Sarah said, opting to grab a luggage cart instead. Between the two of them, she'd managed to pack everything into one large suitcase and their carry-on. But she'd also had to bring Parker's car seat along, and she simply did not have enough hands to manage everything.

When their bag and the car seat came around, she snatched them from the belt and dumped them on the cart with the carry-on. Everything was a little harder with a tiny human attached to your hip, but Sarah had become so used to doing things one handed that she navigated them out of the terminal toward the pickup point without crashing into the flurry of people coming and going.

"Auntie Kate?"

"Yeah, we're gonna go find Auntie Kate."

And as soon as they cleared the main doors, there she was. Sarah's very best friend in the world, Kate Cardiff, leaned against a post, looking more like a rancher's daughter than ever. Or maybe that was just how a large-animal vet dressed in their natural habitat.

Kate's face broke into a wide grin as soon as she spotted them, and she lifted her hand to wave. Parker kicked his legs excitedly.

Kate was the most effortlessly beautiful person Sarah knew. She stood there in baggy jeans, a plaid shirt that Sarah suspected belonged to this new boyfriend of hers and sturdy, tan work boots. They were a complete study in opposites. Kate had always been tall and lean, maintaining a strength that came from a life of ranch work. Sarah was average height and curvy, a fact that had become even more pronounced since her pregnancy with Parker. And while Kate's blond hair was pulled back into a neat ponytail, Sarah's dark curls spilled in a tangle around her face. Despite their differences, Kate had always felt like the closest thing to a sister Sarah would ever have.

Kate was an only child, and Sarah had a half brother from her dad's previous marriage whom she'd only met a handful of times. Neither of them really knew what a sibling was. But when they'd met in college, things had just clicked, and it had been like they'd known each other their entire lives.

"You made it!" Kate called.

"For a minute there I didn't think we would," Sarah replied, laughing. She rolled the luggage cart to a stop, and Kate hugged her.

"It's so good to see you."

"We keep saying we won't let it go this long between visits."

"I know—we're the worst."

After graduation, life had taken them in different directions, and they'd spent years surviving on sporadic whirlwind visits and phone calls. Kate had normally been the one to fly out and visit, especially once Parker had been born. This was Sarah's first time back in Michigan since finishing school—and her first time ever visiting Kate's childhood home. It was also the first time her plans didn't necessarily have an end date.

Sarah and Kate were used to having to cram a lifetime of memories and moments into short visits. It was strange now to have time to take things slowly.

"Hi, Parker," Kate said, holding her arms out for him. Unsurprisingly, he went to her without a fuss. Parker spent a lot of time babbling to Kate through video calls, so there was a familiarity there, and Sarah was glad for it.

"Oh, someone's Mr. Snuggles today," Kate said as Parker hugged her.

"Enjoy it while it lasts," Sarah said. "I just traumatized my child, so these cuddles don't come cheap."

Kate chuckled, her face buried in Parker's curls. "What did you do?"

As they made their way to the parking lot, Parker cuddled against Kate, clearly still tired, while Sarah relayed the entire in-flight emergency. She finished with Parker waking up as the plane was landing, terrified and unimpressed with the entire situation.

"He wailed, Kate. Like some sort of demon that had just been booted out of hell. I've never even heard my child make noises like that."

"At least you know you could find him in a crowd if he ever got lost."

"Thank God we got to disembark first, or else the airline probably would have put us on a no-fly list."

"Do you think he'll be okay?" Kate asked. "Jack, I mean."

Kate had recently been through a scare with her own father. He'd suffered a heart attack, which had prompted Kate to move back to her family's ranch, so this story was probably hitting a little close to home.

"You know, I really do," Sarah said. "He was doing well when I left him, and the paramedics had him loaded onto the stretcher in a minute flat. He's probably already at the hospital with a doctor poring over my terribly written report."

"I'm glad," Kate said. "And what about you?"

"What about me?"

"Kind of scary, right?"

Sarah shrugged. "There was a part of me that was hoping there was a doctor on board. I mean, thirty-six thousand feet is not an ideal place for a cardiac event. But it's really no different than walking into the trauma bay in the ER. You never quite know what to expect—you just do what you have to do to plug holes and stop the bleeding."

"So this was a regular old day for you, huh?"

Sarah laughed. "Pretty much."

"Truck!" Parker shouted as soon as they entered the parking lot.

"Yeah, buddy, that's a truck," Kate said.

"Truck!" he shouted excitedly, pointing at another vehicle.

"Boy, he's gonna love the ranch," Kate said to Sarah. "Trucks galore."

"Speaking of loving the ranch, where is Rancher Hotstuff? I'm a little disappointed that he wasn't here to greet us."

Kate threw her head back and laughed. "Nice segue."

"I thought you'd appreciate that."

"Nathan is back at the ranch, helping my father patch up holes in the stables."

"Is it that bad still?"

"The stables are in pretty good shape actually," Kate said. "It's just been difficult to get the lumber we need. The entire town is trying to rebuild."

"Oh, right," Sarah said. "Of course, that makes sense." A bad storm had ripped through Kate's hometown recently, creating a tornado that had left a trail of destruction in its wake. Thankfully, Kate's entire family had pulled through unscathed, including Nathan, the photographer turned ranch hand who had promptly fallen in love with Sarah's best friend.

It was a better love story than any book Sarah had ever read, and she was dying to meet the man in person.

"Besides," Kate said, "I thought it would be safer not to confine you two to a vehicle together for an hour for your first meeting."

Sarah rolled her eyes. "I'm not going to scare him," she said. "Much."

"Lies." Kate kissed Parker's cheek. "Tell your mommy she's lying."

"Lie!" Parker screeched.

"Thanks for that," Sarah muttered.

"I love this aunt thing. I'm going to corrupt him by teaching him all sorts of wicked things."

"Just remember who knew you best while you were in college. I have a lot of stories, Kate Cardiff."

"Can't be worse than what my parents have already told Nathan."

"I'm sure I could come up with a couple."

"Parker," Kate whispered. "Your mommy is being mean to me."

Parker reached out with a pointed finger. "No mean!"

Sarah scoffed. "I'm here all of five minutes and you are turning my son against me."

"What a productive morning." Kate snatched the car seat off the luggage cart, shifting Parker up her hip to balance both.

"Truck!" Parker squealed, seeing the beat-up ranch truck that Kate drove.

"Well, now you're definitely going to be his favorite."

"I had it all planned out," Kate said. "Are you going to help me with this thing, or what?"

"Installing a car seat is the most elite of parenting skills."

"I can see why. This thing has way too many buckles."

Sarah snorted and helped Kate install the car seat in the truck while Parker flopped around the back seat. Then they strapped Parker down, loaded up the luggage and were off. Hatchet Lake, the ridiculously small town in Southern Michigan where the Cardiff family ranch was located, was about an hour's drive from the airport.

Parker was ecstatic to be riding in a truck, babbling away in the back for about the first twenty minutes of the drive. Then he was quiet.

"I think he's asleep," Kate said, glancing in the rear-view mirror.

Sarah hummed in agreement. "He didn't sleep very long on the plane. Maybe an hour."

"Plus he did all that screaming. Probably wiped himself out."

"That too." Sarah stared out the window as the crowded city streets faded to fields of green and gold. "You really grew up with just this as a view?"

Kate smirked, one hand on the wheel as they raced down the empty stretch of back highway. "We can't all grow up in California."

"I always assumed you were joking."

"What? That we were secretly hiding a Starbucks?"

"Wouldn't that be great?"

"I don't think Hatchet Lake would know what to do with a Starbucks. Then again, we just got this fancy resort, so maybe one will pop up soon."

Sarah frowned, and Kate laughed. "It's not funny."

"All you have to do is drive thirty-five minutes from the ranch to the closest Starbucks in the city. Then you can feed your sugary coffee addiction."

After a while the highway came to a four-way stop, and Kate turned onto a road that was aptly named Hatchet Lake Road. The fields on either side of the car were less wild, cut neatly.

"Is that it?" Sarah asked as they approached a large building. "The resort? I didn't see that during my research."

"You mean your night-shift googling?" Kate chuckled. "Yeah, it's new. Mosaic Resort and Wellness Retreat. I think it's some sort of frilly health-spa type deal. You know, small-town peace and quiet. Fresh air. Deep tissue massages."

"Built all the way out here?"

"Town's only, like, a three-minute drive from here, and the lake's not far either. I assume they bought up all this land to expand."

Sarah scanned the building, all polished stone and tall, peaked rooftops. "Looks like it made out okay in the storm."

Kate's lips pulled into a tight line. "Better than the rest of town, that's for sure."

Kate slowed as the road suddenly became a traffic jam. There were large vehicles parked on the shoulder and in fields, with dozens of people in matching red shirts milling about.

"What's going on?"

"We've got some volunteers in town to help with the cleanup. It's usually only ever this busy when the tourists are here for the summer."

Sarah noted that the volunteers were scattered about town, patching holes and moving debris. Some had chain saws, cutting up rogue trees that were still splayed across the road. Others were on ladders, fitting new siding to buildings or new shingles to the rooftops.

"Wow," Sarah said. "It's quite a production."

"They've been a big help so far. And my mother's taken it upon herself to feed them all. So the house is going to permanently smell like banana bread. Prepare yourself."

"I mean, I'm not complaining," Sarah said. They left the main stretch of town and drove down another road. There were more downed trees, though most of them had been dragged far enough off the road that Kate could pass.

When they arrived at the ranch, a temporary sign had been nailed under the one that read Cardiff Ranch. The addition said *& Veterinary Practice*. Sarah grinned, happy that Kate had decided to stay on the property with Nathan and her parents.

"The sign looks good," she said.

Kate's answering smile was radiant. "Wait till you see the new one. Everything's still a work in progress, but I'm pretty pleased."

They pulled up in front of the house, and Sarah jumped out, getting her first real glimpse of the property. Green fields. Stamped horse trails. The stables. A whitewashed farmhouse. It was all so picturesque she almost didn't believe places like this really existed. Even as she started to catalog the damage from the storm—missing porch railings, downed trees, shingles and siding and random debris that still needed to be collected—there was a certain charm about the property. It was the kind of place that childhood dreams were made of.

"Mom!" Parker cried, but Kate got to him first, untangling the buckles and hauling him out of the seat without bumping his head on the door frame.

"Hey, buddy," she said. "Look where we are."

Parker blinked around at the unfamiliar surroundings. For a moment, Sarah thought he might burst into tears. Then he spotted another truck, and his eyes lit up. He squirmed out of Kate's arms and made a dash for it.

"I think he approves," Kate laughed.

Sarah unloaded their things, watching Parker investigate the massive tires on the other truck before flopping down in the grass. "I have a feeling I'm going to be doing a lot of laundry while we're here."

"It wouldn't be the quintessential ranch experience if you weren't."

The door to the stables opened, and a man appeared. He was as tall, dark and handsome as the heroes in any of Sarah's romance books. He jogged toward them, and Parker got up from the grass, spooked by the stranger. He raced back in their direction, crashing into Kate's legs, where he promptly decided to hide.

Kate grimaced.

"Oh, I forgot to mention," Sarah said. "He's in a head-butting phase."

"It's like being kicked by a horse."

"Hey," Nathan said, slowing as he approached.

"How's it looking?" Kate asked him, gesturing to the stables.

"It's nothing pretty," he admitted, rubbing at the back of his neck.

"I thought Rusty was supposed to be helping you?"

"He was. Then he took off with Tara to go photograph some property damage for some of the folks they met in town." Nathan shrugged. "Helps with the insurance claims."

"Nathan's friends," Kate clarified for Sarah. "You'll probably meet them later."

"Anyway," Nathan said. "Definitely not adding *carpenter* to my resume, but it's a patch job."

"You can't be good at everything."

Nathan shrugged, then turned to greet Sarah. "So this must be *the* Sarah."

"And you must be Rancher Hotstuff in the flesh," she replied.

Nathan reached out to give her a quick hug, and Sarah returned it. She liked him immediately. His easy nature. His reassuring presence. The way he smiled at her best friend.

"She's staring," Nathan whispered to Kate as he pulled away.

"Don't make any sudden movements," Kate joked, lifting up on her toes to press a kiss to his cheek.

Sarah nudged her. "You did good."

"I think so."

Nathan followed their conversation. "I made the cut, did I?"

"For now." Sarah smirked. "More silent judgment to follow."

"My favorite kind of judgment," he said.

Parker stopped dancing round Kate's legs and looked up at them.

"Hey, buddy," Nathan said.

"Truck!" Parker yelled, pointing at the truck across the yard.

"That sure is a truck. You want to see inside?"

"Yah!" Parker lifted his little hand for Nathan to take, and Sarah could tell Nathan was here to stay. The two of them wandered off to babble about vehicles, and Parker didn't even look back once. Sarah felt oddly abandoned.

"Well, that's adorable," Kate said. "C'mon, let's take advantage of the break and move your stuff upstairs."

Kate grabbed the suitcase, Sarah took the carry-on and they headed into the house. They entered into an open-concept living-room-and-kitchen deal. At the island, Kate's mom was elbow-deep in a mixing bowl. "I wondered when you were going to come in and say hello."

"Hi, Mama Cardiff," Sarah said, pecking the older woman on the cheek. Anne Cardiff had always been one of the warmest and most welcoming people she'd ever met. "Kate told me you've been baking up a storm."

"Oh, you know, just a little bit."

Sarah watched Kate roll her eyes behind her mother.

"I saw that, Katherine," Anne said without missing a beat.

"*How?*" Kate mouthed.

"Where's that son of yours?" Anne asked.

Sarah gestured over her shoulder. "He got distracted by the trucks. He's out there getting his first driving lesson from Nathan."

"You've met the boyfriend?"

"I sure have." Sarah grinned as Anne's eyes lit up.

"He's a nice guy, isn't he?"

"Very nice," Sarah agreed. "I approve."

"I do too. You know, compared to Kate's past relationships—"

"Okay," Kate said, taking Sarah by the arm and steering her to the stairs. "She's only been here for ten minutes, Mom. The two of you do not need to start meddling in anything related to my love life."

"Who's meddling?" Anne called after them.

Kate led Sarah upstairs, where she and Parker would be staying since Kate and Nathan had shacked up in the guest house on the property.

"This is my old room," Kate said, dumping Sarah's

suitcase in a room before sitting on the edge of the bed. "It's small but comfy. Best view of the stables too."

"Oh, I believe it," she said, spying out the window, from which she could see both the stables and the guest house. She watched Dale Cardiff, Kate's father, come around the back of a building with a hose to fill the horse troughs. "Must be cozy since you spent weeks up here pining after Nathan."

"Don't forget I actually loathed him in the beginning. It didn't turn to pining until much later."

"I always knew it would," Sarah teased, glancing down to where Parker was playing in the front seat of the truck with Nathan standing watch. The bedroom window was open a crack, and she could hear him squeal in delight.

"Parker can take the spare room," Kate said. "It's farther from the stairs and at the back of the house, so hopefully ranch stuff won't wake him up at the crack of dawn. Or we can move the mattress in here if you'd prefer to keep him close."

Sarah was touched at how much Kate had thought about their visit.

A crash sounded from downstairs, and they both froze.

"Kate!" Anne called.

"What do you want to bet there's batter all over the kitchen?" Kate reluctantly stood up. "You unpack. I'll keep an eye on my mother and Parker."

"Thanks," Sarah said, dragging the suitcase over to the bed as Kate disappeared downstairs. She usually wouldn't unpack this much for a vacation, but this was more than a simple vacation. This was time for her to figure out the next phase of her life, and she wanted to be comfortable. She didn't know if they would be here for a week or for three. She just knew she liked the sound of Parker's laughter as it drifted up from downstairs.

As she unpacked, her phone started to buzz. She glanced at it and sighed. It was her mother. Sarah had always considered herself a pretty self-assured person, but that all went out the window where her mother was concerned.

"Hi," Sarah said, stuffing the phone between her ear and her shoulder as she carried a stack of clothes across the room, destined for an empty dresser drawer.

"When were you going to tell me you moved?" her mother asked impatiently.

"How's California?" Sarah replied instead. She'd grown up in the echoing halls of her parents' Malibu estate but had barely been back since leaving for college.

"Stop trying to change the subject. When did you move?"

Sarah had never gotten used to these jarring conversations. "What are you talking about, Mom?"

"I called and couldn't get a hold of you—"

"I was on a plane. I had no service in the air. We just landed and got sett—"

"I called the sitter, you know, and she told me you and Parker packed up and left. She had no idea where you'd gone, only that you'd quit your job and taken off."

Sarah owed her babysitter in Washington an apology and a bottle of wine for fielding that phone call. Bonnie Schaffer could be a menace in person, but over the phone all bets were off. "It's much less dramatic than that. And I didn't quit my job. My contract ended."

"So you're unemployed and my grandson has nowhere to live?"

"We're not homeless, Mom. We're on a...vacation of

sorts." Sarah picked up a tiny sock that had somehow lost its pair during their travels.

"A vacation where?"

"We're visiting Kate in Hatchet Lake for a while."

"Didn't you tell me they recently had a tornado there?"

Sarah suddenly regretted telling her mother that one piece of information. "It's fine. Everyone was fine. Things are being cleaned up—".

"Cleaned up? Sarah, do you really think that's an appropriate place to take your son?"

Her mother's words climbed right under her skin. It was like getting a sliver in the nail bed, and Sarah retreated. "Okay, Mom, Parker's calling. I have to go now."

"Sarah—"

"Look, I'll have to call you later. Bye." Sarah hung up before her mother could respond. She let out a heavy breath, already developing the same kind of headache she got after a night of drinking.

The only thing more difficult than treating a man for a possible heart attack at thirty-six thousand feet was fielding a phone call from her mother. Frustrated now, Sarah took the rest of the clothes from the suitcase and dumped them into the dresser, shoving the drawer closed. Leave it to her mother to stress her out more than a plane ride with a toddler and a medical emergency ever could.

Chapter Three

"She thinks I'm a terrible mom!"

"No, she doesn't," Kate said, turning the truck off the property. They were currently headed into town with a dozen loaves of banana bread to be delivered to the volunteer crew. After waking up on the ranch and spending the morning running around after the horses and every truck on the property, Parker had finally gone down for a nap. Anne had offered to watch him for a while so Sarah and Kate could make a delivery run.

"Are you sure?" Sarah had asked. "He can be a bit of a handful when he wakes up."

Anne had practically shooed them out of the house. "I raised that one," she'd said, gesturing to Kate. "And a bunch of horses. And kept an eye on her father at the same time. I think I can handle one little boy. Besides, if you two don't go and unload some of this, we won't be able to access the kitchen soon."

Now the entire truck smelled like bananas and chocolate chips.

"Your mother does not think you're a terrible mom," Kate said again.

"She does!" Sarah insisted. She was still stewing over the phone call she'd had with her mother yesterday. "You should have heard her—the way she was going on, you would think I'd dragged Parker into an active war zone."

Kate burst out laughing. "It was not that bad."

"I'm serious. Every time she calls there's this…undertone of judgment. Like I'm not doing it right."

"Doing what right?"

"I don't know," Sarah complained. "Life?" She stole a piece of banana bread out of one of the containers and took a bite. With her mouth full, she said, "Gosh, this is really good."

"I know—but don't tell my mother, or we'll never get her to stop baking." They followed the long stretch of quiet highway for several minutes until a sign for town marked their arrival. Kate turned onto Main Street, slowing to a crawl as she navigated the truck around volunteers and emergency vehicles and piles of debris slated for the dump.

Sarah watched it all with the same sort of fascination with which she watched a busy ER. Each volunteer belonged to their own small crew with their own designated tasks. It sort of reminded Sarah of triage points. She turned back to Kate. "Do you think I'm a terrible parent?"

"Do I—what? Are you kidding me? I can't believe you asked me that. You are an amazing mom! And you know what?" Kate said, expertly reversing the truck onto an empty patch of gravel. "You are allowed to take a break from things. To take some time to figure life out. I'm speaking from experience now."

Sarah leaned her head back against her seat. "Yeah, I guess you just went through the whole life-altering-decision thing."

"And it took a while for me to figure out how I felt about it. I'm still figuring things out. How to set up my vet practice. How Nathan fits into the picture."

"I'm happy you're happy," Sarah told her.

"And I'm happy you're here. I'd be happier if you didn't let these things with your mother bother you so much."

Sarah let out a huff that was somewhere between a laugh and a hum of resignation. "Story of my life." They shared a smile, then Sarah passed Kate a container of banana bread. "How do you want to do this?"

"I find it best to sort of dump the goods and run before they can descend on it." The corner of Kate's mouth quirked. "C'mon. They have a lunch tent where we can leave everything."

Sarah followed Kate out of the truck, loaves of banana bread tucked under her arms. She made her way past a large white trailer that was labeled Command & Control. Brightly colored tents were scattered about, each one housing various supplies. Sarah assumed one of these would be the lunch tent. Trucks with matching logos drove back and forth, transporting people and debris. She noticed that the red-shirted volunteers all had their names written on the fronts of their T-shirts. On the backs, their shirts read TEAM REBUILD: Disaster Response.

"This is an entire operation," she said. She'd done lots of emergency and trauma training as a nurse, and the tents and trailers and organized chaos reminded her of all the disaster simulations she'd been a part of.

"It really is," Kate said, carefully stepping over some wires that ran along the ground. "They showed up almost immediately after the tornado. They've been on the ground ever since, helping clear roads and rebuild infrastructure."

Sarah was impressed.

"Kate!" a voice called.

"Ryan, hi," Kate said as a man dressed in some sort of police uniform jogged over.

"Can I help?" he asked.

Sarah and Kate each gratefully unloaded some of their baked goods.

"This is Deputy Ryan Mullens," Kate told Sarah. "We went to school together way back in the day."

"Don't make me sound that old," Ryan joked.

Kate smirked. "This is my friend Sarah. She's staying up at the ranch with us for a while."

"Ah," Ryan said to Sarah. "She's gonna put you to work, I bet."

Sarah laughed. "Not sure how much use I'll be. Animals aren't really my forte. Especially something as big as a horse."

"What do you do?"

"I'm a nurse."

"Oh, you'll be fine, then. I mean, what's a patient with a few extra legs?"

"Right?" Sarah chuckled. "I'm sure I could figure it out."

The radio on Ryan's hip crackled to life, chirping something about a tractor and a backhoe. "If you'll excuse me, ladies, it sounds like I've got some traffic to unjam."

They watched him walk away with a stack of banana bread.

"Was that the Ryan you had a crush on in high school?" Sarah asked.

Kate nodded. "He's in charge of the coordination between the town and Team Rebuild's command-and-control center." After a moment she added, "He's also single, in case you were wondering."

Sarah bit the inside of her cheek to keep from smirking. "I wasn't wondering. I was just being nice."

"And I was just offering a few tidbits of important information like any good friend would do."

"Mmm-hmm," Sarah said, following after Kate again. They reached the lunch tent, which was a simple tarp stretched out over a couple of long, rectangular tables. An assortment of mismatched chairs had migrated around them.

Kate plopped the banana bread down on one of the tables. Sarah did the same.

"Do I smell chocolate chips?" a man asked. He was incredibly tall, with a booming voice and a killer smile. He had a tool belt strung over his hips and a hard hat tucked under his arm.

"You sure do," Kate said. "Enjoy."

Sarah grinned as the man and a few other volunteers dug in, cutting slices and complimenting Anne Cardiff's baking with full mouths. Anne would be pleased. Sarah glanced around as one of the volunteers struck up a conversation with Kate. While they talked, she wandered between the tents, noting the sheer amount of equipment that had been amassed to help with the rebuild. Construction was out of her comfort zone, but one tent in particular caught her eye.

The roof of the tent was white with a big red cross in the middle. A medical tent? Sarah wondered what kind of medicine they could get up to in the middle of this operation. As far as she'd been told, no one was injured much beyond some bumps and bruises, so it wasn't like they were digging out survivors after the disaster. She assumed the tent was for general first aid, then.

As Sarah drew closer, she spotted a frazzled-looking girl, no older than twenty, turning over boxes as a man stood at the edge of the tent, clutching a bloody cloth in his hand.

"Um," the girl said. "I had a box of gauze here—I'm sure of it. Give me a second. Oh, here!" She tugged on a pack of gauze, but the box went flying, dumping supplies all over the ground. The girl dove after it.

"Are you okay?" the man asked. "If you hand me the gauze I can probably help."

"I'm fine!" She resurfaced with half a dozen gauze packs. "Now, um, I guess we should put this on it. Uh, do you want to sit down? Or no, maybe I should sit down? Wait. I have to clean it first."

She began rifling through the supplies again, and Sarah couldn't take it anymore. She'd wandered even closer, drawn in by the helpless look on the girl's face and the oddly perplexed, maybe even amused look the man gave her.

"I'm sorry," she said, drawing their attention. "Do you mind if I cut in?"

Wide-eyed, the girl shrugged.

Sarah quickly used some hand sanitizer and pulled on a pair of gloves from an open box on the table. They were too big and her hands swam in them, but she would make do. She took a couple gauze packs from the girl and tore them open.

"Here," she said, taking the man's hand and gently shifting the blood-stained cloth. She got a look at the cut on his hand. It wasn't very long or deep. As long as they could get the bleeding under control, he likely wouldn't need stitches. Sarah pressed the fresh gauze to the wound, holding pressure by squeezing his hand between both of hers.

"Hi," he said, that perplexed look drawing his brows together.

A smile stretched across his face, and Sarah couldn't help but notice it was a very handsome face. Clean-shaven. Rich brown hair sweeping to either side of his forehead, just long enough to run your fingers through. And a pair of dark hazel eyes. This was exactly the kind of face that Sarah used to take home at the end of the night before Parker was born.

"You don't work here," he said.

"No," Sarah admitted. "Was it that obvious?"

"The lack of a red shirt sort of gave you away," he said, gesturing to his own shirt.

"Guess I did a poor job of infiltrating."

"Terrible," he said. "I'm Desmond Torres."

"Sarah Schaffer." They made their best attempt at an awkward shake with their unoccupied hands. It took a ridiculous amount of effort for Sarah to stop staring into his eyes. "Um, what did you do to your hand?"

He gestured with his head in a general direction. "Cut it on the metal hinge of a door that had seen better days."

Sarah lifted the gauze up to see how the bleeding was doing. His hand was still covered in dried blood, but the bleeding had stopped.

"A bit of a mess, isn't it?"

"I've seen worse," she assured him. It was nothing compared to the kinds of things that came through the ER.

"You're a nurse?"

"How did you guess?"

"Never met a doctor that was any good at wound care."

Sarah smirked. "And you've been around a lot of doctors?"

He shrugged. "Maybe I just get a lot of wounds."

Sarah narrowed her eyes at his playfulness. A nice face and a good sense of humor. Oh, she definitely would have taken him home.

"Sit," she instructed, directing him to a chair. "And hold this." She left him to hold the gauze pad to his hand while she prepared the table in front of him. "Do you have any sterile drapes?" Sarah asked the girl who'd bent down to finish picking up the supplies she'd dropped earlier. Her shirt said Melanie. As she jumped back to her feet, she looked more scared than confused by Sarah's question. "Or anything that could work to cover the table? Just to keep the area clean."

"Oh, sure," Melanie said, pulling out a drape from a package.

Sarah unfolded it along the table, and Desmond laid his hand down. Under the table Sarah spotted a cardboard box filled with dressing trays. *Perfect.* She took one of those and looked around for some saline. "Hand me that bottle, please."

Melanie passed her a small bottle of saline that Sarah cracked open and added to the dressing tray.

"I'm going to clean it off first," she told Desmond. "There's a lot of dried blood. Once it's clean, I'll dress it, and you should be good to go."

"Sounds like a plan."

Sarah uncovered the wound, picked up a pair of tweezers and a small cotton ball soaked in saline, and began cleaning the area.

"I'm so sorry," Melanie said, hanging over Sarah's shoulder as she apologized profusely to Desmond. "I'm not usually here alone. I'm really just supposed to be shadowing. Learning, you know? But we were short-staffed and the other guy needed a break, so I said I'd look after it. I didn't think anything would happen, and then you were here and there was all this blood—"

Sarah stopped cleaning the wound and looked up. She watched Melanie's face pale to the color of the gauze. Heard the slight tremor in her voice. "Okay," Sarah said, letting go of Desmond's hand and dropping the tweezers. She was out of her chair and shoving it under Melanie just as the girl's legs gave out. "Let's take a seat."

Desmond half rose out of his chair.

"Stay there," Sarah ordered him. "Don't contaminate my clean field."

"Yes, ma'am," he said, smiling at her in amusement.

"Melanie, you okay?" Sarah asked, reaching for the girl's wrist to feel her pulse. Now *this* felt more like the ER, having to divide her time between patients, always being pulled in the direction of the most serious one.

"Yeah," Melanie said, giving her head a shake. "I got really dizzy all of a sudden."

"Might have been some light-headedness from all the blood." Melanie's pulse was a bit quick, but nothing out of the ordinary. Sarah found an instant ice pack in one of the boxes and cracked it. She wrapped it in a clean drape and pressed it to the back of Melanie's neck. "Hold this here."

Sarah went back to the boxes, shifting through the supplies until she found a package of juice boxes. She pulled one free, opened it and told Melanie to drink. "Feeling any better?"

"Much better. Thanks."

"Good," Sarah said. "Just stay there and rest for a bit."

Melanie nodded, closing her eyes and relaxing back into the chair. Sarah changed her gloves and returned to Desmond. She finished cleaning the blood from his hand, pressed fresh gauze to the wound and then found a sticky dressing to hold it in place.

"You're pretty good at this," Desmond remarked. He was looking up at her, his eyes trained on her face. Sarah could almost feel the heat of his gaze. It was why she'd spent the last five minutes hyper-focused on her work. If she let her eyes drift to his, she'd get distracted.

"You think so?"

"Not just this," he said, wiggling his fingers. "I sort of meant everything." His chin jutted out toward Melanie, and Sarah's eyes traced a path along his strong jaw and down his neck.

She took a deep, steadying breath. Pretty soon she was going to need some medical attention herself. "I usually work in the ER," she said, "so jumping between patients sort of comes with the territory."

"Guess of all the days to get hurt, this was the one to do it."

Her eyes found his then, and something fluttered to life in her chest. "If you think this is impressive, you should watch me throw in an IV."

Desmond pretended to shiver. "With talk like that, I'll be itching for a reason to come back."

"Sadly this was a onetime offer."

"Moving on to bigger and better things?"

"Something like that." When Sarah was confident his dressing would survive the day, she cleaned up the rest of the supplies and dumped the used stuff into the trash.

"Well, then I will count myself lucky to have been

your patient." Desmond reached out with his good hand again for another clumsy shake. It might have only been her imagination, but she thought he lingered, the pads of his palm rough against hers, his skin flushed and warm.

Or maybe she was the flushed one.

"Oh, one more thing," she said, ignoring the sparks jumping in her chest. Thankfully years of practice fell into place like muscle memory, and she gave him the infection-prevention spiel. "If there's increased pain or redness or fever, you should get it checked out by a doctor. And I'd recommend coming back tomorrow and having whoever is here change your dressing. Make sure it's healing okay."

"Sure thing," Desmond said, letting her hand go, his fingers skimming her palm. "Anything else?"

"Maybe consider a tetanus—"

"—shot? Yeah, I'm up-to-date," he said. "Not the first piece of rusty metal I've been bested by."

"Well, that should heal up nicely, then."

Desmond smiled at her. "It was good to meet you, Sarah Schaffer."

Mesmerized by his eyes, Sarah could only nod, willing her racing heart to settle.

"God, he's attractive," Melanie muttered as Desmond walked away.

Sarah barked a laugh and turned to face her. "You focus on finishing your drink there before you make yourself light-headed again."

Melanie's cheeks pinked, but she pursed her lips, catching Sarah's eye. "I'm not wrong."

"I didn't say you were."

They shared a conspiratorial smile. A shadow crossed Sarah's peripheral, and she turned to see both Kate and an older woman approaching.

"Here you are!" Kate said. "I lose you for five minutes and you've already set up a *MASH* tent?"

"Ha!" Sarah said, using some sanitizer on her hands again.

The other woman carried a clipboard in one hand and a large thermos in the other. She had a short gray bob and thick-rimmed glasses. She looked like the nononsense clinical instructors Sarah had worked with in nursing school who'd mostly terrified her at the time. The phrase *Don't talk to me until I've had my morning coffee* was printed on the side of her thermos. The fact that it was now afternoon didn't bode well for that.

"Sorry," Sarah said. "I got kind of sidetracked."

"This is Lori Milne," Kate said. "She's one of the project managers for Team Rebuild."

"Hi," Sarah said, reaching out. She'd shaken a lot of hands today.

"I was a little concerned when I saw a stranger running the medical tent, but Kate told me you're an ER nurse, so I'm less concerned now."

Sarah nodded.

"Where do you work?"

"I just finished up a contract at UW Medical Center in Seattle. Sort of between contracts right now."

"Well, you know, Team Rebuild is always looking for good volunteers if you're interested. I'm not sure if you've noticed but our medical team is a little understaffed at present."

"Oh, I'm only passing through," Sarah said. "Might not be in town long. But Melanie's doing a great job holding down the fort."

"Just keep me away from the blood," Melanie piped up, giving Lori two thumbs-up.

Lori grimaced, and Kate hid a smirk behind her

hand. "Well," Lori said, "hopefully Evan should be back from break any minute. I'll stay with Melanie so you can head out."

Sarah traded places with Lori.

"But if you change your mind," Lori called after her, "you know where to find us."

Sarah waved. "I'll keep that in mind. Thanks."

Kate bumped her shoulder as they walked back to the truck.

"What?"

"You wander off and take over their medical tent?"

"I didn't take it over."

One of Kate's brows rose to a point.

"Okay," Sarah relented. "It was a little chaotic. I thrive in chaos—you know this. And that poor girl had no idea what she was doing."

"You're lucky Lori let you leave," Kate joked as they reached the truck. "Did you have any interesting patients?"

"Nope," Sarah said, her thoughts immediately returning to Desmond. "A cut. One fainting spell."

"So just the usual Sarah Schaffer day?"

"Exactly," she said, trying not to dwell on those dark hazel eyes or the lingering feeling of Desmond's hand in hers.

Chapter Four

"So, what did you do with the apartment?" Kate asked as they walked down Main Street the next day.

"Packed it up," Sarah said. "Moved everything into storage. I'll have the movers go back once I know where I'm going next."

"Doesn't that get expensive? Moving everything across the country all the time?"

"Uh, yes. That's why it's usually in my contract."

"Smart."

"But I travel light. Packed two pairs of scrubs, my stethoscope and Parker. That's all I really need to start over."

Sarah held Parker's hand so as not to let him loose in the construction. He gaped, mostly at the steady line of trucks that rolled past them and the red-shirted volunteers on rooftops and on ladders, nailing down new shingles and replacing doors or windows. The diner was in the worst shape of the block, the entire front window missing. Yellow caution tape stretched across the opening, and Sarah could see the glass that sparkled on the floor. A pair of volunteers were inside, documenting damage. Thankfully, the diner was not their destination.

Kate led them down the street toward the hardware store. Wilkes & Sons Hardware was etched onto a sign above the door. Except for the strips of siding missing from the upper part of the building, the store looked almost untouched. Kate had ordered a new sign from the owner of the hardware store to replace the temporary one posted at the entrance to the ranch. Colm Wilkes was probably in his late sixties, with a full salt-and-pepper beard and the bushy eyebrows to match. He wore a pair of thin-rimmed glasses perched on the end of his nose, which he looked over as they approached.

Colm leaned over the counter and looked down at Parker. "Hello there, young man."

Parker shoved his head between Sarah's legs. "He's playing shy."

"I've got two grandsons of my own, and I still remember when they were that small. Believe it or not, they listened better back then."

Kate snorted. "See what you have to look forward to?"

"Don't remind me," Sarah said.

Colm laughed, then beckoned them to the back of the store. As they walked farther down the aisle, the hardware seemed to fade, replaced by hand-carved woodworks. There were rocking chairs, small stools, coffee tables, side tables, planter boxes and cutting boards. And that was just what Sarah could see in her immediate surroundings. She could tell the tourists would go wild over everything. Against the wall, Colm had a bunch of finished signs. Sarah spotted the one they were after in a heartbeat. Cardiff Ranch & Veterinary

Practice was displayed on a massive wooden sign in a looping, hand-painted scrawl.

"She is a beauty," Kate said, staring at it.

Sarah smiled at how happy she sounded. Parker stood beside Kate, unsure of what they were doing but desperate to be included.

"What do you think, buddy?" Kate asked him.

"Truck?" he asked, pointing to the sign that was easily double his height.

"Yeah, we're gonna put it in the truck," she said.

"Truck!" Parker repeated, bounding down the aisle.

"That's my cue," Sarah said, chasing after him. She caught him by the entrance, fiddling with the doorknob.

"I do appreciate the business," Colm said as he and Kate walked back to the front desk to settle the bill. "Everyone's a little shook up still, and they've been avoiding Main Street for the most part."

Sarah felt a pang of worry for the old man and his business. The tornado and subsequent destruction had driven off the last of the tourists for the year, according to Kate, and despite running a hardware store, it was clear that Colm made a good chunk of his income off his woodworking business. Sarah couldn't even imagine how the other townsfolk were coping.

"I'd only use the best," Kate said with a smile.

Colm dipped his head. "I'll have the boys get it in the truck for you since you've got the little one to run after."

"I'm parked over there." Kate gestured down the road. "We couldn't get any closer with all the construction."

"Luke, Caleb?" Colm called.

A pair of shaggy-haired teenage boys appeared from a room behind the desk.

"We heard you," one of them sighed before scurrying

to the back of the store. They muscled the sign down the aisle and out the door, bickering the entire way.

"Hey, knock it off," Colm shouted after them. "Sorry," he said. "Their parents don't want them running around town right now, with all the debris everywhere, so they're stuck at the store with me for the weekend. Probably end up killing each other by the end of it."

"That's smart," Kate said. "There's still downed trees and power lines and random furniture everywhere."

"Yeah, well, you try telling a teenager anything, and suddenly you're an enemy of the state."

Sarah rolled her eyes as Kate glanced at her. She was fully aware that she needed to cherish these moments with Parker. The days when he actually wanted to be with her would apparently be short-lived.

Kate paid, and they said farewell to Colm, heading out after Luke and Caleb. As they made their way back to the truck, there were even more red-shirted volunteers milling about. In the crowd, Sarah spotted a familiar face. Or maybe it was the familiar bandage work that caught her eye as Desmond lifted his hand to wave.

"Someone you know?" Kate asked, raising her brow.

"One of the patients from yesterday."

Kate gave him a surreptitious up and down. "Maybe you should go check on that."

Sarah snorted as Kate stepped away to help Luke and Caleb get the sign in the bed of the truck, but Desmond was already walking toward her.

"Hey there," he called. "Didn't think I'd see you in our neck of the woods again so soon."

She could see the top of the Team Rebuild command trailer from where she stood, so she supposed she was in the center of the chaos again.

"Did you change your mind?" he asked. To her confused look, he added, "I heard Lori offered you a spot on the team."

"Oh, not quite." She gestured to Parker where she held tight to his hand. "I sort of have my hands full right now with this one. So…"

"So," he said, stopping directly in front of her. He was tall enough that she had to tip her head back to look him in the eye. He stood there for a moment, smiling, and it sort of dazzled her.

"Ouch," Parker said, pointing to Desmond's hand.

"Yeah, that's an ouch, but I still have this hand. And you know what it's good for? Giving high fives." He held his hand out, and after a moment of consideration, Parker pressed his palm to Desmond's. "All right!"

Grinning, Parker dove for Desmond's knees, but Sarah managed to catch him in the act. "Sorry," she said. "He's in a headbutting stage. I feel like I need to tape a warning sign to him."

"Ah." Desmond chuckled. "The best of all the stages."

"Oh, the very best."

Sarah let him go, and Parker made a beeline for Desmond's knees again. Desmond caught him this time, scooping him up under his arm.

"You're asking for it, pal," Desmond said. Parker squealed in delight as Desmond flipped him upside down once before placing him back on the ground.

"You're setting impossibly high standards for me."

"Just letting him know who he's messing with," Desmond said, pretending to flex. He didn't need to pretend. Sarah could tell by looking at him, particularly at the way his shirt clung to his arms, that Desmond was the kind of man who carried an unassuming strength. His eyes and his smile were the first things you noticed. They charmed you easily, so you hardly took note of his muscle or his build. But the man could have been on the front of one of her romance novels. Sarah's hand almost itched to run up the front of his shirt, to feel the defined muscle under the fabric.

Thankfully, Parker chose that minute to pick up a handful of rocks and throw them into the sky, so Sarah quickly squashed those thoughts before they could run away from her. "Oh, no," she said. "We don't throw rocks."

Parker lifted his hand. "Ouch!"

"Yeah, you're going to hurt yourself." She picked him up and swung him onto her hip.

"Hey," Kate said, walking over. "We're all loaded up."

Sarah nodded. "Uh, Kate, this is Desmond. His shirt probably gives it away. But he's volunteering with Team Rebuild."

"Hi," Kate said.

"I've seen you around," Desmond said. "You're the one who keeps bringing all those baked goods."

"That's courtesy of my mother. But if you don't like them, don't tell me—because she's not going to stop baking anytime soon."

Desmond laughed, then turned to Sarah. "You keep looking at my hand."

Better than gazing foolishly into your eyes, Sarah thought to herself. "Because that dressing is practically falling off."

"Hey, they did their best. At least Melanie didn't faint this time."

"That *is* an improvement," Sarah said.

Watching the bandage sag irritated her like nothing else. In its current state it was protecting him from exactly nothing. Not from infection. Not from the elements.

"You could fix it," he suggested.

"I've already been accused of hijacking the medical tent once."

"I don't think they'd mind."

Kate held her hands out for Parker, inclining her head in the direction of the medical tent. "You go," she said. "I'll take Parker and run this sign back to the ranch. Call me when you're done, and I'll come get you."

"Are you sure?" Sarah asked.

"Oh, definitely. I'm going to use Parker to distract my mother from her recipe book."

Sarah said goodbye to her son, then passed Parker over. "Call me if he gets out of hand."

Kate kissed the side of his head. "He would never misbehave for his Auntie Kate." She took him to the truck, leaving Sarah and Desmond alone.

"Are you going to put this bandage out of its misery now?" Desmond asked.

"Yes, c'mon. Let's go steal some supplies."

They picked their way through the crowd. Sarah spotted Melanie at the tent, eating her lunch, and a young man with jet-black hair kicked back in a chair, scrolling on his phone. That must've been the Evan that Lori had mentioned yesterday.

"You're back!" Melanie said, jumping out of her seat, and Sarah wasn't sure if she was talking to her or Desmond.

Evan put down his phone. "Dude, what did you do?" he said to Desmond, gesturing to his hand. "We just wrapped that."

Desmond shrugged. "It's rough out there. But I brought reinforcements with some actual skill."

Evan smirked. "Oh, so this must be Sarah. All I've heard today from Lori and Mel and Desmond is how great your wound-care skills are. Too bad you had to work on the whiniest patient on the team."

Desmond lifted his hand, gesturing to the sagging bandage. He quirked a brow at Evan.

"What do you want from us?" Evan exclaimed jokingly. "Melanie is a newbie, and I'm a paramedic. I don't make things look pretty. I just patch holes." The radio on his waist began to chirp, requesting medical support, and Evan picked it up. "See, this is an actual problem we're going to attend to. C'mon, Melanie. Keep your bandages, Torres."

Desmond rolled his eyes, chuckling under his breath as Evan and Melanie hurried away after the call. "Guess you're in charge now," Desmond said to Sarah.

"Guess so." She gestured for him to take a seat. "Let's hurry before Lori finds me."

Sarah sanitized her hands, secured the supplies and got to work pulling down the old bandage. Her phone buzzed on the table. It was a text from Kate saying that Parker had fallen asleep on the way home.

"He is the spitting image of you," Desmond said, noticing the lock-screen photo of Parker on her phone. "Except for the—"

"Eyes," Sarah finished. "Those belong to his father."

"And his father…"

"Is not in the picture. Never has been," Sarah said curtly. It happened all the time. People always wanted to know where the other half was. She supposed it was a normal question. Or, at least, people thought it was normal. But she also grew tired of answering it all the time, and maybe for that reason she was a little short with him. "Sorry," she mumbled. "It's a single-mom thing."

"No, it's my fault for prying."

Sarah pursed her lips, struck momentarily by his

gaze. Maybe she was thinking too much about his eyes and not enough about the bandages in front of her. She got back to work.

"How's it looking?" Desmond asked.

"Good," she said. "No signs of infection. Does it hurt?"

"Not too bad," Desmond said.

Sarah prodded his hand. "How about now?"

"Well, if you're gonna do that."

Sarah laughed. He watched her as she cleaned and wrapped his hand again. Like last time, his gaze bore into hers whenever she looked up, setting her skin on fire. She made sure not to glance up again until she was done.

"Good as new," she announced.

Before she could consider what his answering smile meant, they were interrupted by a clipboard-wielding Lori. "I knew we hadn't seen the last of you."

"Just following up on my patient," Sarah said, clearing up the supplies.

"Once is a favor. Twice is asking for a job. And if you're asking..." Lori said. "I'm offering." She stood on her toes and threw her arm around Desmond's shoulders. "C'mon, you're really going to say no to faces like these? All these hardworking volunteers? We need you, Sarah. Desmond needs you."

"I really do," he said, holding up his hand.

Sarah laughed. "This feels like a setup."

"I am not above begging," Lori said.

Sarah bit her lip, considering the offer again. She had to admit, she did like stretching her nursing muscles a little. And compared to her usual work environment, this one was pretty low-key. Probably something she could volunteer a few hours of her time for if she could figure out a schedule for Parker. The more she thought about it, the more she actually liked the sound of it. And not just because it would mean she'd probably bump into Desmond every now and then. Maybe a little volunteering would be good for her while she figured out which contract to take next.

"If you can be flexible with the schedule, I can probably make something work."

"Welcome to the team," Lori said, tossing her a red Team Rebuild shirt.

"And you were just carrying this around?" Sarah said, smiling at the now-familiar logo on the shirt.

"I spotted you before I came over and figured I should come prepared. But honestly, I wasn't going to let you turn me down this time. Drop by the command trailer when you have a minute tomorrow, and we can talk details."

"Sounds good," Sarah said, waving as Lori hurried off to no doubt sort out a myriad of other problems.

"Guess we'll be seeing more of each other," Desmond commented.

"Guess so," Sarah said.

He stretched his fingers, holding out his bandaged hand. "It really is a work of art. I almost feel like I should be paying you for your time."

"Like all nurses, I accept payment in coffee."

"I'll remember that," Desmond said. "But until then, how about a ride home?"

Chapter Five

A light drizzle had started, turning the cornfields into an ocean of frosted gray gold through the window. Sarah traced the raindrops across the glass until they fell out of sight. She sat in the front seat of a borrowed Team Rebuild truck beside Desmond. Jordan, the man with the radiant smile she'd met in the lunch tent that first day, sat in the back. They'd collected Jordan on the way to the ranch, picking him up from a job site outside of town. At first she thought Desmond was simply doing the guy a favor considering the turn in the weather, but Sarah had quickly realized that Desmond and Jordan were more than volunteer buddies. They were also best friends. She could tell by the way they bickered over the radio.

"So, how'd you end up volunteering for Team Rebuild?" she asked Jordan once they'd settled on a soft rock station.

"Sorta got dragged into it the same way you did,"

he said, leaning between the front seats to punch Desmond in the arm. "By this guy."

"That is not true," Desmond said, rubbing at the spot. "There was no dragging of any kind. It was a mild suggestion."

"He's right," Jordan admitted. "After I got out I was looking for some sort of community again—"

"Got out?" Sarah asked.

"From the military," he clarified. "A lot of us are former or retired military of some kind. Me, Des, Lori. Once you leave that kind of organization you start to miss the camaraderie. The sense of purpose. The desire to serve. Volunteering for Team Rebuild helps fill the gap. Plus you've never met a group of men and women who could mobilize faster."

"Lori is starting to make a lot more sense now," Sarah said.

Desmond and Jordan laughed.

"Oh yeah, she's an officer through and through."

"Okay, I get it if you're retired," Sarah said. "You'd have extra time on your hands to volunteer. But how does the average person drop everything and show up in some random community?" Both Desmond and Jordan were clearly too young to be retired.

"I started a renovation business when I left the military," Desmond said. "Jordan and a couple other buddies came to work for me. We take turns rotating through Team Rebuild projects, lending our skills where they're necessary. The others hold the fort down back home."

"Where is home?" she asked as she pointed out the sign for the ranch. Desmond made a turn onto the gravel drive.

"Where *isn't* home?" Jordan countered. "When you've

been posted around the country as much as we have, one state is pretty much the same as the next."

"We're based out of North Carolina right now," Desmond said as they pulled up in front of the farmhouse. "Jordan wanted to relocate the business to Florida, but he got outvoted. He's still bitter about it."

"You stacked the vote against me." Jordan got out of the truck and turned back to Sarah. "One piece of advice—never bet against this man."

Sarah smirked as Jordan closed the door. "Is that true?"

Desmond shrugged. "Maybe a little. Nice place."

"It's Kate's. Well, her parents' place. But she's just bought into the ranch to build up her vet practice."

As they exited the truck, she spotted Nathan on his way back from the stables.

"Hey!" he called.

Sarah walked toward him, Desmond and Jordan on her heels.

"You've got a hole in your roof there," Desmond said, glancing up at the stables.

"We've got a few of those," Nathan said. "I'm Nathan Prescott. Kate's boyfriend. Amateur ranch hand. Failed carpenter."

"But photographer extraordinaire," Sarah clarified. "This is Jordan and Desmond."

"We volunteer with Sarah for Team Rebuild," Desmond said.

"*With* Sarah?" Nathan repeated, surprised. "Since when?"

"Since today." She held up her new shirt. "And it's not a big deal."

"I don't know," Jordan said. "Our project manager is pretty pleased with herself for recruiting Sarah."

"It's just a little gig," Sarah clarified. "To help keep my nursing skills from getting rusty."

"Well, congrats," Nathan said. "Anne will be pleased. Now she'll have a direct access point within the organization to funnel all her baking through."

Sarah snorted. "You know, Desmond and Jordan might know a thing or two about patching holes. Maybe they could give you some advice."

"Oh yeah?" Nathan said.

Desmond nodded. "You want to show us around?"

Nathan waved them toward the stables.

"I'll head inside and send Dale your way. I'm sure he'll want to be a part of this." Sarah jogged up the stairs and into the main house. Anne was watching the guys out the window, relaying all the happenings to Kate, who sat on the couch.

"You brought him home?" Kate said, her head tilting in Sarah's direction.

"You *know* him?" Anne said to Sarah before glaring at Kate. "You didn't tell me that part."

"I was getting to it."

"His name is Desmond," Sarah said. "And actually, *he* brought *me* home. The details are important here. He also brought his friend Jordan."

"What are they doing?" Kate wondered.

"Talking shop with Nathan. Something about patching holes in the stables. I'm supposed to be sending Dale out there."

"Dale!" Anne whisper-yelled down the hall.

The man emerged from his office, scowling at being beckoned. If Sarah hadn't been told that Dale had suffered a massive heart attack a few months ago, she'd never have known.

"Why are you whisper-yelling at me?" he asked.

"Parker's sleeping." Anne pointed out the window. "There are people in the stables who want to talk to you."

"Volunteers from Team Rebuild," Sarah clarified. "They're looking at all the holes."

Dale didn't need to hear any more. He slipped his boots on and hurried out the door with Kate calling after him, "Take it easy, Dad!"

"And they're qualified to do that?" Anne asked. "Look at holes?"

Kate snorted.

"Look at them. Patch them." Sarah shrugged. "Apparently they own a renovation business back in North Carolina. How was my child?"

"Oh, he's got me wrapped around his finger," Kate said. "You know how I know? Because his foot is currently jammed into my kidney but I'm afraid that if I move it'll wake him up."

Sarah leaned over the back of the couch, smiling at the way Parker was flopped on the cushions, his little feet pressed against Kate's side. "Yeah, he tends to do that. I think it's for warmth or something."

The oven timer beeped, and Anne hurried over to take her baking out.

"What is he *really* doing here?" Kate asked as Sarah slumped down onto the couch beside her.

"It's all very harmless, I swear."

Kate nudged her. "Is anything ever harmless with you?"

Sarah glossed over that comment. "Oh, I got a job. Well, a volunteer job." She passed Kate the red shirt she'd been carrying.

Kate held it up. "'Team Rebuild Medical Staff.'" A grin pulled at the corner of her mouth. "I knew you'd impressed Lori when she saw you yesterday. Should have known she wouldn't let you go very easily. That woman is determined."

"Very," Sarah agreed.

"You accepted the role, then?"

"Maybe. I'll have to see if I can figure something out with Parker."

"There's nothing to figure out," Anne said, surprising them both by appearing behind them. She leaned over the back of the couch, putting a gentle hand on Sarah's head. "You go help out. I'll keep an eye on the little guy when you're off doing your thing."

"Are you sure, Mama Cardiff?"

"Very sure."

"I told them they had to be flexible with the schedule. That I could only do a few hours a day."

"Sarah, don't worry about it. It's the least I can do if you're going to be volunteering to look after the folks that are fixing up our community."

When she said it like that, Sarah felt like less of a burden leaving Parker with the Cardiffs for a few hours here and there.

"Don't try to talk her out of it," Kate said. "If she's distracted by Parker, there won't be muffins in every inch of the fridge."

"Why are you complaining? You don't even live here anymore," Anne said.

Kate tipped her head back to look at her mother. "I'm worried they're going to start spilling over into the guest house fridge soon."

"Oh, you," Anne muttered, walking away.

"So you really think it's a good idea?" Sarah asked Kate.

"I'm fully on team If It Makes You Happy, Do It. So, does it?"

"Yeah, I think so."

"Well, then, as long as it makes you happy, I say give it a shot. If there happens to be an extremely attractive man that works for said organization too, well, that's just a perk of the role."

"That is not why I'm accepting the position," Sarah said.

Kate barked a laugh.

"Well, not entirely." Sarah wiggled her eyebrows.

"I knew it. Also, your kid sleeps through everything."

"Yeah, he could sleep through a freight train running through your living room. Apparently he only wakes up when he's on airplanes with strangers."

Sarah and Kate both turned on the couch as Anne hurried to the front door with a container full of baked goods.

"Oh God," Kate said. "She's starting to meddle."

"What?" Anne complained, throwing the door open to peek off the porch. "I'm just going to feed them a little. There's no harm in that."

"Nice try, Mama Cardiff," Sarah said. "Desmond's just a patient. Now a coworker."

"A very handsome patient and coworker."

"Isn't there, like, a rule about dating patients?" Kate asked.

"Who said anything about dating?" Sarah said. "Besides, I barely did anything. Stuck a Band-Aid on his hand and sent him on his way."

"Oh, there they are," Anne said, waving them down.

Sarah dropped her head into her hands.

"Now you know what I had to deal with while I was getting to know Nathan. C'mon, we'd better go supervise this interaction," Kate said. "Or else you might not want to show your face at that medical tent after all."

Sarah got up and pulled Kate to her feet. As they did, Parker stirred, bolting out of his nap. "Mom?"

"Hi, buddy." Sarah held her arms out for him.

"Oh, sure, you get the nice cuddles. I got the kidney kicks," Kate said.

Parker nuzzled against Sarah as they followed Anne onto the porch. Sure enough, Desmond, Jordan and Nathan were on their way back from the stables with Dale.

"Well, don't you look like a hardworking bunch," Anne called as they approached.

"I've got some reinforcements now," Nathan said. "Dale's on board, so Desmond and Jordan are going to come back tomorrow with the right tools and lumber. Help me do the repairs properly."

"And that's okay with Team Rebuild?" Kate asked.

"We'll run it by Lori," Desmond said. "But I don't think it'll be an issue since it's a shelter for the horses."

Jordan shot them a thumbs-up. "Lori loves horses."

"Well, isn't that lovely," Anne said. "Oh, here!" She hurried off the porch to pass off her baking. "We have some extra."

"Some?" Kate muttered in disbelief.

Jordan accepted the container gratefully. "You're the one supplying all the banana bread? I've died and gone to heaven."

Anne beamed.

"You're gonna have a hard time getting rid of him now," Desmond warned. "Nothing the man loves more than home cooking."

"Well, you're both welcome here anytime," Anne said. "You bring the appetites, and I'll set the table."

"I will hold you to that," Jordan called on his way back to their truck, already shoving banana bread into his mouth.

"He and Rusty could start a club," Kate murmured to Nathan. They grinned at each other, and Sarah again felt like she was missing out, not having met either of Nathan's friends yet.

"Well, we're off," Desmond said. "I'll see *you* tomorrow," he told Sarah. "Bright and early at your new post."

A pleasant buzz filled her chest. It was a curious feeling. Maybe there was something there. The spark of attraction, of course, but also a growing respect for this man who'd offered to help her best friend. She admired him, she realized suddenly, so she was just going to have to work harder at getting these pesky feelings to behave.

"Bye!" Parker shouted from Sarah's arms, surprising them all.

"Bye, buddy." Desmond waved, then followed Jordan to the truck.

"Well, Parker seems to like him," Kate noted.

"Parker likes everyone," Sarah said, kissing his head before setting him down. He scrambled down the porch steps. Kate, Sarah and Anne watched Desmond climb into the truck.

"Don't tell me we're all just gonna stand here and gawk at the man," Nathan said.

Kate nodded. "That's exactly what we're doing."

It was after dinner when an olive-green Volkswagen van rolled onto the ranch and Sarah finally got to meet the two people that Nathan considered his closest friends in the world—Rusty and Tara. They had followed him to Hatchet Lake to photograph the summer storm systems and hung around when he'd fallen for Kate and subsequently decided to make a life for himself at her side.

Seeing the trio together, gushing about spontaneous pictures they'd taken with the perfect lighting in the most remote of places, really sold Sarah on wanting to be a travel photographer. That was until she remembered that she possessed zero creative instincts. An art teacher in high school had once called her midterm project "a valid attempt"—and it was supposed to be a self-portrait.

Rusty burst out laughing as Sarah recounted the story. "Well, sounds like you found your calling in the end."

"True," Sarah said. "I don't need any creative vision to be a nurse."

"I don't know. That bandage job you did on Desmond seems like it took some creative ingenuity," Kate commented.

"Arts and crafts," Sarah said. "Parker could do that."

Hearing his name, the toddler poked his head up from where he was currently digging in the garden. Probably looking for bugs. He was going straight to the bath as soon as they were done outside. His little brow furrowed for a moment, but he'd obviously decided that mud and bugs were more fun than whatever Sarah was talking about, so he went back to work destroying one ecosystem at a time.

"*Oh*," Rusty said. "Who's Desmond?"

"We're not sure yet," Kate answered. "Either Sarah's crushing on him or he's crushing on Sarah."

"No one is crushing on anyone," Sarah clarified.

"He drove you home," Kate protested.

"As if that's a measurable indication of anything."

"He heard me say that I would pick you up when you were done. He went out of his way for you."

Sarah rolled her eyes and took a sip of her beer.

They'd settled on the porch of the guest house, sharing a few after-dinner drinks as Kate and Nathan caught up with Rusty and Tara. The group seemed to have enveloped Kate, and Sarah was glad her best friend had found a little community of her own.

"This town is full of gorgeous, burly men," Rusty said. "I might never leave."

"Now you're cool with ranch life?" Nathan said.

"He meets one attractive farmer," Tara explained, "and suddenly he's Old MacDonald."

"I could pull off plaid and overalls."

The group snickered, and Sarah found herself falling a little bit in love with this dynamic. Rusty was as exuberant as his red hair, easily matching Parker's energy at his most high-strung and filled with witty one-liners. Sarah got the impression that he didn't take anything in life too seriously, and he was exactly the kind of friend you wanted around in a crisis. Tara was almost his polar opposite. She cracked the occasional smile and offered scandalous glimpses into Rusty and Nathan's past ventures around the globe, but Sarah suspected it was her steady, observant nature that made her a good photographer.

"You want another?" Kate asked as she collected her own bottle and Nathan's.

"I've still got plenty," Sarah said, tipping her bottle in Kate's direction.

"That's not like you."

"Um, I grew up a lot since birthing this one," Sarah said, gesturing to Parker.

"We're home tonight. I think you can let loose a little."

Sarah smirked. "You want to deal with drunk Sarah and a whiny Parker at bedtime?"

"You know what, good call," Kate said, heading inside to get more beers. "You just sip yours."

"*I* want to see drunk Sarah," Rusty said.

"Watch it, or you'll be cut off too," Tara warned him. "You're as bad as a toddler when you're drunk."

"She doesn't like children," Rusty stage-whispered to Sarah.

Tara nudged the back of his head. "That's not true. They just make me nervous to be around."

Sarah found that funny. "Nervous how?"

Tara shrugged. "I don't know what to do with them. I grew up in a really artsy family. I was around adults all the time. Always felt distant from kids my age. And now they sort of freak me out. I mean, I can photograph them. Appreciate the cuteness from a distance. But when I have to directly engage with them beyond, 'Okay, now smile,' I feel like I have no idea what I'm doing."

Rusty nodded along with everything. "Basically we've deduced that Tara has the personality of a cat."

"I was the same way in the beginning," Sarah admitted. With the strained relationship she had with her own mother, she'd never really thought about having kids of her own. "Honestly, I didn't think I had a maternal bone in my body. But then Parker showed up, and I figured it out. I find it best if you don't overthink it. Kids don't really know any better. Parker would be friends with a rock."

Nathan choked on his laugh. "Kate'll love to know how easily replaceable she is."

"Kate will love what?" Kate asked as she returned, handing Nathan another beer.

"Nothing," everyone chorused at once.

"Oh, sure," Kate said. "Talk about me when I'm not here."

"What do you think we've been doing for the past three months?" Rusty said. He didn't look up from his hand as he said it.

"What are you doing over there?" Sarah asked him.

"Surgery," Rusty said, holding up a pair of tweezers.

"He got a sliver as he was gawking at the farmer," Tara explained.

"I was lining up a shot with my camera," Rusty countered.

"Of his…never mind," Tara said, glancing at Parker.

"Give it here," Sarah said, holding out her hand for the tweezers.

"Are you sure?" Rusty said. "You're, like, half a beer in."

Sarah scoffed. "You're going to reach your bone before you dig that out." Rusty slumped toward her and handed over the tweezers. "Are these clean?"

"If you mean did I pour half a bottle of rubbing alcohol on them before using them, then yes. Who knows how long they've been in that first aid kit."

"Perfect. Sit down," Sarah said, patting the porch step next to her.

"Okay." Rusty glanced around at the others before looking Sarah dead in the eye. "Now that it's just the two of us," he joked, "on a scale of you-don't-interest-me to where's-the-nearest-horizontal-surface, how attractive is this man who drove you home?"

"Oh," Sarah said without missing a beat. "He's definitely a would-do-you-up-against-a-vertical-surface kind of attractive."

Rusty gaped at her for a moment. "My God, where have you been all my life?"

Sarah threw her head back and laughed.

Chapter Six

It was a cool morning sheltered beneath the first aid tent, the clouds full and threatening rain, each gray inch blocking out the sun. After providing Lori with all the necessary paperwork and agreeing to a schedule, Sarah had started her first official shift with Team Rebuild. Thankfully, she'd been licensed to work as a nurse in Michigan upon graduation, and by some miracle, she'd upkept her license yearly since then. In the end, it was easier to pay for her Michigan nursing license even though she wasn't living here than to have to jump through the hoops of the licensing process again if she ever returned to work in the state. For once, her desire to constantly move from job to job and state to state was working in her favor. Now she was dressed in her red Team Rebuild shirt, and the thrill of it still hadn't quite worn off. It was the same thrill she got every time she started working at a brand-new hospital. There was something truly special about loving her job.

Melanie had traipsed into the tent twenty minutes after Sarah, looking like she was still half asleep. She pulled the hood of her sweatshirt over her head until her eyes were obscured and threw herself down into a chair.

"Not a morning person?" Sarah asked as she started to properly assess the supply situation in the tent. She hadn't wanted to poke and pry too much before; she'd just used what was absolutely necessary to treat Desmond's hand and Melanie's fainting spell. Now that she had the official green light, she was going to tear this place apart and organize it.

Melanie grunted in response, pulling her knees up to her chest.

"She won't be coherent for at least an hour," Desmond said.

Sarah looked up to find him standing there, charming grin and all. She chuckled. "Good to know."

Desmond produced a cup of coffee and handed it to her.

"I didn't think you'd remember."

"What? That I committed to paying you in coffee for your excellent nursing care? Or that it was your first official day on the job?"

Sarah accepted the cup gratefully. "Both?"

"Well, it's the lunch tent's finest brew."

"As a nurse who used to work a lot of night shifts, my tolerance for truly terrible coffee is surprisingly high."

"Then drink up," Desmond said. "Can't be any worse than what you'd dig up in a hospital staff room."

Sarah looked over her shoulder at Melanie. If anything, she needed the coffee more than either of them.

"Oh, she doesn't drink coffee. We've tried that on her before. Best just to let her walk around like a zombie for a while."

"Right. One zombie assistant. Should we take a look at your hand while you're here?"

"You're the boss," he said. "Whatever you want."

Sarah gestured to a seat, and Desmond sat himself down in it. She carefully unwrapped the bandage and inspected the wound.

"What's your assessment?"

"Honestly, it looks great. No signs of infection. I'd say you're good to leave it open to the air to finish healing. But since you run around here all day, moving debris and whatever else Lori has you doing, I'd suggest we put a light dressing on it to keep it clean while you're working. And I'd recommend wearing work gloves for some added protection." Sarah glanced up at him. He was biting the rim of his coffee cup, his teeth grazing the edge of the paper. Immediately her thoughts turned wicked, and she couldn't stop imagining an assortment of other things she might like his teeth to graze over.

"Good plan," he said. "Let's do it."

Glad for something constructive to distract her brain, Sarah gathered her supplies and set to work.

"Looking good, X-ray!" Jordan crowed, appearing at Desmond's side. In his arms he held a stack of boxes.

"Are those for me?" Sarah asked.

Jordan nodded. "Special delivery."

Sarah pointed to the end of the table. "Could you put them over there?"

"You got it," he said, stacking the supplies in a neat pile. Then he turned back to Desmond. "Looks like your hand is all healed up."

"Thanks to Sarah," Desmond agreed. "I'd have been sidelined without her."

"Must be magic in your fingers," Jordan said as Sarah

removed her gloves. "My mom always said people with magic in their fingers do one of two things."

"What's that?"

"Heal or cook."

"Well, I certainly don't cook," Sarah said.

"Then we're a match made in heaven."

"Here we go," Desmond complained with a fond smile.

"You cook?" Sarah asked him.

Jordan beamed. "I know my way around the kitchen. I know my way around the barbecue. And I've got an apron that says *Kiss the Cook.* I'm as legit as they come."

Sarah crossed her arms, eyeing Jordan from across the table. "Why do I feel like that's a pickup line you've used in a bar before?"

Desmond snickered. "Because it is."

The next thing Sarah knew, Jordan had Desmond in a headlock that pulled them both to the ground.

"The first aid tent is not equipped to set broken bones," Sarah muttered, doing her best to ignore them. "Just so you're aware."

"Desmond!" Lori called from the command trailer.

Desmond and Jordan broke apart, both of them grinning like fools. There was something untroubled and childish about them when they were together. It wasn't something Sarah was used to finding in a man that she found as attractive as Desmond. Not that she was thinking about him like that.

"Now you're in trouble," Jordan muttered, jumping up and pulling Desmond to his feet.

Desmond ran his uninjured hand through his hair, pushing back the unruly strands until they parted neatly on either side of his forehead again. Sarah picked up a clipboard to hide the obvious fact that she was staring until Desmond raced off to chat with Lori.

Sarah let out a breath that rattled her lips and attempted to tackle the boxes Jordan had delivered. They were sealed with so much tape she probably could have shipped them to the moon in one piece.

"Here, let me," Jordan said, flipping out a multi-tool from his pocket.

"Thanks. Why Ray?" Sarah asked him.

"What?"

"You called Desmond 'Ray' earlier."

"Oh, nah," Jordan said. "X-ray. Short for…well, whatever the heck *X-ray* stands for."

"Is that, like, a nickname or something?"

"Or something," Jordan said.

Sarah stared at him expectantly.

Jordan got the box open and handed her a few packages of new gloves. "Desmond and I were deployed overseas together. I was infantry. He was a medic. There was this running joke in camp about Desmond. That's where the name came from."

"What was it?"

Jordan grinned a bit, and Sarah knew it was a memory tainted with both good and bad. "Whenever Desmond stepped out beyond the wire with a section, he always brought someone back destined for imaging. So the name X-ray became a thing."

"Oh," Sarah said, not quite sure whether she should smile or frown.

"No," Jordan said quickly. "It's not like that. What I mean is…most healthcare staff didn't leave camp. They stayed inside the wire. But the medics did. *Des* did. They were the ones out there with the soldiers. And when you went out with Desmond, you knew he was going to bring you back. Didn't matter what happened or where your section ended up, you knew you were safe with him because he always got you back in time." Jordan huffed a laugh. "Sometimes the people he brought back weren't even the people he left with."

"*Oh*," Sarah said again, a shiver sliding down both her arms.

"He doesn't like to talk about it like that, but he saved a lot of lives while he was over there."

Sarah didn't know what else to say. She was surprised on a lot of fronts. Yesterday, Jordan had mentioned they were former military, but she hadn't realized that Desmond was a medic. If that was the case, what was he doing hanging around the first aid tent? He could have easily done his own wound care. In fact, why wasn't he in charge of Medical? He clearly had more than enough experience.

"Where do you want these?" Jordan asked, unpacking the boxes like it was nothing. All those years of service, all those experiences.

"Uh, over there," Sarah said, pointing to a vague spot behind her.

"I'll start building a wall around Melanie," Jordan said. "See how long it takes her to break free."

"I heard that," Melanie muttered darkly.

Sarah held up her coffee cup. "I'm going for a refill. Don't do anything dangerous while I'm gone."

"I make no promises," Melanie said.

Sarah had only taken a few steps before Desmond caught up with her.

"Did Lori fire you?" she asked.

"Nah, she loves me too much. She does want me to drive out to pick up one of our teams though. They've been sawing trees on one of the farmsteads." Desmond fell in line beside her. "So, what sordid details did Jordan give away about me?"

"How do you know we were talking about you?"

He grinned. "You just told me."

Sarah rolled her eyes. She'd walked right into that one. "He explained why he calls you X-ray."

Desmond didn't have anything to say to that.

"You told me you were in construction," Sarah continued. "That you have a renovation business together."

"I am. I do. *Now.*"

"So, the whole medic thing was…what?"

"A past life," he said.

"That's quite the career change." She couldn't help but wonder why.

"I once worked with this social worker who told me we have six or seven careers over the course of our lifetime."

"And what number are you on?"

Desmond grinned. "Eight."

"Can I ask why you didn't stick with it?"

He nodded. "It's nothing soul-shattering. Like most of the people who came back from overseas, I saw a lot of stuff while I was deployed. Impossible things. Some terrible things. But a lot of medical miracles too. Holes in arteries that were plugged with fingers to keep people from bleeding out. Bodies literally held together with staples and tape. By the time my deployment was winding down, I'd had my fill. The rush, the adrenaline, it starts to eat at you after a while. And somewhere along the way that thrill that you feel as you're trying to save a life, it became anxiety. I knew it was time to pull back then. I still like medicine. I just didn't want to be the one making those life-and-death calls in the field anymore."

Sarah could understand that. For as much as emergency medicine thrilled her, there was inherent risk in it. Unpredictability. Uncertainty. As good as the teams were that she'd worked on and as many people as they'd saved, there were still some they didn't save. And somehow, those always outweighed the good. If you didn't find the right balance, it could unravel you.

"So you finished your deployment, and then what?"

"I released from the military. Thought about what I wanted to do next. I'd done a little construction in my late teens with my dad before I joined up. I was pretty good at it, even. And I knew a bunch of former military folks that needed work on the other side. The business sort of sold itself, really."

"And you like it? Renovating?"

"I still get to fix things," Desmond said. "Just far less life-and-death. And when we get that itch to go out and do something truly important, we put our names down for Team Rebuild. It's been a pretty good experience so far."

The radio on his hip started to crackle, a sharp request coming through.

"This is Desmond. Lori, say again?" He held the radio closer to his ear.

"Are you with Sarah?" Lori crackled.

"Yes," he said. "We're almost at the lunch tent."

"We've got a medical response request from one of the sawyer teams," Lori said.

"The one I was supposed to pick up?" Desmond asked.

"Yeah," Lori confirmed. "Reports of an injury as they were clearing a tree from the road."

"Did they say what kind of injury?"

"Report's still coming in but sounds non-emergent."

"Understood. Sarah's on her way."

The radio quieted.

"I'll throw a go bag together," Sarah said.

Desmond nodded. "I'll drive."

They both turned and hurried in opposite directions. *Non-emergent* meant non-life threatening, but that didn't mean they should dawdle.

"I'll meet you at the first aid tent with the truck!" Desmond called over his shoulder. "Two minutes."

Sarah darted between volunteers, muttering, "Excuse me," so often that she was out of breath by the time she reached the first aid tent.

"What's going on?" Jordan asked.

"Request for medical in the field," Sarah said, finding a go bag under the table. She opened it, scanning the supplies, adding a few more things. "Desmond's going to drive me out."

"I better come too," Jordan said. "In case you need some muscle." He grabbed the portable stretcher, and Sarah tossed the AED onto it. She had no idea what kind of situation they were walking into. With chain saws involved, she thought of the worst things. Severed limbs. Blood and bone and body parts that would need to be kept on ice. She'd seen her fair share of accidental finger amputations in the ER. The fact that they'd called for a Team Rebuild medical response and not an ambulance forced Sarah to reel in her imagination.

"Do you want to come?" Sarah asked Melanie. "Might be a good learning opportunity."

"Is there gonna be a lot of blood?"

"I wouldn't say a lot," Sarah said honestly. "But there could be some."

"I think I might stay here. Hold the fort down."

Sarah scribbled her number onto a piece of paper and handed it to her. "If anything requires more than a Band-Aid and you get overwhelmed, call me. Okay?"

Melanie nodded. "Thanks."

A horn blared, and Sarah turned to see Desmond roll up in that Team Rebuild-branded truck. Jordan was already running toward it, throwing the stretcher into the bed of the truck. Sarah chased after him.

She climbed in beside Desmond, and he navigated out of the camp and down Main Street. It didn't take long for Sarah to spot the red shirts. They were gathered on the side of the road where a large uprooted tree had been sawn into moveable chunks.

"Medical?" one of the volunteers asked as Desmond slowed and rolled down the window. He nodded, and the woman pointed them on. "It's Greg. We set him down over there."

Desmond pulled ahead, past the tree, and Sarah got her first glimpse of their patient. He was stretched out on the grass, his head thrown back, eyes squinted in pain. But no one was screaming, and there was no immediate sense of panic. Most reassuring of all was the distinct lack of blood.

Sarah hopped out of the truck, throwing the go bag over her shoulder.

She approached Greg, doing a quick scan of him and the surroundings. The other volunteers backed off.

"Hi…Greg?" she said. "My name's Sarah. I'm a nurse. Can you tell me where it hurts?"

"My ankle," he gasped.

Sarah let out a massive breath of relief. Trying to control a bleed out here was not her idea of a good time. It was almost as bad as a heart attack at thirty-six thousand feet. An ankle injury she could handle.

She looked down at Greg's right leg. His ankle was visibly swollen, already puffing up over his sock. "What happened?" she asked, pulling his pant leg back gently.

"Hit a divot in the field. I didn't even see it. Caught

my foot and I twisted wrong, and next thing I knew I was on the ground."

"Okay," she said, scanning for any obvious sign that it was broken. No exposed bone anywhere. No fracture pressing against the skin. It didn't rule out a break—it just meant that she couldn't see it. Sarah gently pressed against his swollen skin, checking to make sure his circulation was still strong. No issues there. "Hear any snaps or pops when you fell?"

Greg shook his head.

"Any numbness or tingling now?"

"No, just pain."

"Is there pain all the time or only—"

"If I move it," he said. "Yeah."

"And did you try to walk on it after it happened?"

"Tried to get up, but when the pain spiked, the guys said I should sit and wait until the medical team got here."

Sarah smiled. "Well, I don't see any obvious signs that it's broken. But we probably need to get some additional help to rule that out."

Desmond inclined his head, and she stood to speak to him.

"What are you thinking?" he asked.

"I'm guessing a mild sprain. He probably needs to be off his foot for a few days. A pair of crutches might help him get around. Definitely no more field work for the next week or so. But he really should have someone else look at it to confirm. Maybe an X-ray if they're more concerned."

Sarah glanced from Desmond to Jordan. "Want to help me get him in the truck?"

Jordan jumped into action, helping Greg to his feet. Together they toddled to the back seat.

Desmond pulled away as the radio on his hip crackled to life with Lori's voice asking for a report. "We're on scene now. Patient is being loaded into the truck. Sarah thinks we have an ankle sprain."

Lori's voice chirped back. "Take him to the hospital for assessment."

"What about the medical tent?" Sarah asked. "Melanie's alone right now."

Desmond relayed the question.

"I'll have Evan come in early to cover," Lori responded. "Keep me posted."

With that, Sarah climbed into the truck beside Greg, grateful to have both Desmond and Jordan along for the ride.

Chapter Seven

Sarah had propped Greg's foot up on the center console between the front seats to keep it elevated while they drove. She'd used a rolled-up blanket to keep his leg from being jostled side to side, a trick she'd learned after recertifying her first aid training for the umpteenth time.

"Greg, when this is all over, we're gonna talk about the importance of foot powder in your boots, man." Jordan cracked the window, and Desmond snorted. Even Greg laughed, though he was clearly uncomfortable.

Sarah had smelled worse than stinky feet in her time as a nurse. Heck, she had a toddler. Strange and unusual smells were par for the course.

While Greg grimaced in the back seat beside her, she dug around in her go bag for some Tylenol or ibuprofen to take the edge off his pain and swelling. After her second pass, she realized that she hadn't tossed any into the bag, too concerned about packing gauze and wound-care supplies. Even with Lori's assurance that the injury was non-emergent, Sarah had still expected something far worse than a possible sprained ankle.

She'd expected blood.

She'd been prepared for blood.

"Turn here," Jordan said, reading the directions off his phone for Desmond. Jordan had been placed in charge of navigation since Sarah was occupied with first aid and Desmond was behind the wheel. According to Google Maps, the closest local hospital was still twenty-seven minutes away.

Sarah watched as the fields rolling along either side of the road turned to grass, then to packed earth and finally to stretches of pavement and brick buildings. The hospital was located between the airport and Hatchet Lake, which meant it was likely the same hospital Kate's father had been at when he'd had his heart attack.

They passed a strip mall housing a small family-owned restaurant, a convenience store and a gas station. The farther into the city they drove, the more Hatchet Lake felt like something out of a storybook. Sarah hadn't recently thought about McDonald's or Starbucks or any of the regular places she usually stopped at to feed her caffeine addiction before she went in to work a series of twelve-hour shifts. At the ranch or even in town, it was easy to forget these places existed. People got their coffee at the diner when it was open. They drank their beer at the local pub. Everything was quaint and quiet and more personal.

Sarah wasn't sure if she liked the idea of everyone knowing her name, but as they pulled into the hospital parking lot, she suddenly remembered what it was to be a small fish in a big pond. Desmond drove around the lot twice before a spot opened up. There were patients and employees in scrubs and first responders everywhere.

As Sarah climbed out of the truck, she looked back at Greg. "You stay put," she said. "I'm going to go track down a wheelchair, then we'll get you checked in."

He nodded once, then reclined back in his seat.

"I'll come help you," Desmond offered.

They hurried down the sidewalk toward the amalgamation of buildings. The main building was a muddy brown color with slim tinted windows in the front. A tall gray addition poked up from behind, like a mountain towering over the rest of it. The sign for the emergency department was highlighted by bright red neon letters. They glowed even in the daytime, and Sarah could tell that the ER was in the older part of the hospital.

"Over there," she said.

Sirens wailed as they entered the waiting room, and Sarah was immediately hit with two distinct smells. Bleach and vomit. She wrinkled her nose as a custodian mopped in a corner, clearly cleaning up a mess someone had left behind.

There were dozens of chairs with speckled green seats staggered about the room. The TV mounted in the corner only switched between the Weather Channel and the local news. It was the same in every hospital. She walked straight past seated patients and up to the triage window. Before she even reached the window, a door popped open and a nurse wearing bright blue scrubs waved her over.

"I was told to keep an eye out for the red shirts." Sarah glanced from herself to Desmond. She supposed the Team Rebuild shirts were like flashing signs outside of Hatchet Lake. "Lori called ahead," the nurse clarified. "Said you were bringing someone in."

"He's in the truck," Sarah said. "I think we need a wheelchair."

The nurse directed them to an alcove with wheel-chairs, and while Desmond went back to the truck to retrieve Greg, Sarah started the check-in procedure. There were a lot of questions she couldn't answer since she wasn't the patient, but she gave them whatever info they needed on behalf of Team Rebuild and confirmed Lori's number in case they had any follow-up questions.

By the time she was done with her part, Desmond had wheeled Greg into the waiting room and the triage nurse had arrived to escort him into the back.

"You two have a seat," she said. "We'll keep you posted."

Sarah sat down, and Desmond sunk into a chair next to her. "Waiting rooms are the worst," he muttered. "Feels like prison for the sick."

"This one's not that bad. You've got TV." She pointed to a vending machine. "Snacks. What more could you ask for?"

"Those snacks have probably been expired for years."

Sarah laughed. "No way. They're the one thing in here that actually gets updated regularly. The nurses totally raid the vending machines on the night shift."

"You'd think there would be a chicken-soup vending machine considering it's a hospital."

"There are zero medicinal benefits to eating chicken soup when you're sick."

"Tell that to every mom everywhere."

Sarah laughed again. That was so easy to do around Desmond, she realized. Sitting here in the ER, waiting on Greg, she didn't feel anxious or bored. Being with Desmond was nice. Even if the waiting room did still sort of smell like puke. "I think most people would rather have a beer than chicken soup anyway."

Desmond glanced around. "You know, I think you're

right. This crowd would totally enjoy a beer at the Pint Pub with Old Joe."

"Ah, so you've already met the surly owner I've heard so much about?" Sarah had been given the run-down by Kate, and she knew that Joe had owned and operated Hatchet Lake's only pub since the beginning of time. Thankfully it had pulled through the storm with little to no damage, meaning it had become the hub of activity and sustenance while the diner was under construction.

"First thing Jordan and I like to do when we travel is have a beer with the locals. It's a good way to get to know the people."

"Too bad the diner is still closed." Sarah had also been hearing about Diane's famous pancakes and pies since she'd arrived. "It sounds like exactly the kind of place I'd love to take Parker for breakfast."

"We'll get Diane back up and running in no time. Probably should have started with her repairs," he joked. "Her lunch menu might have been better than the pub's."

The same nurse poked her head out of the triage room door and beckoned to them. Unsure, Sarah and Desmond followed her into the back of the ER where patients were assessed and treated.

"Greg said you might be able to help with the history," the nurse said, looking over her shoulder at Sarah. "You were on the scene?"

"We responded to the call," she said. "Is he already in with the doctor?"

"Not yet. Managed to get him down to X-ray first."

"That was fast." Sarah must have looked surprised because the nurse just laughed.

"Doc called in a favor with Imaging. They cut their lunch short for him."

"It's nice to know people," Desmond said.

"It really is," the nurse agreed. "You know any good people? 'Cause we could really use a few more nurses running around this joint."

Desmond playfully put his hands on Sarah's shoulders. "She's our only one, and you can't have her."

"Might have to keep her as an offering to Radiology."

"Looks like we're gonna have to Bonnie and Clyde our way out of here with Greg," Desmond joked.

He had such easy rapport with strangers, and Sarah liked that about him. She'd always found that her job was easier when she got along with the other staff, and easy banter went a long way to solidifying those relationships. Sarah had never been the kind of person to struggle with filling silences or talking to new patients. As a kid she'd gotten in trouble in school for talking too much, but now she considered it one of her superpowers.

The only thing about being an adult was that she'd learned to turn her power on and off to avoid annoying everyone within a six-foot radius.

"If you want to just wait here," the nurse said when they reached a small exam room. "Patient should be back any minute, and the doc's already got his chart."

"Thanks," Sarah said. "Sorry—what's your name?"

"Sheila."

"Thank you, Sheila. We really do appreciate all the help." Sarah was very aware that they could have been sitting in the waiting room for hours.

Sheila smiled, asked them to wish Greg a speedy recovery when they saw him and hurried off to Triage once more.

Sarah peeked inside the room, noting a bed with plain sheets and an assortment of medical instruments fastened to the wall. Though the room maintained the older finishes common to the rest of the ER, it had also been plastered with so many posters on good hand hygiene that the walls were almost nonexistent. It was chaotic in a familiar sort of way.

"Hey there," a man called as he made his way toward them. He threw his gloves into the trash and used some sanitizer on his hands. "Sorry, I was just finishing up with someone. Heard Team Rebuild had a patient for me?"

"We sure do," Desmond said, stepping forward to shake his hand.

"Doctor Beckett," he said. "But call me James."

"Sarah," she said as he reached for her hand next. She noticed he wore sharp rectangular glasses. They were a few shades darker than his hair, which was graying at the temples despite the fact he couldn't have been much older than Sarah herself. Clearly he was just one of those men who went gray early and wore it well. The little bit of salt-and-pepper gave him a distinguished charm. Sarah liked to think that she was good at reading doctors. She'd worked with enough of them to be able to pick out the ones who were short-tempered or stuffy. But James exuded warmth and patience. He was the kind of doctor she never would have hesitated to call at two in the morning to ask for orders. She liked him instantly.

"Want to give me the rundown?" James asked.

"Fifty-year-old male complaining of acute pain in his right ankle. Able to weight bear with some discomfort. Visibly swollen. Said he twisted it in a divot in the field where they were working."

"No visible bone deformity?"

Sarah shook her head. "Hoping you could help us rule out a fracture with the X-ray."

"I called in a favor," James said, whispering like it

was the hospital's biggest secret, "so it should be back anytime."

"We heard," Desmond said.

James frowned, and Sarah laughed. "The nurses know all," she told him.

"Can't get anything past them," he agreed. "They usually know my lunch order before I know it myself."

A call bell went off and didn't stop.

"Busy place you got here," Sarah remarked. "Sheila said you guys are short-staffed?"

"We had a lot of nurses leave at once, some unexpectedly. A couple got poached by the ICU. One went off on maternity leave early. One went back to school to become a nurse practitioner. Happy for them all. Bad timing for us." He sighed and smiled despite himself.

Sarah could understand why he was trying to get them in and out quickly, which made her appreciate him calling in a favor all the more. "Team Rebuild appreciates everyone's time."

"I'm happy to do it," James said. "It feels like the least I can do to help out after what happened. The ER manager talked about sending a team down to support Hatchet Lake after the storm, but we didn't have the staff to spare long term. I was a little disappointed, honestly. It's been a while since I've done any kind of field medicine, so the skills could have used some work."

A wheelchair appeared at the end of the hall.

"Ah," James said. "You must be Greg, the ankle guy."

"That's me," Greg muttered. "Tripped over my own two feet, and here I am."

"Come on back," James said. "We'll get you sorted out." James took over from the nurse and wheeled Greg back to the exam room. When the door closed, Sarah wandered down the hall. A few more call bells sounded.

Sarah could hear people being told not to bend their arms as their IV pumps went off.

Desmond looked around, tapping his foot. "Doesn't it bother you?"

"What?"

"Everything beeping at once?"

She shrugged. "You learn to tune it out. To hear what's actually important."

"How do you know which bells are important and which aren't?"

"I don't know," Sarah laughed. "You can just kind of tell when someone is going to code versus when they want more ice for their water. It's like a sixth sense."

Desmond smirked but his foot kept tapping, and she gently pressed her hand to his arm. "Hey, you can go wait with Jordan in the truck if this is bothering you." He'd told her why he'd left medicine. Maybe just being around the chaos of the ER was enough to heighten his anxiety.

"Oh, the incessant dinging is driving me up the wall," he confirmed. "But not in that way. More like the way it does when you get put on hold and a loop of music plays. I actually don't mind the chaos. There's no stakes when I'm not in charge of decisions that affect people's lives, so being here doesn't bother me. Not like that at least."

Sarah nodded.

"You were worried about me?" he teased.

Sarah rolled her eyes. "I already have one patient on my hands. I didn't feel like adding you to the list."

His entire face scrunched playfully. "I think maybe you just care about how I feel."

"I will leave you here and tell Jordan to drive away."

"You wouldn't dare."

Before they could determine if she really *would* dare, the door to the exam room popped open and James and Greg appeared.

"What's the verdict?" Desmond asked.

"Doc says I've got a mild sprain. Gotta do this RICE thing."

"Rest. Ice. Compression. Elevation," James repeated. "And no chain saws for a while."

"You're on desk duty, pal," Desmond said, taking the wheelchair from James. "I'll get him settled in the truck and run this back to you."

"Thanks—again," Sarah said to James.

"No trouble." He handed her a folded-up piece of paper. "That's a copy of my report in case you need to file it. If the ankle is bothering him, he can take some medication for the discomfort and the—"

"Swelling," Sarah finished for him. She grinned. "I'll make sure he does."

She turned and followed Desmond out of the ER. While they'd been inside, Jordan had made a coffee run, and Sarah could have kissed him right there, smack on the lips. She cradled her Starbucks between her hands and grinned the entire ride back to Hatchet Lake.

When they returned to camp, they stopped outside the command trailer to talk to Lori.

"How's our patient?" she asked.

"Down and out," Sarah said. "He's gotta rest his ankle."

Lori peered through the open truck window at Greg. "You can work admin with me," she joked. "I need help with all these incident reports I keep having to file."

Greg glared at Lori, unimpressed, and Sarah under-

stood that look. Paperwork was the bane of her existence, but as a nurse there was a never-ending pile of it.

Lori turned to Sarah. "And I'll need a write-up
from you."

"Of course. I'll do it before I leave for the day."

Lori turned to Jordan then. "You mind filling Greg's
spot for the afternoon?"

"Sure thing," he said.

Lori nodded. "Are you two good with the patient?"

Desmond shot her a thumbs-up. "We've got it."

While Sarah retrieved some ice packs and a pair of
crutches from their supplies in the first aid tent, Desmond got Greg situated in the lunch tent with his leg
propped up on a pillow. Sarah found them and passed
the ice and crutches off to Greg before returning to the
first aid tent to finish up her report for Lori. She relayed
the event to Evan, with follow-up instructions for Greg.
"Make sure he doesn't keep the ice on too long. And
remind him to take some meds if he's in pain."

"I've got it," Evan said. "Go home to your kid."

Sarah smiled. When she was all packed up, Desmond
was still hanging around.

"Busy first day, huh?"

"I thought you were on your lunch break?"

"I am, technically. I was actually wondering if you
wanted to grab a bite before you head back up to the
ranch."

"I could eat," Sarah said. The caffeine had awak-
ened her appetite, and it was only then that she realized
that she was running on coffee and a slice of banana
bread today.

"The lunch tent usually has something," Desmond
said. "But we could always go to the pub if you want a
break from Team Rebuild stuff."

Was he inviting her on a lunch date?

Sarah's lips twisted at the thought. Lunches in staff lounges or break rooms or even in lunch tents with colleagues were nothing new. Sarah was used to sharing her lunch hour with a myriad of coworkers. But lunch elsewhere with a single coworker—and someone as attractive as Desmond—was more than that.

He was asking her out.

She usually had qualms about starting something with coworkers. She liked to keep her work life and her social life separate. That way there were no messy feelings in the way of doing a good job.

But this isn't a job, some sly part of her brain whispered.

Technically, no. It was a volunteer position. Short-term. She wasn't on a contract here. She could have lunch with Desmond without worrying about work complications.

"Unless you've got to get back to Parker," Desmond added.

Sarah checked her phone. "I've got some time to kill before Kate comes to get me," she said. "Let's go."

They made their way through the menagerie of tents and stopped in at the pub. It was your typical dark, dingy haunt with sleek wooden tables, old peeling vinyl booth seats and cobwebbed corners. Sarah liked it immediately. A man, probably this Old Joe she kept hearing about, stood behind the bar. He was wiry and thin, with a gray beard and a permanent furrowed look upon his brow.

"Sit anywhere you like," he called. "I don't care."

Desmond raised his hand in greeting and led Sarah past a few diners to one of the empty booths.

After a moment, Joe wandered over to take their order. "What can I get you?"

"What do you have?" Desmond countered.

Joe looked back toward the door that likely led to the kitchen. "I can do a burger and fries today. This isn't Diane's, so don't go expecting miracles. Though she did drop off some pies, so there's that."

"A burger sounds good," Sarah said.

"I'll have one too," Desmond agreed.

"Good, 'cause that's all the kitchen's making." He shuffled away without asking about drinks but a moment later returned with two beers and slid them onto the table without a word.

Sarah burst out laughing as soon as Joe left. "I like him."

"He's a character," Desmond agreed. "Straight shooter. He tells you how it is, and that's that."

"The world could use more people like that," Sarah said.

"You think so?"

She nodded. "I like to know where I stand with people."

"You know," Desmond said, "me too."

He smiled at her, and a giddy flutter came to life in her gut. She stamped it back down. "So, do you miss it?"

"What?"

"The medic thing. You were a big help earlier with Greg, getting us to the hospital. I know you said you moved away from it for a reason, but you don't really ever lose those skills."

"Trying to recruit me to the first aid tent?"

Sarah laughed. "I mean, Melanie would probably love that."

"And what about you?"

Sarah's laughter faded, and it felt as if sparks crackled between them. Her eyes narrowed mischievously. She remembered his comment from the hospital earlier, when she'd thought he might've been anxious standing in the middle of the ER. *You were worried about me... Maybe you just care about how I feel.* Regardless of how she'd felt, he was not going to get her to admit that out loud, so she turned the tables on him. "Over the last three hours I've come to realize that as a former military medic, you were more than capable of changing your own bandages this whole time."

Her tone was still playful but accusatory. She wanted him to know that she was onto whatever game he was trying to play.

"It's true," Desmond said, taking a sip of his beer. "I am very good with a pack of gauze and some tape."

"So you just wanted to make me work harder?"

"That's not really my style."

"Then what?" she asked, tracing the condensation on the rim of her glass.

"Maybe I just wanted an excuse to see you again."

Those sparks turned to flames, and Sarah felt her entire face light up. Thank goodness for the dim lighting. "My nursing services are in high demand."

"I could tell. You almost got poached by the hospital. Pretty soon I'm going to have to start booking an appointment."

"Probably," Sarah agreed. "I'll definitely need to get myself a secretary."

Joe appeared at the end of their table, dropping two large plates in front of them. Sarah took a deep breath, using the distraction to clear her head. She wasn't used to this. When it came to her love life, Sarah was very up-front. She was usually the one doing all the flirting and making the first move. But Desmond was dishing out as much as she was.

Sarah took a bite of her burger. "This is actually really good."

"I think Joe's secretly got a five-star chef back there."

"It's always the dives that have the best food."

Desmond agreed. "I should have ordered something for Jordan."

"It'd be cold."

"There's a little kitchenette in the cabin."

Sarah quirked a brow, asking the question around a mouthful of food. "What cabin?"

"The resort was kind enough to offer a bunch of rooms to Team Rebuild to house the volunteers. But there's too many of us, so some of us are being housed in the cabins down by the lake."

"I wondered where they were hiding all of you," Sarah said, taking another bite of her burger.

"I've heard the cabins are usually full of tourists well into October, when the leaves change, but the tornado scared most of them off. Others left after they realized the town was in such rough shape. Worked out for us, but also means it's a short tourist season. On top of the repairs a lot of these people need to their properties, I think it's going to be a little bit of a rough year for most."

They'd moved on to safer topics now, and Sarah felt the flutters in her gut ease. She thought about Colm at the hardware store. About all the handcrafted furniture that wouldn't be seen again until next summer. Thankfully Kate's livelihood was in need all year long. Even more so after the storm, by the sounds of it—she was always rushing off to check on some animal or visit some farm or tag along with Doc McGinn, the resident livestock veterinarian that she was replacing when he retired. Kate and the ranch would be okay—Sarah was sure of that.

Hopefully the rest of Hatchet Lake would too.

"You never answered my question," she said.

Desmond raised a dark brow. "Which one?"

"Do you miss being a medic?"

"I do," he said. "But every day I find one more thing to be grateful for on this side of things. And I'm glad for all the experiences that brought me right here to this exact moment."

"This is a moment for you?"

"How could it not be? Successful ER trip. Having lunch with a new friend."

Sarah watched the way his lips rolled over the word *friend* and the smile that broke across his face afterward. Her heart began racing as she lifted her beer. "To more moments, then."

He clinked his glass against hers. "To more moments."

Chapter Eight

Watching Desmond and Rusty dangle from the rafters of the stables while Nathan passed sheets of plywood up a ladder wasn't exactly the kind of moment she'd had in mind when she'd made that toast in the pub, but apparently that was what they were doing today.

"Everyone be careful," Sarah said as a piece of old wood came crashing down in an empty stall. "I've hit my max ER-visit allowance for the week."

"It's all about controlled chaos," Desmond said, flashing her a smile from above. He tossed another piece of old wood down to the ground. The horses had been relocated to the pasture for the afternoon, so at least they didn't have to worry about the animals.

"I've already clocked out for today," Sarah said, hoisting Parker higher on her hip. "There will be no Band-Aids handed out."

"What if I just have a boo-boo that needs to be kissed?"

Sarah's lips twisted as she stared up at Desmond. She

didn't know whether to blush at his boldness—here he was, flirting with her surrounded by a bunch of their friends—or whether to accept the challenge and flirt right back.

"Depends where it is." She arched her brow. Challenge accepted.

Desmond dipped his head as if to say *Point to you*, then reached to help Rusty steady a piece of plywood against the wall.

"Watch that corner," Kate said from the bottom of the ladder. She held it steady for Nathan as he climbed up, her grip turning her knuckles white.

Jordan returned from outside with a tool belt cinched to his waist and scurried up the ladder with the kind of grace Sarah had thought only dancers possessed. He had a piece of plywood tucked under his arm, cut into a triangle to fit the corner they were repairing. Somehow he hoisted himself onto the rafter beam. When Jordan finally joined them, Kate moved the ladder closer to where they were working so they could easily climb down again.

As promised during their earlier visit, Desmond and Jordan had returned to the ranch with tools and extra lumber supplies to help Nathan properly repair the damage to the stables. Rusty had taken a break from his photography to lend a hand, and between the four of them, Sarah had hope that the stables would finally be set to rights.

Nathan's temporary patch jobs had worked to keep out the elements, but Dale didn't think they would survive the winter.

Parker kicked, wanting down, and Sarah let him go, only to catch him as he bolted straight for the ladder. He whined and fussed, determined to climb the thing.

"I don't think so, mister," Kate said, scooping him up and blowing kisses into his cheek. "We've got enough men dangling from the ceiling right now."

Parker reached out with the grabby hands that were usually a precursor to a meltdown. "I should probably take him back inside," Sarah said. "No need to tempt him with this giant playground."

"I also don't want to be here when someone inevitably drops a hammer on their foot," Kate said. "Waiting for it to happen is stressing me out."

"Is it because you really love me?" Nathan called down to her.

Kate smirked at Sarah before cocking her head in the direction of the door. "Come get us when you're done," she called over her shoulder. "We'll be in the house."

"Is your mother cooking?" Jordan asked.

"You know it."

He whooped, then got back to hammering a sheet of plywood into place.

Sarah and Kate wandered back to the house, slow enough that Parker could stop to investigate every single weed in the yard. "Is Tara coming by?" Sarah asked.

"Tara's gotten herself a gig with Team Rebuild."

"Oh?" Sarah said.

"Looks like you weren't the only one Lori poached." Kate laughed. "She's apparently taking photos for their social media now. She really has a knack for that side of marketing."

"She was helping Nathan with the ranch's website too, right?"

"Yeah. Nathan's already shown me some mock-ups. It looks fantastic."

"When are you hoping to go live with it?"

"Probably when I'm ready to fully take over the case load from Doc McGinn."

"And when do you think that will be?"

"Doc wants to hang up his stethoscope in the new year. Probably four to five months from now. So I have a good amount of time to get the renovations done in the stables."

"Soon you're going to have to start calling him something else," Sarah said. "People are going to start calling *you* Doc."

"Speaking of doctors, I heard you met one."

"How on earth did you hear that?"

Kate chuckled. "Small town. News travels fast. Bad news travels even faster and brings everyone out with baked goods. Your ER run was major news."

Sarah reached down and accepted the blade of grass Parker had pulled from the field for her. "The doctor's name was James. He was great. So were the nurses. They apologized for not being able to help out more. I guess they'd wanted to send a team down after the tornado but were too short-staffed to give up the people."

"Oh, that's nice of them."

"What you should be asking me is what happened *after* the ER run."

Kate tipped her head and leaned down to cover Parker's ears.

Sarah laughed. "It's not that scandalous."

"I never know with you." Kate released Parker, and they climbed the porch. He took off through the front door with his scraggly handful of weeds, running straight for Anne's knees. "He's gonna be a heartbreaker."

Anne pulled him up onto a stool beside her, where she was prepping dinner.

"Mom," Kate sighed. "I told you not to do anything big."

"This isn't a big thing. It's pork chops and salad. And maybe a few sausages and a couple baked potatoes." She handed Parker a bottle of salad dressing. He slammed it down onto the counter. The fact that nobody flinched told Sarah everyone was getting used to having a toddler in the house, and it warmed something inside her. She wasn't used to this. She wasn't used to having other people around.

It was always just *her*.

Her running between shifts at the hospital and the babysitter's.

Her taking time off when Parker got sick.

Her trying to figure out the best place for him to grow up.

It was nice to feel like she was part of a team, for however brief a time.

"How's it going in the stables?" Anne asked, helping Parker add the dressing to the salad bowl.

Sarah watched his little face scrunch up in concentration. "We're taking a break from watching the men dangle from the rafters," she said. "I've already had one Team Rebuild emergency room visit to contend with this week—I don't want to add another one."

They moved to the living room, and Kate leveled her with a stare. "Okay, spill. What happened after the ER visit?"

"Well, we brought the patient back to the command trailer. I had to write up a report for Lori, which was really long and involved—"

"Get to the good part!"

Sarah giggled as Kate's eyes widened comically. "You're so impatient."

"You can't dangle this kind of thing in front of me

like a carrot and then not expect me to be hanging on your every word."

"Well, once we'd wrapped up for the afternoon, Desmond asked me to lunch."

The corner of Kate's mouth lifted. "Why am I not surprised? I saw the way he was looking at you the first time we met. Where did you go? There's hardly anything open in town right now except for the—"

"Pub," Sarah finished. "Ambience was great. Service was even better."

Kate snorted, throwing herself down onto the couch. Sarah joined her. "Joe is the living embodiment of the Grinch. We love him for it, but the service was probably abysmal."

"The burger was good though," Sarah reasoned. *So was Desmond's company,* she wanted to add, but she was currently trying hard not to flush at the memory of him gazing at her from across the booth.

"You had a good time," Kate said, sitting up.

"What?"

"This is usually the part of the conversation where you start to tell me all the reasons you and said date could never work. You *like* this guy."

"First of all, it was a lunch date. Between coworkers."

"Mmm-hmm," Kate said.

"Second of all..."

"That's what I thought," Kate cut in. "You have nothing to complain about."

"Give it time," Sarah said. "I'm sure I'll find something."

The front door flew open, and Nathan rushed inside, breathing heavily, followed closely by Jordan and Desmond. They'd clearly just run from the stables. Sarah and Kate were on their feet in an instant.

"Good news." Nathan beamed proudly. "Holes are patched."

Kate frowned. "You scared the crap out of us, coming in the door like that."

"Sorry—it started to rain." Nathan wrapped his arms around her, kissing the side of her head. "Just waiting on your seal of approval. Do you want to grab your dad and come take a look?"

"Eat first," Anne insisted. "Everything will be done in another five minutes."

Dale appeared from the back door with a plate in his hand. He'd obviously been put in charge of the grill.

"We'll just take a peek," Kate said. "Be back in time for dinner."

Anne was already cutting up a sausage for Parker.

Jordan wandered over to the counter, inhaling deeply. "Something smells amazing."

"That's my smoked sausages," Dale said. "I do them myself."

"With cherry wood chips?" Jordan asked, taking the fork Anne offered him with a slice of sausage on the end. He took a bite. "This is phenomenal."

"I've got a smoker out back," Dale said. He headed for the door, waving Jordan after him.

"Should we wait?" Kate asked.

Desmond shook his head. "We've lost him. That man will talk about good barbecue for hours if you let him."

"All right, then," Kate said. "Let's go see your handiwork."

Nathan took Kate by the hand, practically dragging her back out the door. Sarah followed slower as Parker toddled after them. Desmond hung back enough that they fell into step beside each other. It was hardly raining.

"I'm happy to see you've walked away without any injuries," Sarah teased.

"C'mon, a professional like me?"

"We literally met while I was bandaging your hand," she reminded him.

"And you're sure I didn't orchestrate that entire meeting?"

Sarah had come to realize that Desmond was just a shameless flirt. Well, she might have met her match, but he'd also met his. "I hope your construction skills are better than your flirting."

"Gotta step my game up, huh?"

Parker shoved his way between them, taking Sarah's hand. "Take note," she told Desmond. "This is how it's done."

He barked a laugh as they reached the stables.

They could hear the whinnies of some of the horses. Shade and Tully had already been relocated to their stalls now that the construction had ceased.

"Take a look at this," Nathan said, waving his arm toward the rafters. "You'd never even know gale-force winds ripped a hole in the roof."

"It looks great," Kate said. She glanced back at Desmond and mouthed, *Thank you.*

Desmond nodded, leaning against a stall. Shade came over to investigate him, and Desmond turned, giving her neck a scratch.

"You've been around horses before?" Kate asked, noticing Desmond's ease.

He nodded. "I had friends with a farm growing up. We got up to all sorts of things. Used to ride the horses all over the property. Fell off my fair share of them as well."

"You know who's never been on a horse before," Kate said, turning and eyeballing Sarah.

"Really?" Nathan said, surprised. "You're best friends with the horse girl. How does that make sense?"

"It makes perfect sense," Sarah said.

"I've tried to convince her," Kate said. "She won't have any part of it."

Desmond smirked. "Sounds a little like you might be afraid."

"I'm not afraid of the horse," Sarah insisted. "I'm afraid of being up there." She gestured to Shade's back. "Two completely different things."

"Don't you want to teach your son to face his fears?" Desmond asked.

"I'm teaching him to avoid things where he's likely to get a concussion."

"I don't think anyone here would let you fall."

The way Desmond looked at her made every inch of Sarah's body flush. She tucked her hair behind her ear, hoping to pass it off as nerves.

"You could tick it off the bucket list," Kate said to her.

"Riding a horse is not going anywhere near my bucket list," Sarah assured her. Parker ran up to Shade's stall and held his arms out for the horse. Sarah picked him up and nuzzled his cheek. "Not anytime soon, mister."

"I've just had a brilliant idea for a photo shoot," Nathan said. "Parker and the horses together. Think about it—Cardiff Ranch, the place where dreams begin."

Kate cracked a smile. "That's going on the website, is it?"

"As part of my personal testimony."

Kate snickered at him. "I'll finish up in here and get the horses settled. Why don't you take Desmond back to the house before my mother starts hollering out the door about feeding him?"

"On it," Nathan said. Desmond followed him out of the stables, and Sarah hated to admit that her gaze followed Desmond until he was out of sight.

"I see why you like him," Kate said.

"Yeah," Sarah muttered. "Wait, what?"

Kate leaned against the door of the stall. "You and Desmond? It's, like, an actual thing."

"It's not a *thing*," Sarah said.

"I know you said the lunch was just between coworkers, but I'm pretty sure I felt some real sparks."

Sarah gave Kate a pointed look. "Like that's anything new. During undergrad you used to joke that I could have flirted with a napkin at the bar."

"Okay, well, I'm thinking about hiring him to do the renovations on the stables. These repairs turned out great, and I really need an office in here. And space for more supplies. Maybe an area for exams."

"All the things a good livestock vet needs," Sarah agreed.

"Exactly. I just didn't want things to get awkward."

"Why would it be awkward?"

"I don't know? You two seem like you might be getting close."

Sarah wrinkled her nose. "I don't do *awkward*. Or serious. You know that."

"Of course. You're the queen of cool."

"Right. So, if you want to hire him for the renovations, then hire him."

Kate nodded, hanging a loose halter back on the wall. Parker whined as soon as he realized the horses weren't coming out of their stalls again.

"No more horses for today," Kate said. "We can see them tomorrow."

Parker threw himself down onto the ground, immediately wailing at the top of his lungs.

"That's dramatic," Kate muttered.

"Toddlers are spontaneous one-man theatrical productions. In the middle of the grocery store. On the floor of the doctor's office. You never know when you're going to get a show."

Kate sighed, bending down next to him. "I know, autumn's a rough time to be alive. The whole world is changing."

"Yah," Parker said in between his wails.

Kate snorted, and Sarah turned away, trying not to laugh. It was good for him to hear the word *no* on occasion. As much as she wanted to give him the world, there were limits.

When Parker realized that they were in fact done with the horses, he climbed to his feet and threw himself at Kate. She picked him up. "The screaming I could live without, but this?" she said, cuddling him close.

"I know. Just when I think I'm ready to pack him up and ship him back to the manufacturer, he does something cute. It's a lost cause."

"Say, 'Bye, horsey,'" Kate told him.

"Bye," Parker said, waving.

Sarah spared one more glance at the stables, her chest immediately warming at the thought of Desmond spending more time here. Kate might have wanted him for the renovations, but Sarah wanted him too—in a nonserious, very casual sort of way.

Chapter Nine

"You're still in Michigan?"

Sarah resisted the urge to grind her teeth in response to her mother's question. She'd been dodging her phone calls for days, trying to avoid having this conversation. But it had gotten to the point where Sarah was certain her mother was going to muster the local authorities to track her down if she didn't respond soon. She took a deep, steadying breath before replying. "Yes, we're still in Michigan. We're still staying with the Cardiffs."

September had quickly given way to October, and Sarah had no immediate plans to leave. Parker was happy, and Sarah was busy with volunteering. Besides, the Cardiffs didn't seem to mind having them around. And if she happened to see Desmond every day at work and occasionally at the ranch, well, then that was an added bonus.

"And how long do you plan on intruding on Kate's family?"

"I don't know," Sarah said. "Maybe I plan on becoming a rancher and wearing overalls and rubber boots for a living."

"Sarah, don't be ridiculous."

"I don't know, *Mother*. Until they kick me out, I guess."

"Look, if you need money—"

"God, Mom, I don't need money. That's not why I'm still here." Besides the necessities and day care, Sarah had actually been very frugal during her last nursing contract. She had more than enough in her savings to afford a few months away from a hospital job. "I'm volunteering with the disaster-relief organization that came down to help the town rebuild."

"Volunteering?"

"Yes, I'm volunteering as part of their medical team."

"And who is watching my grandson while you're doing this?"

"Parker is fine. He's hanging out at the ranch with Anne or Kate or whoever else is around."

"So you're spending all day working without getting paid while your son is running around waiting to get kicked by a horse?"

Sarah wondered if she could get away with accidentally hanging up. "Parker is perfectly safe. And *unpaid* is the definition of a volunteer, Mom. It's no different than all the luncheons and committees you've organized over the years."

"Sarah, that's a few hours of my time. You have a son to raise."

It was as if her mother had conveniently forgotten that she'd also had Sarah to raise when she'd been living this *Real Housewives* life. "I literally do not have time for this conversation with you."

"You're the one who's been avoiding me for weeks, and *you* can't make the time?"

Sarah pinched the bridge of her nose. "I'm sorry— I've been really busy."

And she had. Between Team Rebuild stuff and spending time with Parker on the ranch, her days were almost as full as when she worked a contract at a hospital. The only difference now was that Sarah didn't spend half her time driving around between the babysitter's and work. Now she got to go straight home and see her son, knowing that he was happy and well cared for. The Cardiffs were practically family. They treated her and Parker as such, and that feeling of security was not something Sarah was in a hurry to abandon.

Potential jobs filtered through her email daily, but Sarah had yet to bite at any of the contracts. Even now, she could hear Parker giggling downstairs. How could she possibly take him away from this?

"Too busy for me," her mother muttered. "Too busy for your son apparently."

Sarah's hand tightened around the phone. "Parker's just fine. Don't you worry about him."

Kate appeared in the doorway. She winced, hearing Sarah's half of the conversation.

"I don't like that you're currently unemployed with no plan other than to stay at the ranch and volunteer. I mean, that's very admirable of you, Sarah, but is this really the smartest decision?"

"Well, it's a good thing you don't have to like it," Sarah said. "I have to go now."

She hung up before she could say anything that she would regret and tossed the phone down onto the bed. Crossing her arms, she turned to look at Kate.

"Okay, so, Parker threw his meatloaf on the floor,"

Kate said. "Clearly that's not a winner. Good news is he was polite about it and screamed 'No, thank you' as he did it. So, manners are going really well."

Sarah laughed as she collapsed onto the bed. It was an almost hysterical sound.

"You okay?" Kate asked, wandering into the room.

"Oh, yeah, I'm just ruining my life and Parker's life. I've made one big mess apparently."

"Classic Bonnie," Kate said, slumping down beside her. They both looked up at the glow-in-the-dark stars on the ceiling.

"I don't know if I want to cry or shake something." Every phone call with her mother ended the same way. And each time it left Sarah irritated and snappish. She didn't want to feel like that for the rest of the night, and she especially didn't want to be around Parker when she was so frustrated.

"I vote we shake something," Kate said. "Like a full-body shake. We should let off some steam the same way we used to in college."

Sarah snorted. "We're too old to shake like that now."

Kate needled her gently. "I think we've still got it. Plus the pub never gets as lively as the bars we used to go to, so it's not like we'll throw our backs out or anything."

Sarah cackled, sitting up on her elbows. "Oh, you're serious?"

"I am very serious. C'mon, forget about Bonnie and come have a drink—or a few—with me. Girls' night."

Sarah bit her lip. Girls' night sounded like a good distraction from the way she was currently feeling. But Sarah didn't do girls' nights anymore. Not since Parker had been born.

"I don't know," she said.

"We'll put Parker to sleep before we go, and my mom will babysit," Kate said. "You'll be home and tucked into bed before he even notices you're gone."

"I'm pretty sure I used to be the one convincing you to go out past your bedtime. When did you become the bad influence?"

Kate grinned at her. "When you became a mom."

The pub wasn't exactly the downtown bars of Sarah's youth, but between the locals looking to burn off some steam after the long work week and the Team Rebuild volunteers, it was far livelier than it had been that day Desmond had brought Sarah for lunch.

As it was, Sarah and Kate had to worm their way through a crowd to reach the bar.

"Hey, Joe," Kate called, waving at him.

He glanced over, immediately jumping Kate to the front of the line, which Sarah took to be more about local privilege and less about luck.

He offered up a beer, and Kate held up two fingers.

After a moment, Joe delivered them two beers, and Kate told him to open a tab.

"That kind of night, is it?" Joe asked. He hardly looked at them, doing a hundred things at once as people called their drink orders at him.

"Definitely that kind of night," Sarah said. She picked up her beer and knocked it against Kate's before taking a sip.

"In that case…" Joe said, pouring them both a shot.

"Thanks," Kate said.

Sarah didn't hesitate throwing it back. The sooner she forgot about her mother's judgment, thinly veiled as concern, the better she would feel. "It's packed in here," she said, lips puckering.

"Those Team Rebuild folks can really party."

"I don't think these are all Team Rebuild people," Sarah said. She hadn't exactly met everyone volunteering in Hatchet Lake yet, but she'd chatted with a fair few of them while getting coffee in the lunch tent. None of these faces were ones she recognized.

"Mostly college students," Joe said. "They sometimes come down from the city on the weekends to skip out on the crowds. They usually have this place to themselves."

"That's genius," Sarah said.

"It's annoying is what it is. I have to run around making sure they all have a DD so I don't have to have them camped out in the pub all night sleeping it off." He grimaced—but clearly couldn't deny they were good for business. If Sarah remembered anything from her partying days, it was the loyalty they had to their favorite drinking establishments.

Joe made his way down the bar, filling orders. Kate and Sarah staked out a pair of stools where they could nurse their beers and listen to the college drama unfold. Over a fifteen-minute period, they'd watched two couples break up, a new relationship take shape and some kid try to pass off a fake ID.

"You get outta here," Joe warned him. "I'm not gonna tell you again. And if I see you back here, my next call is gonna be to our deputy." The group of college students booked it out the door, and Kate smirked.

"He acts miserable about it, but I think he secretly loves catching the fakes. He's been doing it since I was young enough to start drinking." Kate frowned at her beer. "I think Joe's secretly immortal. Like how people think Keanu Reeves hasn't aged."

"I could see it," Sarah said, eyeing Joe over her beer.

She said it so seriously Kate started snickering. "Don't tell me you're tipsy off one shot."

Kate waved away her accusation. "Keep them coming."

Sarah signaled Joe, and two more shots appeared. "I feel like we should offset these with shots of electrolytes."

"Probably." They clinked their glasses and drank. "Think Parker will let us sleep in tomorrow morning?"

"Not a chance in hell."

The crowd at the bar steadily thickened, until it was three people deep and Sarah was sweltering. Suddenly, Kate took her hand, pulled her off her stool and dragged her to the back of the pub. There was a free booth in a dingy corner that Kate had eyeballed. They reached it at the same time as Deputy Ryan Mullens.

Now *he* was a familiar face that Sarah saw on occasion around the Team Rebuild camp. Ryan was still heading the town's rebuilding efforts, meaning that he spent a lot of time in and out of the command trailer coordinating with Lori.

"Mind some company?" he asked. He wore jeans and a button-down shirt tonight, clearly off duty.

"We're having a girls' night, but for you I'll make an exception," Kate said.

"Like I do whenever I spot you speeding down Main Street?"

Kate opened her mouth to protest, then thought better of it. "I'm not saying anything."

"You're a smart one, Cardiff."

"Night off?" Sarah asked him as they piled into opposite sides of the booth. Working in the ER, cops were pretty frequent fliers, bringing in patients for assessment, so she wasn't unused to their presence. But hanging out with Ryan felt different. There wasn't the accompanying stress and uncertainty. He was friendly and good-natured, like everything and everyone else in this town. Maybe that came from growing up in the same community you now looked out for.

"Something like that," he said. He glanced around at the rowdy patrons. "We'll see how the night goes."

"Joe's already kicked a few kids out."

"He usually does," Ryan laughed. "We're getting to know them so well I've got some of their parents on speed dial back at the station."

Sarah smirked. Small towns never failed to amuse her.

"Is this where we're hanging out?" someone asked, and Sarah looked up to see Jordan. "I'm not intruding, am I?"

"Only on ladies' night," Ryan said, but he moved over to make room at the table.

Jordan rubbed his hands together. "Perfect. I love hot gossip. It's like currency around here."

Kate chuckled, and Sarah could almost hear what she was thinking. *So much for girls' night.* But as far as company went, Sarah didn't mind the added distraction. It wasn't often now that she traipsed out to a bar, so it was nice to spend some time with this odd group of friends and coworkers, even if she'd just seen some of them earlier in the day.

"Refill?" Sarah asked as she heard the empty bottles clink against the table. Kate and Ryan had devolved into talking about their childhood, snickering over ridiculous stories about the things they used to get up to. She got a resounding *yes* to the question of more alcohol, so she headed back up to the bar, parking herself on an empty stool. It was less crowded than it had been earlier, but the drink orders had grown more complicated, and Joe was surrounded by liquor bottles.

A young man slid onto the stool next to Sarah, eyeing her from beneath a mop of blond hair. He turned his head then, giving her an obvious up and down, before twisting on the stool to face her.

He had a boyish smile that reminded her so much of Parker that for a second she wanted to march right home and swaddle her son in her arms.

"Can I buy you a drink?" the young man asked, and Sarah almost choked on her beer.

Sarah wasn't unused to this kind of attention. But she and Kate had rules. Girls' night meant you arrived with your girls and you left with your girls. And as much as free drinks were nice, she didn't much feel like entertaining anyone right now. Especially this kid. Because that was what he was to her. He had to be twenty-one. Maybe twenty-two. Sarah felt ancient beside him, like her joints might seize and her skin might turn to ash if he looked too close. She almost laughed at herself then. When had thirty become so old?

"Thanks, but I think I'm good," she said, gesturing to the rest of her beer.

"C'mon," he said. "One drink, maybe a dance?" He held his hand out to her, but Sarah wasn't interested. She could tell by the flush in his cheeks that he was maybe a few too many beers in anyway. She'd seen her fair share of college kids rolled through the ER, hooked up to fluids all night while they slept off their hangovers.

She shook her head. "No, thanks."

His face fell, but there was something in his eyes that told Sarah he wasn't done asking.

Then they were interrupted.

"You're in my seat."

Sarah looked over her shoulder to find Desmond looming over the boy. He gave his head a flick. At first Sarah thought the kid might argue, but he eyeballed Desmond again, perhaps with a clearer mind, and this time he thought better of refusing. He slumped off the stool and disappeared into the crowd.

"I think you hurt his feelings."

Desmond shrugged. "You hurt them first when you turned him down."

"Well, what was I supposed to do? Lead him on?"

"No way. A little rejection is good for him. It'll build character." He grinned. "We all had to go through it."

"You got rejected?"

"All the time."

"I find that hard to believe."

"Then envision a scrawny, shy, tongue-tied kid. About forty pounds lighter. With a face full of acne. I could barely work up the courage to talk to a woman, never mind find the money to be buying them drinks."

Sarah leaned her head on her hand, purposely letting her eyes roam and linger on all the muscle hidden by his shirt. "Yeah, I didn't have that problem."

Desmond laughed silently beside her. "You were always just full of confidence, weren't you?"

"Always."

"Could pick up whoever you wanted."

"Anyone," she agreed.

"Got all the guys to buy you drinks."

"Never spent a dime."

"And I'm sure you enjoyed every minute of it."

"The highlight of my early twenties."

"Be honest—you would have rejected scrawny little me."

Sarah paused then. It was hard to imagine Desmond

like that. The man beside her had started flirting with her about two minutes into their first meeting, and something in her had been hooked. She didn't like to admit it—and maybe it was only the alcohol talking—but there was something addictive about Desmond. Something that kept her coming back for more. And no matter how nonchalant she tried to be, seeing him at work or on the ranch was always the best part of her day.

If they'd met back then, Sarah wanted to think she would have seen past all his insecurities. That they would have been friends at least. But she knew twenty-one-year-old Sarah hadn't been that kind. She'd been shallow and frivolous. Like most kids, she'd been looking for a good time. Nothing more. Nothing less. It had taken a job in the real world and one very unexpected pregnancy to get her to grow up.

"To be fair, you probably didn't want to know me back then."

"That I find hard to believe."

"Believe it," Sarah said, getting to the bottom of her beer.

"All right, then how about I buy you a drink *now*?" he asked.

Sarah shook her head. "How about I buy *you* a drink?" She lifted her hand to wave Joe down.

"Almost seems like you're hitting on me," Desmond teased.

"Maybe I am."

"Well, maybe I like that."

Sarah had to bite her lip to keep from grinning at him. Joe slid a couple shot glasses down the bar toward her, and Sarah handed one to Desmond. A few people grumbled at her.

"I think we jumped the line."

Sarah shrugged. "Perks of being friends with a local."

"Feels illegal."

"Should I do it again?" Sarah asked, putting up her hand.

Desmond grabbed her hand and yanked it back to the bar. He didn't let go. "Are you trying to get me drunk?"

"Is it working?"

Desmond threw back the shot. "Probably gonna regret that in the morning. But that's a tomorrow problem now."

"Technically it's a today problem," she said, glancing at her phone. It was already after midnight. Who would she have to sacrifice to get Parker to sleep past six?

"You're right."

"I do tend to be right a lot."

"Is that so?" He shifted his stool closer.

"Are you surprised?"

"Somehow not at all." He leaned toward her, and she felt compelled to close the distance. He was like a magnet, drawing her in. She could see the flush in his cheeks. The vast shadows that were his pupils. She was suddenly hot all over, fighting the urge to climb out of her clothes. "Want to get some air?" he asked.

"Why? Do I take your breath away?"

Desmond covered his face with his hand, softening the tension that had built between them. "That was so bad."

Sarah took his hand, and the heat she felt sparked to life. She wanted to be shallow tonight. She wanted to do things without thinking them through first. Mostly, she wanted to kiss him. But she was definitely not doing that for the first time in here, surrounded by drunk college kids and a band of coworkers. She tugged, and Desmond followed her to the door.

Outside, the cool air cleared her mind and invigorated her all at once. The door closed behind them, and the din of the pub faded away.

She turned back to Desmond, and his eyes winked under the flickering light above the pub door. The space between them felt so charged, Sarah struggled to breathe. She took a small step back. She wanted him. Wanted to kiss him. Wanted his hands everywhere.

She pulled at him gently, and something darkened in his eyes. He took a step, leaving the halo of light that surrounded him, following her into the shadows. He stalked her until her back hit the wall, bumping up against the side of the pub.

The door opened and closed on occasion, but Sarah paid it no mind, hoping the patrons were too drunk to notice them or too occupied to care. Desmond's hand traveled down the length of her bare arm. It was warm for an October night, so she'd left her jacket behind. Gooseflesh spiraled beneath his touch, and a delicious chill zipped across her body. Sarah pressed into his heat, into the warmth of his arms and surged up, meeting his lips.

Desmond's hands fell to her waist, squeezing, his fingers brushing the skin by her hips. He held her to him so firmly her knees could have given out and neither of them would have noticed.

Desmond's lips dragged across hers, then their tongues met. He tasted like alcohol, and Sarah groaned into his mouth. She never wanted this to end. The dizzying, intoxicating feeling of falling for someone. A throat cleared, and with great effort and restraint, Sarah tore her lips away.

Kate stood there, arms crossed, her face twisted in amusement. "I thought you might have gotten whisked away by one of those college kids. But it looks like you didn't need rescuing after all."

Desmond stepped away from Sarah—not far enough that she lost the heat of him, but far enough not to tempt either of them again. "We were just getting some air," he said.

Kate's teeth bit into her lower lip to keep from laughing. "I see that. Well, since we're all here, getting some air, is this a bad time to ask if you'll come do some renovation work on the stables?"

Sarah was still trying to catch her breath.

But Desmond smiled, all business. "I'd love to."

"Good," Kate said. "Come by the ranch sometime, and we'll talk details."

Desmond nodded. He glanced back at Sarah quickly, and her entire body felt like Jell-O. "Definitely took my breath away," he whispered so only she could hear. Then he was gone, and somewhere between her alcohol-addled thoughts, Sarah was trying to decide if she'd just made a fool of herself.

Kate came up and looped their arms together. "I missed *this* Sarah."

"Me too," she admitted. "But we can only let her out on occasion. You know what they say about too much of a good thing."

Chapter Ten

By the time Monday rolled around, Sarah was still nursing a bit of a headache, and she wondered if she had, in fact, had too much of a good thing that night at the pub. Apparently once you turned thirty and had a kid, your body rejected any combination of fun and alcohol.

"You can't still be hungover!" Melanie said.

"Enjoy your youth," Sarah declared. She had an ice pack over her eyes, her legs kicked up on one of the collapsible tables they used for work. "It's all downhill from here."

"Oh, please. You're, like, what, thirty?"

"You add ten years after the first kid."

Melanie scoffed. "As if. I heard a bunch of college guys tried to hit on you."

Sarah removed the ice pack from her head. "And who told you this?"

Melanie shrugged. "Jordan."

Sarah didn't have to wonder where Jordan had heard

it from. He and Desmond were practically attached at the hip. She *did* wonder just how loose Desmond's lips had been. If he'd spilled all the juicy details about their shadowy kiss outside the pub. Sarah's head might have been pounding all weekend, but that part was clear as day. Melanie didn't mention anything, though, so even if Desmond had said something, Jordan had wisely chosen to keep it to himself.

"Want to toss me those bandages?" Melanie said.

Sarah picked up the box and handed it off. "What are you doing?"

"Making room. Lori said she spotted our supply order on the truck that came in this morning."

Sarah sighed and rallied. Time to shake off her old age and actually do some work. An autumn chill spilled across the camp, sweeping orange-and-yellow leaves beneath the tents, and Sarah pulled her vest tighter.

The squeak of a dolly announced Jordan's arrival, and Sarah looked up to find him rolling a stack of boxes across the field.

"I didn't know we ordered this much," Sarah said as Jordan carefully set the stack down. It towered over her by at least a foot.

"There's a couple more loads on the truck," Jordan said.

"I think Evan got a little out of control with the order form," Melanie said. "I'm guessing it's the last order though, so he was probably trying to be thorough."

"Oh," was all Sarah could muster. She hadn't really been thinking about what would happen when Team Rebuild packed up. Of course, she knew it would happen eventually. Every day the town looked a little better than the day before. The debris was being hauled away. There were no longer trees to dodge in the middle of the road. Homes had been repaired. Ranches had been boarded up. Even Main Street was coming along—Diane's diner was the last big project to tackle there, and Sarah had heard nothing but good things from the volunteers. Team Rebuild was close to achieving what it had set out to do; it only made sense that they would be leaving soon. Sarah just wasn't ready. She looked from Melanie, her reluctant, blood-averse sidekick, to Jordan and his ever-present smile. In a short time, these people had become constants in her life, and she didn't know how she was going to say goodbye.

Thoughts of Desmond filtered to the forefront of her mind, and she immediately pushed them away. That wasn't something she wanted to tackle right now.

"Here," Jordan was saying as he passed Sarah a clipboard. "I need you to make sure everything on the list matches what's in the boxes. If the order is right, sign the bottom. I'll be back in a few minutes with the rest of it."

Jordan shoved the boxes up against the side of the tent so as not to be in the way of where they were working. Sarah walked around the table to investigate. "I don't even know where we're going to put it all," she called out to Melanie. "There's enough to stock an entire hospital here."

"That's okay," Melanie said, her voice muffled as Sarah was swallowed up by the boxes. She ripped one open and counted more gloves than they would use in a year.

"What was that?" Sarah called back.

"Everything either gets donated in the end or packed up and taken along to the next call."

Sarah wondered if the hospital would take it. She might've been wrong, but judging how things had gone during her short stint at the first aid tent, there was no way they would burn through this many supplies. She didn't think the hospital would turn down anything so long as it was unused and unopened. She could always send an inquiry to James. He'd put his number on the report he handed her when they'd taken Greg to the ER. She'd written it down and kept it in the first aid tent in case they had to get in touch with him again.

"Supply day, huh?" a smooth voice said.

Sarah's pulse quickened before she'd even turned around. Desmond stood there, dressed for the weather, wearing sturdy hiking boots and a navy jacket over his red Team Rebuild shirt. Sarah had the urge to dip her hands between the zipper and run them along the sturdy planes of his chest.

She remembered the warmth of him.

The strength.

The feel of his hands at her waist.

She let the dizzying thoughts be whisked away by the sight of coffee. He held a steaming cup in each hand.

"Looks like you could use this," Desmond said, passing her one.

"How did you know?"

"Oh, I could see the tower from across the field." He gestured to the boxes. "Figured I should get to you before you ended up buried beneath it."

"Good call," she said, taking a sip.

Part of her had been uncertain about how this interaction would go. She'd let her mind drift here on occasion as she'd whiled away the weekend with Parker and the Cardiffs. What would they say to each other? How would they act? As a rule, Sarah chose not to let awkwardness dictate her life. She'd perfected pleasant detachment for situations such as this. But Desmond stirred up feelings Sarah didn't normally carry around with her after she'd been kissed silly by a stranger. Perhaps it was because Desmond wasn't technically a stranger anymore. Or maybe it had just been a *really* good kiss. She banished those thoughts as quickly as they appeared, taking a long drag of coffee.

Then she put the cup down on the ground near the edge of the tent and reached up for the next box in the pile.

"Here, let me," Desmond said.

He slipped by her, so close their clothes brushed. All she could think about was the pressure of his lips against hers and the fine silk of his tongue brushing the inside of her mouth.

God, she was in rough shape. Flirting was one thing. Kissing was something else. But more… *More* was dangerous. More was trouble. And though Sarah had once been skilled at taking more without letting her heart get involved, Desmond was already a little too close for comfort.

He snagged the box easily, placing it on the ground beside her.

"Thanks. Jordan's got me on a tight schedule," she joked, picking up the clipboard again. "Said he'd be back with more boxes."

"No trouble. I always offer to help out those less fortunate. Especially in the height department."

Sarah's jaw dropped. "Excuse me," she laughed. She'd never even thought of herself as that short, but compared to Desmond, she supposed she was. "I can reach my own boxes, thank you very much."

"That's good to know," he said. "For a minute I thought you might have just been using me for my height."

"That probably *is* all you're good for," she agreed.

He was flirting with her again.

And she was flirting back.

Danger and trouble be damned. It came so naturally with him. Felt so easy. Sarah hardly realized she was doing it. Hardly noticed until the giddy butterflies erupted in her gut, swarming in a mass that beat against her chest in time with her pulse.

That was the part that worried her the most. Since when had she cared enough for butterflies?

Those same butterflies staggered to a halt suddenly, like they'd crashed up against the unyielding strength of her ribs. She couldn't do this. She couldn't let herself get attached. Sarah Schaffer *did not* get attached. Butterflies were relationship-type thoughts, and she didn't do relationships. The men in her life were given passing glances, and that was all. They came and went at her discretion, never staying for very long and she certainly didn't let them have anything to do with Parker. Sarah bit her lip to keep from cursing out loud. She was already breaking all sorts of her own rules when it came to Desmond.

Now it was time to pull back.

"Can we talk?" she asked him, inclining her head behind the tent, where the tarp was neatly pegged to the ground. It wasn't exactly a closed door, but between the tarp and the boxes, it was the best she could do for a little privacy out here in the open. She needed to firmly reestablish the boundaries she had put in place for herself after she'd gotten pregnant, but part of her—the foolish part filled with all the butterflies—also needed him to understand why.

With his brows drawn together, Desmond nodded and followed her around the tent. "Everything okay?"

Sarah set her clipboard down on a box and crossed her

arms. She needed the barrier between her heart and his.

"I wanted to talk about what happened the other night."

He frowned.

"Outside the pub," she clarified.

"Oh, *that*," Desmond said, a small smile tugging at the corner of his mouth. "Sorta thought I might have imagined it."

Sarah smirked. She couldn't help herself. "Only in your dreams, huh?"

"Apparently not."

"Look," Sarah said, getting a hold of herself before she could let his flirting distract her. "I realized that I came on a little strong. I just wanted to say that I like you—I really do. I just don't want to give you the wrong impression of what that was."

"So what was it?"

"Desmond, we both know you're not here to stay. Not once you finish with Team Rebuild and whatever renovations Kate has in mind. And it's only a matter of time before I pick up and leave. Could be tomorrow, could be next week. It just depends when the right contract comes along."

"Okay," he said, still confused.

"What I'm trying to get at is that Parker is my priority. He always is, always will be." She exhaled, watching him take in each word. "I just didn't want you to read more into the situation than what was there. The night at the pub was fun. But that's all it was. A bit of fun."

Desmond nodded slowly.

He didn't react the way she'd had people react in the past. Rejection was a complicated territory. Sarah had found it full of denial and anger. Sometimes even bitter resentment. That was why she usually preferred to keep things short and sweet.

"Are you okay?" she asked, curious more than anything about his silence.

"Sorry," he said, shaking his head as if breaking from a trance. "I just didn't come prepared for a conversation like this first thing in the morning." Sarah took a small step back, but Desmond caught her arm. "But I do like to know where I stand with a person. It's better than wondering all the time."

"For what it's worth, it's not a *you* thing, it's definitely a *me* thing," Sarah said.

Desmond's smile returned. "Isn't that line supposed to come at the end of a relationship?"

"See, that's what I'm trying to avoid."

He tilted his head. "The *R* word?"

"I don't do serious. It's a take-it-or-leave-it kind of stance."

"So you're not saying you regret it," Desmond clarified. "Kissing me the other night. You just don't want me to take it too seriously?"

"Exactly."

"Interesting."

"What?"

"Nothing—I'm just figuring you out."

Sarah bristled, though it wasn't unease that filled her but a warm, tingling heat that started in her cheeks and ended at the bottom of her stomach. She took a step away, putting a short stack of boxes between them. "Well, stop that."

"Why?"

"'Cause 'figuring out' is for serious people."

"And we're not serious people?"

Sarah eyed him over the boxes. Desmond leaned against the stack, grinning mischievously. "I do have work to do," she told him.

He gestured toward the clipboard. "I'm not stopping you."

"You are actually."

"Why?" He walked around the stack, coming to stand before her. Sarah picked up the clipboard and clutched it to her chest. He leaned toward her, almost as if he were going to kiss her. "Am I distracting you?"

The question was spoken so quietly that the words were breathed across her neck. Sarah felt that warmth in her cheeks spark and flame. "Something like that."

"Let me just clarify a few things, and I'll let you get back to your very important clipboard."

Sarah settled him with a look but gestured for him to continue.

"You like me but not in a serious sort of way."

"Sure."

"And you liked kissing me."

"Are you fishing for compliments?"

"Answer the question."

"Why?"

"For science. You liked kissing me. Yes or no?"

"Yes," Sarah said, feeling a familiar tension building between them. It felt like the night at the pub just minus the alcohol. He needled his way beneath her skin so easily. The problem was she couldn't get him out.

"So, in a strictly hypothetical, *nonserious* sort of way, if my lips were to find their way onto your lips, would you be interested?"

The question, in all its ridiculousness, shot straight to her core, every inch of her skin aching with desire. Sarah suddenly wished they were alone. She'd drag Desmond onto the first horizontal surface she could find.

She'd made it clear to him that she didn't do serious relationships, and he clearly understood that. The fact that he was still asking her these questions told Sarah that he wasn't opposed to some fun of the *nonserious* kind. They'd both been working hard. They could enjoy themselves as two nonserious, consenting adults.

"So?" he asked again. "Is it something you might be up for?"

Sarah took a deep breath. She really did like him, and she didn't want this thing between them to end quite yet. If a few more weeks of volunteering for Team Rebuild was all the time they had left, then Sarah wanted to make the most of it. "I could be convinced," she said. "If the mood was right."

"'The mood,'" Desmond said, smiling with all his teeth. "I can work with that." He took a step back, giving her a flirty glance.

"Stop," Sarah warned, looking around to be sure no one was watching them. She scoffed at the way he now openly ogled her. "You're not even trying to hide it."

"If you storm away in frustration, you won't even notice me staring."

"Maybe I'm waiting to watch *you* leave."

"Well," Desmond said, "what the lady wants, the lady gets."

He made a show of turning on the spot, smirking the entire time. She let her eyes roam as he headed off to work. What was the harm now? They'd both admitted there was attraction there and that a repeat performance of what had happened outside the pub wasn't off the table as long as it stayed casual.

So what if her heart galloped at the sight of him.

So what if the thought of his lips on hers made her entire body ache.

Sarah might not want anything serious with Desmond. But it was clear to her that she certainly still *wanted* him.

Chapter Eleven

Despite their mutual declarations, Sarah and Desmond had found themselves pulled in different directions for most of the week. Sarah was occupied with the first aid tent, while Desmond had been asked to help out with renovations at the diner. His days ran long, and Sarah spent her afternoons on the ranch with Parker. Lunch breaks and morning coffee dates became a thing of the past.

If Sarah didn't know better, she'd think he was avoiding her.

But she did know better.

Besides, it wasn't like they were a couple or anything. She didn't *need* to see him.

That assertion did nothing to stop her massive smile when she returned to the ranch on Friday to find Desmond there, discussing renovation plans with Kate.

"Thought you two might have gotten lost," Kate called to her.

Sarah unbuckled Parker from his car seat and set him loose. He ran right for Kate. Sarah had taken Parker into town to fill the truck up with gas. She liked being able to do these little things around the ranch. And though Anne and Dale repeatedly told Sarah that they weren't a burden, she always felt a little better for being able to help out with a chore or two.

"We might have had a treat before we came back," Sarah said.

"I can tell," Kate laughed, catching Parker and hoisting him onto her hip. His mouth was covered in chocolate. "Did you have fun?"

"See horses," Parker said, making grabby hands at the stables.

"Auntie Kate is busy," Sarah said, walking over. "We'll see the horses later."

"Auntie Kate actually just finished," Kate said, smiling down at Parker. "Desmond and I were finalizing the plans for my new office."

"Sounds fancy," Sarah said.

"Oh, it will be." Kate put Parker down and took his hand. "Let's go say hi to the horses before dinner." They disappeared inside the stables, leaving Sarah alone with Desmond.

Alone felt like such a charged word now, and she fought the flush that crept across her skin, focusing instead on the sketch pad in his hand. It was already marked up with lines and figures. He held a measuring tape in his other hand and had a pencil tucked behind his ear. "How are the plans looking?"

"Good," he said. "We just finished going over the interior. I've got some measurements to take out here though. Gotta make sure we're not expanding into anything important."

"Want some company?" Sarah asked.

"Sure," he said, setting off. "How are your math skills?"

"Watch me do some pediatric dosage calculations, and you'll swoon."

"Have you treated a lot of pediatric patients?"

"I took a short stint in a children's hospital when I was younger," Sarah said. "I've tried to stay away from pediatrics since I had Parker. Everything about nursing and kids is harder once you have your own."

"Harder to separate your feelings from the medicine," Desmond agreed. "I get that."

"Did you ever have any pediatric patients?" she asked. "While you were deployed."

"A few," Desmond said. "Sometimes we ended up with civilian patients on base. Kids were always the hardest to see in there."

Silence stretched between them, and Sarah considered the difficult things he must have experienced while deployed. She couldn't even begin to understand it, but she reminded herself never to take this life she had with Parker for granted.

When they reached the end of the stables, where the fence that surrounded the pasture started, Desmond handed Sarah one end of the measuring tape.

"If you could be my anchor," he requested, positioning her just right. Her skin tingled beneath her shirt where the pads of his fingers touched both her arms. "I think Kate's office will expand out from here."

Once he was satisfied with where she stood, Desmond took the free end of the measuring tape and dragged it along the stables.

"Will there be an exam area?"

Desmond nodded, moving diagonal to Sarah and then walking along the grass until he'd hit every corner of the invisible room he was building. "I'm gonna throw up a bigger addition right about here, just off the office, with large swinging doors. That way there will be room for someone to drive right up with a horse trailer or whatnot."

Desmond let the measuring tape retract, following it right back to her.

"Sounds like a big job."

He shook his head. "Shouldn't take that long once the supplies arrives. Nathan's offered to help, so I even have an extra pair of hands."

"Not Jordan?"

"He's gonna head back home once Team Rebuild starts winding down here."

"Oh," Sarah said, masking the disappointment she felt. Kate's project might keep Desmond busy a little longer, but if Jordan was going, Desmond would leave soon after. Sarah frowned. What did she care? She was out of here soon too. She needed to stop thinking about Desmond and the last time he'd kissed her. It wasn't good for either of them. He'd gotten in her head when he'd teased her about doing it again.

Now she was waiting for it every time she saw him, expecting it.

And it wasn't like her to pine after a man. Even one like Desmond.

"Thanks for the help," he said, taking the measuring tape from her hand.

She let it go, let their fingers brush together, the touch lingering far longer than it needed to. He took a step closer, until they were sharing the same inch of space. Maybe Sarah wasn't the only one pining. Maybe Desmond wanted to kiss her just as badly, right here in the open, where anyone could see.

Where her *son* could see.

Sarah lifted her hand suddenly, catching him in the chest. She imagined Kate and Parker walking around the corner of the stables, spotting her wrapped up with Desmond. Kate wouldn't think anything of it. She'd probably find it funny, catching them like this again, but Parker? He was only a toddler, but children picked up on far more than people realized. She didn't know what he would think or the kinds of questions he would have. Questions he couldn't even properly verbalize yet.

She pulled her hand back. "Sorry," she whispered, glancing back and forth to make sure they were still alone.

"Don't apologize," he said. "I was being presumptuous."

A small smile stretched across her face. "It's not that. I just don't want Parker to see us all…"

"Wrapped up in each other," Desmond offered. He'd put some space between them but his hand tugged at the button on her vest, and part of her just wanted him to haul her closer and kiss her already.

"Yeah," she said. "You can't really explain things to a toddler. But they see things. They get used to things. I want this to be fun, but I don't want him to be confused."

"We'll be careful," Desmond said. He glanced over his shoulder to make sure the coast was clear, then pulled her in by the front of her vest, pressing a hot kiss to her lips that left her breathless as he retreated.

Sarah blinked away the fog in her brain, and by the time she'd gotten control of her limbs, Desmond was already walking away toward his truck to stow his supplies.

Kate appeared a moment later, Parker running after her. "You're staying for dinner, right?" she called after

Desmond. "My mother will be very disappointed if you leave before she can feed you."

He turned around briefly to reply. "I would never disappoint Anne."

Kate grinned, then turned to Sarah, her brow arching. "What were *you* doing?"

"Nothing. He's staying for dinner?"

"Like my parents would let him leave."

Sarah followed Kate and Parker back to the house. Inside, the air was thick with onions and potatoes, a hearty stew boiling on the stove while Anne slid an apple crisp into the oven.

"Perfect timing," she said.

"You need us to set the table?" Kate joked.

"No, I already did that. It's time to eat."

By the time Anne corralled everyone to the table, including Nathan, who'd been off with Rusty taking photos, and Dale, who'd disappeared to inspect some random corner of the ranch, and Desmond, who'd gotten caught up in a Team Rebuild phone call about the diner repairs, it was almost a half hour later.

Parker had eaten while the adults were sorting themselves out and was now flopped on the couch, occupied by the television. Sarah found herself seated beside Desmond, and part of her suspected that was Anne's handiwork.

"Your mother is meddling," she told Kate later as they washed the dishes. "Inviting him for dinner again. Sitting me beside him. You didn't tell her about the other night, did you?"

"What, finding you and Desmond lip-locked outside the pub? No. But my mother wants what she wants. She clearly thinks he's good for you." Kate smiled smugly.

"And for once she's not trying to interfere in my life, so I'm fine with it."

Sarah splashed her with soapy water. "You're supposed to be on my team."

"If I have to suffer the ploys of my mother, then so do you."

Sarah rolled her eyes. "Well, you can tell your mother that her scheming is wasted on us. Desmond and I are—"

"What? Just friends? Friends with benefits? This audience would like to know."

"Keeping each other company," Sarah finished flatly. There really wasn't a good word for what they were.

"Oh, you are?" Kate said, both eyebrows disappearing into her hairline.

"Well, we might be," Sarah said. "At some point." They hadn't exactly moved past the excessive flirting and frisky-kisses-when-no-one-was-looking stage. Maybe they never would. Sarah wasn't sure how to feel about that. She certainly liked Desmond enough. And with all the buildup and tension she had to deal with whenever she was around him, if she didn't get to see him naked at least once before he left it would be a damn shame.

"To be continued?" Kate asked.

Sarah smiled. There was a reason they were friends— beyond just the fact Kate and her family had so kindly opened up their home to her and Parker. Kate understood her the way a sister would. It was like they'd been separated at birth, only to be reunited with an inherent understanding of what made the other person tick. "To be continued," Sarah agreed, happy to let the topic rest for now.

"Looks like a nice night out there," Nathan said, bringing in the last of the plates. He and Desmond had offered to clear the table while Sarah and Kate washed. Parker had taken it upon himself to help them and was given the very important task of collecting the forks from the table. Desmond kept watch, making sure Parker didn't make a dash at anyone while armed with a pile of Anne's finest silverware.

Sarah's heart skipped a little in her chest—the sight of Parker offering up a fork to Desmond making her feel ridiculous things. She dropped her hands back into the soapy water, scrubbing until the tips of her fingers ached.

"How about we get a bonfire going?" Nathan asked. "We don't know how many more nice nights like this we're going to have."

Sarah perked up at that. He was right. She'd only lived through Michigan winters while in college, but November was not that far off, and she knew either a cold front would blow snow in early to stay or they'd have a green Christmas. It was one or the other. Even without the snow, the days were getting shorter, the temperature steadily dropping. If she and Parker stayed long enough, she'd have to exchange her puffy vest for a proper winter coat soon.

"That sounds nice," Kate said, abandoning the dishes to raid the pantry for supplies with Nathan. "Desmond, you're welcome to stay…unless you have to call it an early night for Team Rebuild stuff?"

"I actually get to sleep in tomorrow morning," Desmond said, bracing himself as Parker dove at his knees. "I can hang out for a bit."

Sarah couldn't help the quiet chuckle that escaped her at the sight. She caught Desmond's eye, and he smiled, thoroughly distracting her from the fact that the dishwater was going cold. She only started to pay

attention again when Parker crashed into her thigh with
an excited squeal. "Mom!"

"Yes, baby?"

"I helping you."

She reached down and retrieved the one fork Desmond had let him keep hold of, pressing a kiss to the
top of his head. "Thank you. You did such a good job."

Desmond brought her the rest of the forks. "I'm also
helping," he said with a gentle smirk, and the question
in his gaze was clear. Would she bestow him with a
kiss too? They'd already discussed boundaries. Already
closed the door on anything physical when Parker was
around. But she hadn't told him he couldn't tease her.
And *boy* was he taking advantage of the loopholes.

Her gaze fell to his lips, and she imagined grabbing
him by the collar with her soapy hand and kissing him
breathless right there in the kitchen just to prove she
could.

But she couldn't.

She *wouldn't*.

Not with Parker staring up at them like he was.

Her twisted smile straightened. "You're both doing
a wonderful job."

Annoyed with being ignored, Parker wrapped himself around her legs. Sarah braced herself against the
counter and pulled him into her arms. "Hi, baby. What's
wrong?"

Parker immediately reached for the sink, eyeing up
the fizzling soap bubbles. He made a grab for them, lifting his soapy fingers from the sink with a magnificent
grin. He showed them to Desmond, who pretended to
eat the soap off his finger with a big animated *chomp-
ing* sound. Parker giggled, scrunching up his nose.
Desmond was so good with him, so unbothered by the

moments of pure childishness, and Sarah's pulse galloped uncontrollably.

Great, she thought. Another thing to add to the growing list of reasons she wanted to sleep with Desmond Torres. Sarah looked up at him, into those hazel eyes, and caught her breath. They didn't smile at each other this time. He wasn't flirting or being funny or even being silly for Parker's sake. He was simply looking at her, and there seemed to be a lot of unsaid things in the silence. The space between them crackled with an energy that Sarah chose not to name, instead hugging Parker to her like a shield.

Thankfully Kate saved her from having to say anything that made sense of the silence. She grinned from ear to ear as she showed off a box of graham crackers. "It feels like a good night to let Parker try his first s'more."

Prior to having a kid, a bonfire might have entailed some music and a few beers. Now, to Sarah's horror, a bonfire consisted of Parker, his hands and face covered in copious amounts of chocolate, with marshmallows and graham cracker crumbs stuck to his hair.

She must have been doing a poor job of hiding the concern on her face because Kate looked up from handing Parker another gooey marshmallow, laughed and said, "Don't worry—I'll give him his bath tonight."

"He *is* starting to look like a bit of a gremlin."

Parker's eyes went wide, and everyone laughed.

"I think he only turns into a gremlin if you feed him after midnight," Desmond remarked.

"See," Kate said, checking the time on her phone. "It's only eight thirty. Plenty of time."

Sarah made a humming noise in the back of her

throat. By eight thirty at night Parker was usually bathed and had already been in bed for close to an hour. But this was an unusual night, Sarah reminded herself, so she curled up on her camp chair without any more protest and let Parker set marshmallows ablaze from the safety of Kate's lap.

The firepit was a good hike from the main house, surrounded by a thick grove of trees and lit only by the stars. A menagerie of chairs and logs had accumulated around the stone pit, probably over the years, Sarah guessed, as the Cardiffs had hosted cookouts and stargazed. She knew that Kate used to watch the stars with her dad. It was something Kate had always talked about, especially when they'd been away at school and she'd been missing her parents.

Sarah had never stargazed with her own parents growing up, but she could see the appeal now and was glad to be able to give Parker the experience.

Though she'd worried that he'd get a case of the sillies, having so much sugar after dinner, the fresh air seemed to have the opposite effect, and Parker soon ended up on her lap, content to be soothed by the flames, watching the crackling embers that drifted into the sky.

Sarah cuddled him close. She'd spent more than her fair share of night shifts away from him, so she soaked up every ounce of the moment, making up for all the nights she wasn't there to tuck him into bed. He babbled about the stars, and Kate regaled them all with stories that brought the constellations to life.

As night shifted around them, the wind blew gently, the crickets in tune, and Sarah marveled at the fact Kate had grown up here. The quiet buzz of nature, the scent of autumn everywhere. It was enough to make a person consider a life in the country, away from all the chaos and hustle. She might even give up her coffee shops for something like this.

After a while Parker grew still, and Sarah knew he'd fallen asleep.

From across the firepit, Desmond watched her, and Sarah wondered what he saw when he looked at them. Was it the strength of a tiny family? Or was it a lonely woman and her son? Bathed in firelight, he looked like a child of the sun, each sculpted inch of his face caressed by amber shadows. When she finally made it to his eyes, they were the darkest she'd ever seen. But what surprised her most was that Desmond didn't turn away in startled embarrassment the way she'd anticipated. Instead, he held her gaze. Something like longing tugged at Sarah, low in her belly, and she was glad for the shadow of night to hide the flush that crawled across her body.

"Want me to take him in?" Kate asked, stepping between them and effectively ending Sarah's torture.

"Sure," she said, letting Parker be swept from her arms.

"Behave," Kate whispered. "You're not that far from the house."

"When do I ever?" Sarah teased.

Kate smirked as she adjusted Parker on her shoulder. "Keep it PG—my mother will probably be watching out the window."

Nathan followed Kate back to the house, and for a moment Sarah just watched the flames in the firepit crackle and spark. When she looked up, Desmond was watching her again.

"Parker seemed to enjoy himself," he said.

"How could he not, with the amount of sugar Kate just fed him?"

"Perks of being the aunt and not the mom, I guess."

Sarah hummed. "I'll return the favor someday."

Desmond picked his chair up and carried it over to her side of the fire. "You looked a little lonely over here."

"Sure I did." Her pulse jumped erratically despite her nonchalance. "Does that work on all your women?"

"How many women do you think I have?"

"I don't know, a handsome guy like you? There's probably a lineup waiting for you back in North Carolina."

He pretended to bat the idea away. "Contrary to what you might think, I am a one-woman-at-a-time kind of guy. And the last one was sort of rough, so it's been a long while since I've had something serious."

Sarah noted the shift in his demeanor. His smile was teasing, but his tone was regretful. "Tell me?" she requested softly.

"There's nothing much left to tell," he said. He leaned his elbows on his knees, folding his hands in front of him, and Sarah listened with rapt attention. Desmond gave of himself so freely, sharing pieces of his past. She hadn't had to work for any of it so far, but this was something she would have worked for. Even if he'd made it hard, even if she'd had to trudge through the muck, she would have picked away at the layers because she wanted to know what kind of woman had held his heart. But more than that, she wanted to know what kind of woman could have broken it.

In no version of the story in her head was Desmond the heartbreaker.

It wasn't possible.

Not *this* Desmond.

"It can't have been nothing if she was that serious," Sarah said.

He sighed. "Tale as old as time. I thought she was the one, so I proposed. Then I went overseas and came back to them living in our house together."

"*Them*," Sarah repeated, her jaw dropping. "No."

"Them," he said flatly, frowning down at the fire. "She didn't even have the decency to carry on the affair somewhere else. I kept finding his stuff in my cupboards and drawers for weeks."

"He really just moved in," Sarah said, floored by the thought. "Who does that?"

"I asked myself that for months. Asked myself why she did it. You know, she didn't even take the ring off. She only gave it back to me after everything blew up."

"What did you do with it?"

"Sold it. Poured the money into my company. Figured some good should come of it. Then I tried to pretend like my life hadn't imploded while I was off trying to save other peoples' lives."

"Do you know where she is now?" Sarah asked.

"They didn't last that long, if that's what you're fishing for," Desmond said. "I guess when all the fun of trying not to get caught was removed, there wasn't really much to the relationship."

"I mean, that's a comfort at least."

"Is it?" he asked.

"Doesn't it give you a little satisfaction, knowing they didn't make it? She lost you *and* the other guy."

He shrugged. "When I stopped being angry, I was just sad. And then I started asking myself why again. I always wondered if maybe I wasn't supportive enough in the relationship. Maybe I pushed her away. And if it *was* me, would I do the same thing again? Would I ruin the next good thing that came along? I think that's scared me off of dating a little."

Sarah could tell he'd carried that worry like a weight around his neck. She could see it pulling him down now, dragging his gaze to the ground. "Hey," she said, taking his hand. "If you put half as much dedication and enthusiasm into a relationship as you do into your volunteering, then you have nothing to worry about. I see the way you care about people, Desmond. You're here in Hatchet Lake, not because you're getting paid, but because you want to help. I think whoever she was... she was just the wrong person for you."

He sat back without letting go of her hand. His thumb grazed her knuckles. "I dodged a bullet, huh?"

"A big one."

"Still feels a little like I got grazed."

Sarah had dodged her own bullet, so she could understand. Parker's dad had abandoned them from the beginning. And as much as she knew they were better off, it still hurt. Somewhere, deep down, in a place she tried not to acknowledge, it burned.

"I know," she said.

Desmond put a couple marshmallows on the ends of two pokers. "To finding better people," he said, handing her one.

She took the poker and tapped his marshmallow with hers. "To being happy with what we have."

"You don't think you'll find someone?" Desmond asked, surprised.

She shook her head. "I'm not trying to."

Rejection might have been a bitter pill but the aftertaste was strong, and Sarah knew better now than to let herself get swept away by charm or dashing smiles or even handsome faces. Those things were impermanent, running off after the next pretty girl. Those things left a newborn baby boy without so much as a goodbye.

Sarah had carried that rejection with her as a personal blight, wearing it like a battle scar to remind herself that she was strong enough to raise Parker alone. He would never question how much she loved him or why people didn't stick around. And she would raise him to be a better person: kind, patient and generous.

Parker would always know that he was enough, even if it was the only thing she managed to do in her life-time.

"Is that what all that 'serious' talk was about the other day?" Desmond asked.

She smiled in a way that felt like a frown. "Parker never knew his dad, so he doesn't have anyone to miss. But he's getting older now. Old enough to notice things. To remember people. If I bring around a string of guys that Parker gets attached to, it'll be like he's being abandoned all over again when things don't work out. And I don't ever want him thinking he wasn't enough just because that guy chose not to stick around. That's why I keep it casual."

"But what if one of these guys on this hypothetical string is *the one*?"

"I can't risk it." Their marshmallows had been abandoned in the flames, sliding from the pokers and dropping into the ashes.

"But how do you know it's not the real thing if you never give it a chance to get serious?"

"I guess I don't," she said.

"That's a hard way to live."

"But it's a good way not to get hurt."

Desmond pulled his empty poker from the flames and gently nudged hers. "To not getting hurt."

"To not getting hurt," she echoed quietly. They both stared at each other as the realization hit. Here they were, two people with complicated romantic pasts, just trying their best not to get hurt again.

"I don't think we're very good at this," Desmond finally said, driving his poker into the ground.

Sarah laughed because in the midst of the heavy conversation, they'd only managed to burn both their marshmallows. But somehow, with Desmond's declaration, the mood shifted, like they'd gotten the hard stuff out of the way and things could just be easy again.

"We definitely needed Parker's help," she said.

He stretched, checking his phone. "Walk me back to my truck?"

"Sure."

Together they put the fire out, then followed the light from Desmond's phone back to the house. Sarah bumped against him as they walked, but she didn't try to force any extra distance. It was kind of nice, knowing he was there in the dark. Knowing that he'd keep her secrets.

Sarah had never explained any of her worries or insecurities to anyone except for Kate. She never talked about what it had been like to bring a baby into the world alone. Or about how heavy the weight of rejection really was. She'd only ever practiced her brave face in the mirror, never one that was breakable. But something about Desmond made her want to break. To be vulnerable. She wanted to let him hold these pieces of her, the ones that were sharp, carrying her pain, and the ones that were bent, carrying her shame.

He was a good person to hold all those pieces, she realized. He would cradle them carefully without cutting himself because Desmond was the kind of man that stepped over the wire to save lives. He was the kind of man who put on a red shirt every morning and stepped into someone else's worst nightmare.

Knowing that now, she knew these parts of her would be safe with him, and yet that scared her all the more, so she recoiled, burying her pain and her shame back where they came from. They reached the edge of the house and then finally his truck.

Desmond swung the door open but turned back to look at her. "Sarah, I—"

She didn't give him a chance to speak. She worried that it might take an even *more* serious turn, and she wasn't ready for that. She wasn't ready to push him away or step back from this, so she surged forward, pressed up onto her toes and kissed him. She kissed him like she had the other night outside the pub, like no one could see the way every inch of her now fluttered with anticipation.

She *wanted* him.

Sarah let her hands roam, and as soon as she did, Desmond shifted, letting his own hands slide over her shoulders and down her back, feeling along every dip and curve before settling into the crooks of her hips. While his fingers pulled at the edge of her shirt, his lips pulled away from hers to caress the curve of her ear, each breath hot and raspy. *God*, she never wanted him to stop.

The porch light flicked on, and through the fog that now filled her head, she noticed shadows in the doorway. Reluctantly, Sarah pulled away, dropping her hands from the enticing swell of muscle beneath his shirt.

"I should go," Desmond said, breathless against her.

"You should," she agreed, glad she wasn't the only one that needed a puff from an oxygen tank.

"You could come with me," he said, and for a moment she considered it. But then she thought of Parker. Kate would have bathed him and put him to bed. He was probably grumpy now, having been woken up from his nap at the firepit, and he would need her to soothe him back to sleep.

"Not tonight," she whispered. "I have to—"

"I get it," he said, interrupting her with a short but well-timed kiss on the lips. He breathed her in, like it pained him to leave, then climbed into his truck.

Sarah stepped back so he could shut the door, knowing that if she didn't let him go right then she might do something foolish. It was better this way. She needed the space to harden the walls around her heart again. Sleeping with him tonight, despite how much she wanted to, would come with too many feelings.

She needed these walls to stay fully intact.

It was the only way to stop them both from getting hurt.

Desmond could understand that.

He'd been through that kind of pain himself.

Chapter Twelve

Mid-October had brought a surge of activity to the Team Rebuild camp. Sarah had learned that this final push would finish out the remaining Team Rebuild work, and though she was busier than ever—there wasn't a day that went by when she didn't hand out at least five Band-Aids—she couldn't help but notice the sense of loss that had already permeated camp.

"You coming?" Melanie asked as Sarah wiped down one of the work tables.

"Where?"

"To say goodbye."

"Goodbye?" Sarah dropped the cloth she'd been using on the table. She'd already removed one stubborn sliver and cleaned up a nasty-looking paper cut courtesy of a cardboard box this morning. There had been no mention of goodbyes. "What are you talking about?"

"Oh, that's right, you weren't around yesterday afternoon," Melanie said. "The bus is coming."

"Bus?"

"I keep forgetting you haven't done this before," Melanie said with an apologetic smile. "Feels like you've always been part of the team."

Sarah let herself be touched by Melanie's words for a few seconds before waving at her to continue.

Melanie shrugged. "When a group of volunteers completes their site contract, Team Rebuild packs them on a bus destined for the airport. It's tradition for everyone else to gather around and wave them off."

"Oh," Sarah said. Sending people home meant that Hatchet Lake was almost back to its old self. Well, maybe not its old self, but its new and improved self. There were fewer projects to tackle, less new construction happening. Most of the injuries Sarah was tending to now came from assignments called *teardown* and *cleanup*. She should've been overjoyed for the town. Glad that everything had been put to rights. But a dull, aching sadness settled in the middle of her chest and refused to budge.

"Don't worry," Melanie said. "None of your favorite people are leaving yet."

Sarah snapped out of her melancholy thoughts. "And who would my favorite people be?"

"Well, me, obviously."

Sarah clipped a radio to her jacket in case someone needed her, then threw her arm over Melanie's shoulders, escorting her out of the first aid tent. "Obviously."

"And Evan and Jordan." Melanie dropped her voice to a conspiratorial whisper. "And *Desmond*."

"Desmond, huh? Doesn't ring a bell."

Melanie snorted. "Oh, please, you two are the camp's worst-kept secret. Everybody knows."

"Everybody knows what?" Sarah said. She stopped

and looked at the girl. She might have been in her early twenties, but Melanie still spread rumors like a teenager.

"How you two feel about each other."

Sarah rolled her eyes. "Gossip."

"Hot gossip," Melanie clarified. They continued walking, following a line of volunteers out to Main Street.

"We're friends," Sarah said. "And you should have spent more time paying attention to what was going on in the first aid tent and less time focusing on us."

"I was paying attention. That's how I know you two are way more than just friends," she said. "I'm not sure if you've noticed, but the two of you sort of stare at each other with these big doe eyes."

Sarah scoffed, shoving the girl gently.

Melanie snickered. "It's actually pretty cute."

"You're impossible, you know that?"

"It's been said."

They finally stopped when they reached the sidewalk. A large white bus was parked along the street, luggage being loaded into its undercarriage. It looked like every member of Team Rebuild had gathered to say goodbye.

Sarah spotted Desmond on the other side of the crowd and got a sour taste in her mouth that she couldn't quite explain.

Hugs and expressions of gratitude were handed out by the departing members as they climbed onto the bus. Lori made a farewell speech that she'd likely made a thousand times before, but the tears in her eyes were real, as were the comments about resilience and hope and rebuilding after a storm.

Sarah found herself getting more choked up than she'd expected as she clapped along with the rest of the remaining members. It was sad to think she'd no longer see these people in her tent or when she popped over for coffee in the morning to hand off more of Anne's baking. She couldn't quite wrap her head around how people could come into your life, change it for the better and then disappear from it as easily as the bus turned the corner at the end of the street. Then again, she should have been used to that strange feeling of abandonment by now.

A week and a half later, Sarah stood on the same patch of sidewalk, preparing herself to say goodbye again.

She hadn't expected things to move this quickly, but as the work started to wind down, the farewells became almost daily. Since she was currently staying with the Cardiffs, Sarah had volunteered to hold the fort down at the first aid tent, allowing Evan and Melanie to finish up their contracts early and get back to their lives.

Melanie chucked her bags under the bus and raced out of the crowd into Sarah's arms, squeezing her so tight Sarah couldn't even utter the word *goodbye*.

"Thanks for everything you taught me," Melanie said. "I think medical school is out of the question considering the blood thing, but maybe I'll go into research or something."

Sarah chuckled. "I have no doubt you'll be amazing in whatever you decide to do."

Evan stepped forward and shook her hand. "If you're ever in Detroit, let me know."

"I will," she promised. "Take care."

Evan and Melanie climbed onto the bus.

Sarah glanced through the shuffling crowd, spotting Desmond toward the back of the bus, and that sour taste returned. Ignoring the implications of what that meant, Sarah turned as a hulking shadow eclipsed her.

Jordan reached down, almost picking her up off her

feet. Sarah laughed, wrapping her arms around him. She didn't think one hug would be enough to last her, but it was all she was going to get, so she closed her eyes and tried to burn this moment into her mind. His boisterous laugh. His brilliant smile. The way he could become the most popular person in a room full of strangers. The fact that his voracious appetite had made Anne so incredibly happy these past weeks.

He finally let her go, and Sarah could feel the emotion tangled up in her throat.

"So, you gonna miss me, or what?"

"Of course I'm going to miss you! What kind of question is that?" Jordan's contract had ended, and he was headed to North Carolina today, back to his home and the business he shared with Desmond.

"Just making sure I have a place to come back to in case the fools we left in charge of the business let it flop."

Sarah laughed. "I bet Desmond could build you guys a loft in the stables while he's finishing the renovations and Anne would bring you leftovers."

"She'd love that," Jordan said cheekily, and Sarah had no doubt that Anne would. "But in all seriousness," he continued, "make sure you look after Desmond for me. You know, patch up any bumps and bruises he gets while up at the ranch."

Sarah pursed her lips, knowing that Jordan was teasing. "He's looking after himself just fine."

"But I'd feel better knowing I was leaving him in the hands of a qualified medical professional."

"I do happen to be an exceptional nurse," Sarah joked.

"Couldn't be more perfect," Jordan said, and she got the feeling he wasn't just talking about work. But before Sarah could say anything else, Jordan caught her in one last bone-crushing hug, then dashed up the stairs of the bus.

Lori gave a very familiar farewell speech, and the dwindling group of remaining Team Rebuild members clapped and waved until the bus drove out of sight.

Sarah tried to swallow against the pang of emotion. Every farewell was getting a little bit harder, and though Desmond wouldn't be leaving when his contract ended because he'd been hired by Kate, Sarah was mentally preparing herself for that goodbye knowing it would be the hardest of all.

As the crowd dispersed, back to their respective jobs or to the lunch tent, Sarah lingered on the sidewalk, taking a moment to appreciate how much the town had changed in the short time she'd been here. A flurry of brightly colored leaves raced by her feet, the yellows and reds and oranges highlighting the change still to come. For once in her life, Sarah didn't know if she was looking forward to that change.

She hugged her elbows closer, grateful for the extra layers she'd put on this morning, and turned to make her way back to the first aid tent. Volunteering had been an oddly quiet affair these past couple of days. Lori had been her only visitor, and that was mainly to request that Sarah start condensing her supplies.

So, while Evan and Melanie had been packing up to leave, Sarah had organized the surplus supplies into two piles: one meant for donations and one destined to be shipped off to Team Rebuild's next disaster-relief mission. Now that Sarah had completed that, there wasn't much to keep her busy, and she'd taken to wandering around camp most mornings, eager for someone to complain about something as mundane as a hangnail.

She still only volunteered for part of the day so she

could spend time with Parker, but Lori had her cell phone number and she'd agreed to remain on call in case there were any emergencies while she wasn't there. Sarah hated to even think it, but she could really do with a good emergency right about now. At least that would take her mind off of Desmond. The night of the bonfire had been a turning point in their pseudo-relationship, and every private moment they found at the ranch was filled with heated glances and lingering touches.

She could hardly look at the man most days without flushing.

Great, Sarah thought as she reached the first aid tent and slumped into a chair. Now she was going to spend all afternoon thinking about the way his hands felt against her skin, knowing very well that Desmond would be working late at the diner, finishing up renovations.

If there was ever a sign for her to start focusing on her own life, it was desperately pining after a man who she didn't want a relationship with. She'd been very adamant about keeping things casual, and yet here she was reciting his schedule down to the minute. Sarah rubbed at her face. Maybe it was time to start taking a closer look at all those nursing contracts that were piling up in her email.

A figure approached, and Sarah looked up, hoping for a patient to occupy the rest of her shift.

"James!" she said, surprised to see him outside of the ER. She'd texted him pictures of a cut last week. To Sarah, it had looked infected, and she'd wanted to know if he thought she should direct the patient right to the hospital to get it looked at and receive some antibiotics. "What are you doing here?"

"Day off," he said. "I'd never been to town to see the

operation in action, so I figured I should stop by before it's all packed up."

"I didn't know you lived in Hatchet Lake," she said.

"I don't. Well, not quite. I'm actually a little closer to the city, that way my drive into the hospital isn't as far, but I still get to enjoy the quiet of country living."

"Ah," Sarah said. "You got the best of both worlds."

He gestured to the piles of supplies behind her. "Quite the setup you have here."

"Would you like the grand tour?" Sarah joked, gesturing to the tent. "I have my triage station here. This table is my wound-care corner. And this is the chair where I put my assistant when she faints."

"You have an assistant?"

"Used to," Sarah said fondly. "She shipped off home just before you arrived."

"I'm sorry to have missed her, but you look like you got the place running as efficiently as any ER."

"Speaking of the ER," Sarah said. "How would you like a donation?" She gestured to one of the supply piles, and James's eyes went wide. "I've been meaning to ask. It's all new and unopened."

"Well, I'm certainly not going to say no."

"Lori will be happy to hear that."

"You know, I was going to stop by the pub to get something to eat before I head home. Care to join me?"

Sarah glanced around camp. Her shift was almost over, and most of the volunteers had stopped for lunch anyway. "Sure."

As they walked down to the pub, they passed the diner. Sarah lifted her hand to wave at Desmond when she spotted him through the brand-new front window. She lingered long enough for him to wave back, then hurried after James.

Inside the pub, Sarah was surprised to see that most of the tables were full. This had become quite the regular hangout spot for her, one she was particularly fond of, and she pointed to a booth in the back that looked empty.

As she and James got settled, a waitress she hadn't yet met took their order. Joe worked the bar, serving up lunch beers and chitchat.

"So, how much longer before Team Rebuild wraps up?" James asked.

"A few weeks," Sarah guessed. "Definitely by the end of November, I would think."

"You sound sad," he noted.

"I didn't realize how much I liked it. I kind of got into the role on a whim, and I'm only now realizing how much I'm going to miss it."

James nodded. "I did some work with Doctors Without Borders early on in my career. There's nothing quite like the spirit of togetherness you find when most of the team is volunteering their time."

That was definitely part of it, Sarah thought, watching Joe pile take-out containers on the counter. The idea that they were all working toward one goal fostered a closeness that she hadn't experienced with any other job before. She'd do it all over again in a heartbeat.

The door to the pub opened, and a small group of volunteers clad in hard hats walked in to collect a takeout order. Desmond was among them. She caught his eye and smiled, but he was gone before she could wave him over. Sarah didn't take it personally. His entire team was pushing to get the diner finished before Team Rebuild packed up, and though the hours cut into her coffee breaks with him, she had to admit he looked good in a tool belt and those worn jeans of his. Apparently she had a thing for contractors. Or at least, one very specific contractor. Later, she might even get around to telling him just how attractive she found him today.

"What are your plans for after?" James asked.

A grin pulled at her lips. "I have no idea. I should probably start figuring that out."

"You know, we always need good nurses in the ER," he said. "I think there's going to be some movement early in the new year, so they'll probably start the hiring process again soon. If you want, I could put in a good word for you to the manager."

"Oh?" Sarah sipped her drink before answering. "That would mean hanging around here long term."

"What's wrong with here?"

"Nothing's wrong," Sarah laughed. "I just hadn't really thought about it like that. Hatchet Lake was supposed to be a temporary in-between."

"Well, maybe it could be a more permanent thing for a while. You're obviously more than qualified, and we could really use a nurse with your experience on the floor. I have no doubts you could get the job if you wanted it."

Sarah let herself imagine it for a minute. She thought about what life would look like for both her and Parker. She could stay in Hatchet Lake. Raise him in this town. They could visit Kate and the ranch whenever they wanted. Anne and Dale could continue to be a part of his life. She could give Parker more of this small-town, country living she was starting to adore.

The smile on her face faded as she considered what it would really mean to settle down. Sure, they'd have some permanence here, but Sarah didn't know if she was really ready to give up her life as a travel nurse yet.

She would have to do it soon for Parker's sake, but was this the right place to stay?

Now that she was considering it, the decision felt momentous. It wasn't the kind of thing that should be decided over a burger and fries.

"What's the harm in putting in an application?" James said. "At least give yourself some options."

Sarah hummed noncommittally. "Is this why you showed up today? To sell me on a job?"

"You caught me," he joked. "I'm only after that recruitment bonus."

Sarah feigned disappointment. "You doctors are all the same. Just using us nurses for our stellar IV skills."

"It's true," James said, playing along. When they both started laughing, he dropped the act. "Okay, I won't try to sell you on it anymore. But my offer stands. If you want me to put in a good word, I will. Shoot me a text if you decide to go for it."

"All right," Sarah said. "I'll keep you posted."

Chapter Thirteen

James's suggestion weighed on Sarah's mind for the rest of the week, and with every spare second at the ranch, she contemplated updating her resume. Today she'd gotten as far as opening her laptop while watching a show with Parker. Now a familiar document stared back at her, but adding Team Rebuild under the word *Experience* felt like too much commitment. Was she really going to apply for this job?

"Hey," Kate said. She tossed a napkin at Sarah. "Help me set the table."

Sarah gladly took the distraction, closing her laptop and promising herself she'd figure out what to do about that later. She leaned over to kiss the top of Parker's head. He wiggled away from her because she was apparently interrupting his view, so she left him to finish the episode and went to help Kate. "When did you get back?"

"Like, fifteen minutes ago. Crisis averted." Kate pulled

up a photo on her phone of a brand-new calf. She'd left the ranch in a hurry earlier this afternoon to assist Doc McGinn with a complicated birth.

"Adorable," Sarah said.

"I agree. I think we should take Parker to meet her."

"Oh, he'd love that."

They made their way into the dining room. Kate and Sarah cleared the table before laying out Anne's choice of dishware. A lasagna had been baking all afternoon, and the entire house smelled divine.

Nathan walked through the front door with Desmond and Rusty minutes before Anne's lasagna was on the table. Tara walked through the door about halfway through dinner, right after Parker had finished licking sauce from all the noodles on his plate and declaring himself finished.

Sarah cleared Parker's mess from the table, and Tara eagerly took his spot.

"Hey, stranger," Rusty complained. "It feels like we haven't seen you in ages. Team Rebuild's got you booked solid."

"How are things going with that?" Anne asked while passing Tara a heaping plate of food.

Tara wolfed down half the plate before responding. "I've been trying to capture as much as I can as the projects are winding down. Look!" She reached for the camera bag she'd strung over the back of the chair. She scrolled through some of her shots, Rusty and Nathan hovering over her shoulder. "I took these the other day when one of the buses was taking people to the airport."

"That's a great one," Nathan said, taking the camera so Tara could finish eating. He flipped it around to show Sarah and Kate.

To Sarah's surprise, Tara had captured the moment

when Jordan had almost lifted her off her feet as they were saying goodbye. This had been right before he'd told her to look out for Desmond. Sarah glanced across the table at him, but he was occupied by the lasagna on his plate.

Sarah reached for the camera to take a closer look. She'd seen Tara in camp on occasion, that camera strapped around her neck. But mostly she'd been off snapping photos of the volunteers filling their respective roles around town.

"You can scroll through them," Tara said, her mouth half-full. "There were some other really good ones I took of the first aid tent."

Sarah flipped through the photos, feeling a smile tug at her lips. With every photo, the smile stretched a little more, until she was grinning uncontrollably. Tara had caught so many sweet moments. Moments that Sarah could remember clearly now that she was looking at the photos. The most interesting part was how candid everything was. The only time Sarah had been asked to smile for a picture was when Tara had wrangled everyone together for a team photo. But Sarah hadn't even known Tara was there for the rest of these. She supposed that was what made her such a great photographer in the field, especially when they were off shooting wildlife.

There were pictures of Melanie and Evan messing around at the first aid tent while Sarah told them to sort out supplies. Pictures of her doing a patient assessment. A photo of her and Desmond, the two of them sharing a coffee before the day started. They looked happy together. Sarah's heart stuttered in her chest. There were a lot of photos where she and Desmond were no more than an arm's length away.

"So does this mean you're almost done?" Nathan asked.

Sarah looked up in time to see Tara grin. "I didn't even tell you the best part yet. They offered me a contract to do another social media stint. Apparently there's a bad storm blowing through the East Coast right now."

"A bad storm, huh?"

"Hurricane, I think. Anyway, Team Rebuild is gearing up to send a group out there to help with the cleanup as soon as it winds down." Tara reached for her camera as Sarah passed it back across the table. "I leave next week to help document the event."

"How long?" Nathan asked.

"I should be back in a couple of months."

"We'll miss you around here," Anne said, "but they're lucky to have you."

Team Rebuild *would* be lucky to have her. They were lucky to have *all* the amazing people who dedicated their time away from their regular lives to help.

Sarah glanced across the table at Desmond again. He still wasn't quite engaged. She could chalk it up to exhaustion—he'd been doing double duty finishing up with Team Rebuild while also making a good start on Kate's renovations. But Sarah knew it wasn't just that. Desmond had been off since the day Jordan had left, and she wondered if he was missing his best friend. Or maybe something was going on with the business back in North Carolina. Jordan had been home long enough now to give Desmond a proper update. But Desmond had also been distant with her, something she hadn't really expected after the way things had been going with them, so maybe it had nothing to do with Jordan or North Carolina. She'd tried her best not to read too much into it—that was what serious people did—but she couldn't shake the nagging feeling that she was at the root of this problem.

Sarah waited until after dinner to say something. While everyone was busy corralling dishes to the kitchen and Parker was quietly watching a show on the couch with Dale, Sarah slipped out the front door and made her way to the stables, where she'd watched Desmond escape to.

She found him halfway up a ladder, his measuring tape out and a pencil between his teeth. He retrieved it and marked something onto a wooden beam.

"Hey," Sarah said, trying not to startle him. The last thing she needed was for him to fall. She was only trying to talk, not provide the mechanism for bodily injury.

"Hey," he said without looking at her. He made his way down the ladder before moving to sort through some of the deliveries that had arrived for the renovation. Skids of material and lumber had been showing up for days, and Parker was becoming obsessed with the big trucks that kept rolling onto the ranch to deliver everything.

Sarah could tell he was busy. She had those moments while she was working too. Moments where you were in your element, solely focused on getting your job done. Like when she was trying to prepare medications for a complex patient. She knew what it was like to have someone interrupt in the middle of that. So her first instinct was to leave him alone. She'd just turn around and go back the way she came.

But she also knew that if she didn't ask him now, that she might never ask. She would let this thing fester between them. In the end it would make everything easier. She and Desmond would part ways, and those pesky things called feelings would have already shriveled up. Unease roiled in her gut at the thought, and she let out a heavy breath.

"Are you okay?" she asked.

"What are you talking about?"

Sarah shrugged, mostly to herself since he wouldn't look at her. "You seemed off at dinner tonight. And you've been kind of distant these past few days. I just wondered if everything was okay."

"Everything's fine."

"Fine?" she said. "So things are okay with Jordan and the business?"

"Yep, they're fine."

Sarah didn't know what to say to that. He wasn't giving her much to work with other than *fine*, which was unusual for him. "Are *we* okay?" she asked, the question weighing heavily on her.

"Why wouldn't we be?"

Sarah bristled then because she could tell by the tone of his voice that she'd hit a nerve—or at least close enough to the problem that he'd grown defensive. Apparently she *was* the root of this problem. Well, at least she knew she hadn't been imagining things. Sarah crossed her arms. "That's a great question," she said, waiting until he finally made eye contact. "Why wouldn't we be okay?"

"I don't know, Sarah. You tell me."

She narrowed her eyes. "What's your problem?"

"I don't have a problem," he said, giving her no indication as to the source of the awkwardness between them.

"I'm just trying to figure out why you're so angry with me."

"I'm not angry with you."

"Frustrated, then. Annoyed. Whatever you want to call it."

Desmond carried an armful of lumber across the stables. "You're turning this into something it's not."

"And you're making this really difficult. I've literally had more mature conversations with my son."

"Sarah, what is this?" he asked, letting the lumber drop from his hands. It clattered to the ground. "What do you want from me?"

"Nothing," she said. "Forget I even asked." She turned on her heel and was almost to the door when she heard him.

"Yeah, go on. Go have some serious conversations with that doctor friend of yours."

Sarah's jaw dropped, and she didn't know whether to laugh or to scream. She turned around so quickly her vision spun. "That's what all of this is about? James?"

Desmond didn't say anything, but his jaw tightened as he worked.

Sarah marched back toward him. "You're jealous of my lunch with James?"

"I'm not jealous," he said.

"So you're being distant and short tempered with me just…for fun?"

"Would it matter if I was jealous? You didn't seem to have a problem rubbing James in my face the other day. But we're nothing serious, right? You don't do *se-rious*. I got that message loud and clear at the diner."

Sarah felt those invisible walls shoot up around her heart. They took the brunt of his words, but she knew there would still be bruises. Most of the fight drained from her then. He actually thought that she'd been trying to hurt him by eating lunch with James. Underneath

Desmond's jealousy was a thick layer of defeat. Defeat she had planted there herself.

"Well," he said, his words just above a whisper. "Am I wrong?"

Sarah shook her head. He wasn't wrong. Not completely. Her arms, which had been braced against her chest for a fight, fell to her sides. She'd never intended to hurt him, and she'd never meant to make him question her feelings for him, but jealousy was a thing couples fought over. And they weren't a couple. They weren't anything. She was almost embarrassed at having to remind herself of that. Even if her lunch with James had been a romantic date, that shouldn't have mattered to either of them.

And yet for some reason it did.

Desmond dropped his hands to his hips, looking down at his feet for a long time before he lifted his head to look at her. "What do you want me to say, then?"

When she couldn't answer that, he turned around, going back to his sorting. He ignored her with such strength Sarah practically felt herself being forced from the stables. Her feet started moving of their own accord, and she only managed to catch herself at the door. "Just so you know," she said, "that lunch was about a work thing."

"Work?" she thought she heard him say.

"James wondered what I was doing after Team Rebuild packs up and heads out. He said they're looking for nurses in the ER and offered to put in a good word if I felt like applying. That's all it was."

Annoyed at having to explain herself—and even more terrified of what his reaction might be—Sarah fled from the stables before he could respond.

Chapter Fourteen

If Sarah was good at anything, it was holding a grudge. She'd been mad at her mother for most of her life, so she'd had a lot of practice, but over a week had gone by since that ridiculous argument in the stables with Desmond, and by mid-November the anger she'd felt had started to fizzle, leaving her mopey and frustrated. The fact that Team Rebuild was officially signing off with Hatchet Lake didn't help her mood either. For the most part, Sarah and Desmond had been able to avoid each other, which was a feat in itself with a curious toddler who was obsessed with seeing the horses every day. Sarah kept busy with Parker in town while Desmond was on the ranch working, and he'd started to decline Anne's offers to stay for dinner.

But tonight was the final Team Rebuild goodbye party at the pub, and despite wanting to say goodbye, Sarah was dreading going. Desmond would likely be there, and she couldn't exactly avoid him if she packed herself into a room like that.

Sarah tossed the jeans she was going to wear back down onto her bed. Maybe she wouldn't go. She'd tell Lori she wasn't feeling well. Pass on her goodbyes through text.

"Okay," Kate said, standing in the doorway of the room. "That's the third time you've kicked those pants around. I don't think the denim has offended you, so what's wrong?"

"Nothing's wrong."

"You've had a look on your face for almost two weeks like someone smeared manure under your nose."

Sarah scoffed. "I have not!"

"The rest of my family might not know you well enough to notice, but I sure do. Now, are you going to tell me or am I going to have to hold Parker for ransom to get it out of you?"

Sarah smiled a bit at that. "Desmond and I had a fight. That's all."

"That's all?" Kate said, coming to sit on the bed.

Sarah sat beside her. "I had lunch with James a couple weeks ago. The ER doctor who helped out with some of our Team Rebuild cases."

"Right."

"He lives just outside of town, and he dropped by to see the setup. But then he asked if I wanted to go to lunch, which Desmond saw, and he got mad about it."

"Mad?"

Sarah shrugged. "Jealous."

She'd been annoyed at having to explain herself that afternoon, but even more annoyed that she'd *wanted* to explain herself. Who was he to make her feel like this? He wasn't her boyfriend. If Sarah wanted to talk to another man or eat lunch with him, then that was her pre-rogative. Either way, James was just a friend and the lunch had been harmless.

Kate smirked. "That makes more sense. What did you and James talk about?"

"Work things, mostly. He said they're looking for some ER nurses. Also said he'd give me a good recommendation if I felt like staying."

"Oh," Kate breathed.

"Right! That's what I basically said. I don't know what I want to do yet. It still feels like a huge decision, especially where Parker is concerned, and now I'm in a fight with your contractor."

Kate burst out laughing. "We're calling him the contractor now?"

"That's what he is."

"I think you might have to admit that you and Desmond are a little more than friends with—"

"With what? There have been no benefits exchanged yet."

"I don't know. That make-out session the night of the bonfire looked pretty hot and heavy."

Sarah scoffed. What *were* she and Desmond? This was the most complicated non-relationship she'd ever been in. Was it enough to say that they were simply attracted to one another?

"If he was bothered enough to get jealous, I think his feelings are more than just—"

"Stop," Sarah said, clapping her hand over Kate's mouth. "I don't want you to finish that sentence."

Kate rolled her eyes, mumbling, "*Fine.*" Sarah pulled her hand away. "Let's talk about work, then."

Sarah groaned. "I don't want to discuss that either."

"Too bad. Here's my two cents about that—if James

is offering to give you a reference, I'm not going to talk you out of staying, if that's what you're waiting for. I like having you here, and I think my mom would literally riot if you try to take Parker from her. He's filling that grandchild-shaped hole that I have yet to fill myself. In fact, if you leave, I might keep him. He's making my life far less complicated."

Sarah smirked. "You can keep Desmond and Parker and all the national inquiries from my mother."

"And where will you be?"

"I don't know yet," Sarah said.

"Somewhere hot, with tiny umbrella drinks?"

Sarah grinned, making a soft sound of agreement, only her ideal getaway was no longer accompanied by visions of chiseled men on white sandy beaches. Instead it had become images of handsome contractors in small towns. She groaned and stuffed a pillow over her face.

"Hey, none of that," Kate said. "You have a party to get to."

"I don't want to go."

"Yes, you do. You want to celebrate and say goodbye to all the great people you worked with."

"Desmond will be there."

"Probably. But you're going to put your big-girl jeans on and handle it. If you don't go, you'll regret it."

Sarah pulled the pillow off her face. "Come with me?"

Kate grinned. "I thought you'd never ask."

The pub was packed from corner to corner, and yet Sarah still managed to immediately spot Desmond. The moment her eyes found his, she knew this had been a mistake.

Sarah attempted to reverse through the crowd, but

Kate was behind her and instead of letting her escape, she directed her to the bar.

While Kate ordered their drinks, Sarah made small talk with some of the coworkers she'd gotten to know. It wasn't until Kate slid a beer into Sarah's hand that she realized she didn't feel like drinking. Not even to take her mind off of Desmond.

Because that was the problem, really. She couldn't get him out of her head, and she was currently torn between ditching Kate and bolting for the door, and marching straight up to Desmond to demand they start speaking again.

She hated this lingering awkwardness between them.

She hated that she felt like the guilty party. Like she'd done something wrong by eating lunch with James.

Most of all, she hated that this celebration felt more like a trial. Like she was about to be marched before the crowd and accused of ruining a perfectly good friendship. Sarah was so caught up in all the things she hated about this evening that she hardly noticed when Kate pushed her into the arms of the first guy to ask her to dance until it was too late. His name was Kai or Kyle. She couldn't really hear him over the beat of the music and the din from the bar. He was a mechanic. Said he was good with his hands. He smirked at her like that meant something. Sarah barely paid attention. She kept glancing at Desmond, wondering what he was thinking every time he caught her eye.

His expression grew progressively cloudy each time Kyle spun her around. And the next thing she knew, he'd left his beer on a table and disappeared. Sarah only caught sight of his jacket again as he slipped out the door. Now she felt guilty not just about before but also for driving him off tonight. Her intention hadn't been to hurt him further. She'd never meant to make him feel like he had to leave.

Sarah thought back to the moment Kate had asked her if hiring Desmond for the renovations would be a problem. Sarah had emphatically told her no. And yet here they were. She had to fix this situation. If not for herself, then at least for Kate. She didn't want to jeopardize the ranch. She knew Desmond was a professional and that he would do a good job regardless of what was happening between them, but she wasn't making their lives any easier.

"Excuse me," Sarah said to Kai or Kyle, leaving him on the dance floor. She darted through the celebratory crowd, straight to the door. Outside, she shivered without her jacket. Squinting into the night, she could see no sign of Desmond.

Sarah went back inside to find Kate at the bar. "Can I borrow the truck?"

"Do I need to find another ride home?"

Sarah shrugged. "Maybe."

Kate handed over the keys. "Good luck."

Sarah hurried outside and started up the truck, following the posted signs across town to the cabins where Desmond was staying. She was disappointed not to find his rental in the driveway. She knocked anyway, knowing that no one would answer. Determined to make this right, Sarah parked herself on the porch steps, waiting for him to turn up.

The night was clear and cold, the stars out in abundance. November had been kind to them for the most part, but she could see her breath churn in the crisp air. Just when her fingers had grown numb and she considered getting back in the truck at least, a pair of headlights came down the laneway.

It was Desmond.

"What are you doing here?" he said the moment he got out of the vehicle. She could tell he was surprised to see her. But there was something else as well. Relief, maybe?

"I wanted to talk."

He crossed the yard and climbed the porch steps. He reached for her hands, and she let him. "You're freezing."

"Are you going to let me in?"

They went inside, and Sarah got her first look at the tiny but homey cabin.

"So, what did you—"

"I'm sorry," she blurted out before Desmond could finish his question.

"For what?"

She lifted a shoulder. "For going to lunch with James. For dancing with that guy in the pub. For hurting you. All of it. Everything. That's not what I'd intended to happen."

Desmond's lips parted, but for a few agonizing seconds, he was silent. Then he said, "You look confused about it."

"I am."

He chuckled, and the sound of it filled Sarah's heart with glee. "What's so confusing?"

"You are. I don't normally do this." She understood it now. She'd felt guilty because she wanted to be with Desmond. She didn't want to be with anybody but him.

"You don't do what?"

"Catch feelings. Real feelings."

The corner of his mouth flickered. "You've said as much before. So what are we gonna do about it?"

Sarah shrugged. "Keep ignoring it for as long as possible."

"It's not gonna work, Sarah. We have to see each other every day at the ranch."

"You're right," she said. "Guess I'll have to get you fired."

He chuckled again, softer this time. "Seems like the only solution. Too bad for Kate. I'm the very best at what I do."

"I'm sure Rusty and Nathan will manage."

"They *are* practically professionals now."

"Photography, construction…it's all the same in the end."

"Oh, definitely," he said. His gaze was heated. He was close enough to touch. All she had to do was reach out. "But what if we ran with it instead?"

"What?" she breathed.

"These feelings. See what comes of them."

"Just for tonight?" she asked, silently making herself a promise she wasn't sure she could keep.

"Tonight," he repeated. "Tomorrow. Maybe early next week."

Sarah laughed at his eagerness, then surged forward. She pulled his face to hers and kissed him hard. She would scratch the itch, and hopefully that would take care of it. She could be with him tonight and get over him tomorrow. *Because that's how problems are solved*, a small part of her brain whispered against the tide of desire flooding her veins.

"Wait," Desmond husked. His eyes were pinched closed, his brow furrowed, like he was thinking really hard.

"What is it?"

"I'm sorry too. I didn't mean—" he started to say, but at that moment Sarah decided she wanted this more than anything, wanted him, and she pulled her shirt over her head, desperate to feel his hands on her bare skin.

Desmond's eyes opened. Apology forgotten, he reached out and claimed her lips again, letting his hands slip into her hair as he continued the kiss. His hands brushed through her curls and melted down her neck and across her shoulders, the tips of his fingers tracing her collarbones. Her body responded instantly, a delicious heat spreading wherever he touched. Then his hands split up, one traveling between the valley of her breasts and across her belly to claim her hip. The other lifted to cup the side of her face, keeping her lips from slipping away from his.

Sarah moaned into the next kiss, hungry for him in a way she hadn't fully let herself appreciate until now. He pushed at her gently, and Sarah let him guide her from the front room. They passed cozy woodworked furniture and a hallway filled with photos. Sarah couldn't focus on any of them long enough to say what they were, but she was sure they were nice. Everything about this was nice.

The way his hand had curved over her backside, grabbing at her jeans, was nice. Actually, it was extremely hot, and Sarah would have said so if she'd had any control over her speech at that exact moment. Instead, all she could manage was the desperate, breathy sounds that kept falling from her lips.

When they bumped up against the edge of the bed, Sarah was surprised. She hadn't been paying enough attention, eyes only for him as he peeled his shirt off. Sarah couldn't help herself. She marveled at the muscle, her fingers itching to sample every inch, but her eyes were faster and for a moment she just stared.

Desmond took her hand and gently placed it on his

chest as if whispering, *It's okay—you can touch*. Sarah didn't need to be told twice. In fact, she let herself be greedy, using both hands to trace over the rounded strength of his shoulders before following the natural dip from his chest to his abdomen.

Only able to go as far as his belt, Sarah stopped, letting her fingers play with the buckle for a moment. Before she could go any further, Desmond kissed her again. Her fingertips brushed lower, and she could feel his excitement through his jeans.

She wanted to get to the *really* good part, and maybe Desmond had the same idea because he bumped against her, forcing Sarah to sit on the edge of the bed. When he leaned over her, she fell back, gasping as his hands stroked their way up her body. A trail of fire burned in their wake, coiling in the pit of her stomach. Everything about this moment was warm and *oh, so good*, and Sarah never wanted to stop burning.

Desmond pulled back, and as Sarah reached for her jeans, she heard the crinkle of a condom wrapper. She smiled to herself as she wriggled out of her pants. Despite the thumping of her heart and the rush of blood in her ears, she knew very well that she didn't want any surprises to come from this night of fun, and the fact that she hadn't even had to ask him only sweetened the moment. She felt the bed dip again, and she lifted her head to meet his eyes. His hair fell over his face, and he swept it back with his hand to see her clearly.

For a few strangled heartbeats she let herself feel what it would be like to *want* him without conditions. He stood there, one knee braced on the edge of the bed, before moving any further, as if asking for her permission. Sarah gave an eager nod, then dropped her head back against the comforter, gasping as Desmond leaned forward and pressed a kiss to her inner thigh.

His lips and tongue were dangerous things, and Sarah squirmed, running her own fingers through his hair. She tugged when something felt particularly good, biting her lip so often that she was dangerously close to drawing blood. When Sarah found that precipice within herself, she pulled at him, wanting his lips on hers, but Desmond was unyielding and Sarah fell hard and fast, almost launching her hips off the bed.

"*Desmond*," she moaned. The sound of his own name was like a summons, and he crawled up her shuddering body, settling his weight above her with a pleased grin. Sarah marveled at the strength of him as she gripped his arms, keeping herself moored in the waves that followed. A storm surged inside her, demanding more, only she didn't know how much more she could give.

Still, Desmond made her want to try. And with him, like this, she thought it might be possible to fall again and again.

Desmond didn't give her heart a moment to rest. Instead, he took her leg and hitched it over his hip. Sarah's nails bit into his skin as they moved together, but he never complained. He merely kissed her harder, until she was sure the imprint of his lips would be forever marked into her skin.

Sarah felt the waves inside her grow unsteady once more, the tension ebbing and flowing. She whispered his name desperately. It wasn't much, and in response he could only moan, perhaps as deliriously tongue-tied as she was as they rocked together. For long moments the only things she could see were the backs of her eyelids as her mouth fell open in a silent series of gasps. Her back arched and her limbs curled around Desmond, and finally she let herself be carried away by the storm they'd created.

After spiraling through the storm, an abyss of nothingness consumed her, and Sarah floated in it. She basked in the tangle of their limbs, in the messy breathing that filled the room, in the way her body fit against his.

Sarah had done this many times before, but it had never felt so right from the beginning. There was no clumsy awkwardness as their hands learned each other. No hesitant smiles as they figured out the mechanics of how they were supposed to fit. The entire night was simply need and passion and desire.

A desire so strong Sarah could already feel it tugging in her belly again as Desmond pulled the comforter around their naked bodies.

And she knew at once that she would have to leave.

She couldn't let herself *want* Desmond that much.

Wanting him like that was dangerous.

Wanting him like that... It would be her undoing.

Sarah kissed him as he drifted off to sleep, first his brow and then the top of his cheekbone. She kissed the very corner of his mouth, careful not to let herself linger. And then, as his breathing evened out, she crawled from the bed and dressed in the dark.

She didn't let herself think about what it would be like to stay the night or what it would be like to wake up beside him the next morning. She didn't let herself hope that they might do this again. Such things were just dreams.

So she closed the door behind her softly and drove back home to Parker.

Chapter Fifteen

Sarah woke up at the ranch, mulling through her hazy memories of last night. Images of hands upon muscles and the gasping sounds of pleasure filled her head as she changed her clothes and brushed her teeth. In the mirror, a flush painted her skin, but she was filled with misery, her dark eyes lost.

Post-one-night stand Sarah never looked like this.

This Sarah looked tortured.

She bent over, spitting her toothpaste into the sink, and splashed some water on her face. *Get over it, girl. Get over him.* It was just sex. Good sex. Great sex, even. Her mind wandering again, Sarah went back to her room and made the bed. She could hear Parker and Kate in the other room. He must have woken up while she was in the bathroom.

As she finished with the bed and headed to the hall, Parker went tearing by her straight for the stairs.

"Excuse me?" Sarah laughed. She was truly being replaced.

"Mom!" Parker crowed, climbing back up the top steps to throw himself at her legs. She picked him up, taking a deep breath, letting the sweet scent of his soap fill her. His cuddle only lasted another moment before he was kicking to be free of her. She'd learned to enjoy every quiet moment along with every rambunctious second. People always told her these days were short, so she set him free, enjoying how happy he was.

Sarah could hear Anne puttering around in the kitchen downstairs, and no sooner had Parker reached the bottom step did she hear the sweet sound of his giggles.

"I didn't think you'd be here this morning," Kate said. "Isn't there a handsome contractor you should be schmoozing?"

Sarah smirked, crossing her arms as she sat down on the top step.

Kate sat down beside her. "How'd it go last night?"

Sarah shrugged, fighting the blush. "We kissed and made up, if you must know."

"Oh, I *must*." Kate nudged her. "And what happened after the kiss?"

Sarah mimed zipping her lips.

"That good, huh?"

"*Yes*, it was that good."

"And?"

"And nothing." Sarah was already sick of contemplating last night. "It was just sex. We got it out of our systems. Now we can all move on."

"Sure," Kate said, grinning as she stood and made her way down the stairs. "Whatever you say."

Sarah followed her, spending a quiet morning with

Parker and the Cardiffs. They baked and ate a late breakfast, and Sarah basked in the close-knit family Kate so freely shared with her. She was truly going to miss moments like this when it was time to go.

After lunch her phone rang. Sarah stared at her mother's number until the ringing stopped. She hadn't meant to ignore it, she just didn't have the energy to deal with her mother right now, but when Bonnie Schaffer called back before dinner, Kate raised a brow, and Sarah took the call.

"Hi, Mom," Sarah said, taking the phone upstairs while Parker was occupied with the TV. They talked of the usual things, landing on the same topics they always did: Parker and the current state of Sarah's working and living conditions.

For the most part Sarah was barely paying attention, hemming and hawing as her mother rambled on. She was in the middle of folding some of Parker's clothes when something her mom said caught her attention.

"I'm not coming back to California."

"Why don't you let me finish talking before you flat-out refuse?"

"Because I'm *not* moving back."

"What's wrong with coming back here? You'd have support for Parker. I have a couple friends on the board at West Hills. I'm sure they could help you secure a job."

"Mom, no. I don't need you to do that."

"You said yourself that your volunteering was over. You need some sort of direction, Sarah. Some sort of permanent plan for your son."

"I have a plan," she spouted, if only to get her mother to stop talking. "I've applied for a job at the hospital here."

"Why would you be staying there?"

"Why not?" Sarah said, unsure herself. "They have an ER in the city with openings. They need ER nurses. That's what I do best."

"You're staying there on a whim."

"It's not a whim."

"This is just another one of your rash decisions."

"It's not." Sarah swallowed hard. "I've thought about this. I'll let you know how the interview goes. Talk to you later, Mom." Sarah hung up quickly, chewing on her lip. It was still swollen from where she'd bitten it last night during… What the hell was she thinking? She hadn't given James's offer much thought until this very moment. She wasn't sure she wanted to stay in Hatchet Lake. She wasn't sure about Desmond. She wasn't sure what was best for Parker. But a part of her wanted to prove her mother wrong, so she'd latched onto the first thing she could think of.

Sarah reached for her laptop and opened her resume file, staring at the jumbled words. With uncertainty coursing through her, Sarah added her Team Rebuild experience, then sent the document in a text to James.

Calling in that favor now, she texted.

James replied almost immediately. I'll give this to the nursing manager during my next shift. Expect a phone call.

Sarah smiled despite herself. At least someone was sure she was making the right decision. Besides, hadn't James said something about leaving her options open? As Sarah made her way back downstairs, she turned at the sound of crunching gravel. She'd grown used to Desmond's truck rolling down the drive at odd hours of the day, but never had her pulse reacted so quickly. Her heart thudded against her ribs with such force,

Sarah swore each of the Cardiffs would be able to hear the echo.

Sarah caught Kate's eye across the kitchen, and with a sly smile, Kate coaxed Parker into playing a game, leaving Sarah free to sneak off for a quiet moment. She slipped on her shoes and grabbed her jacket and hurried across to the stables.

Sarah saw him before he noticed her, but all it took was a quick flash of his hazel eyes to know that all the awkwardness and stress from the past couple of weeks was truly gone. They'd moved past it and landed somewhere else.

He crossed the stables to meet her, his hands immediately diving beneath the open flaps of her jacket, wrapping around her in a way that reminded Sarah of sheets sliding over naked skin. He held her like he knew the planes of her, every dip and crease and curve. He held her like he'd run his hands over all her most secret places. The line of her wrist, the spaces between her fingers, the place where her neck met her shoulder.

Desmond had consumed her with a fire that still lingered in her blood, and his touching her now set those flames alight.

"I missed you this morning," he said, pressing his face to hers.

The spark that had burned between them before hadn't been extinguished, only intensified, and Sarah finally let her lips meet his. She kissed him in a way that would have mortified her mother. She kissed him like he was hers to explore and she was desperate to commit every inch to memory.

Sarah hated to admit that part of her understood his jealousy now.

"You could have stayed," Desmond said.

She could hardly catch her breath. "I had to go. Parker."

"I know," he said. "But I still wanted you there."

The sound of her son's name on her lips cut the lust with a measure of clarity, and Sarah managed to pull away before she started taking off her clothes in the middle of the stables. She put some distance between them.

Desmond nodded once, like he also thought it was a good idea, running the back of his hand across his lips. Sarah waited for the moment to feel strange, for the space between them to grow uneasy, but it never happened. Part of her rejoiced in that.

"I'm sorry," he blurted out.

"What?"

"I meant to say it last night, before we... I didn't want you to think that I didn't care about everything you said. I'm sorry too. For getting jealous. For making you feel like you had to defend the way you spent your time or whom you spent it with. I just..." He sighed. "I really like you, Sarah. And I let it go to my head."

"Maybe it wasn't all in your head," she said, smiling.

"Yeah? Is that why you came to find me last night?"

"Maybe I just wanted to finally get you into bed."

Desmond burst out laughing. He picked up a box of tools and carried them across the stables. "You know, I'm surprisingly okay with that."

He passed by her and kissed her again but chastely, getting back to work without lingering for more. "How was your morning?"

"Pretty good. Though I think I've discovered that Parker would choose Kate over me in a divorce."

"Ah," Desmond said. "Perks of being the fun aunt."

Sarah hummed, losing her train of thought as her phone buzzed in her pocket. It was her mother again. Sarah groaned, swiping the call from the screen, sending it straight to voicemail. When she tried to stash it back in her pocket, her phone buzzed for a second time. Sarah's thumb hovered, she just couldn't bring herself to answer it.

"Do you need me to explain how the buttons work?" Desmond teased, watching her debate answering the call.

"It's my mother," she said.

"And you don't want to talk to her?"

"We've already had one unproductive conversation today. I try to limit our calls to once every other week." Much less if she could manage it. "Besides, she doesn't really want to hear what I have to say."

The ringing stopped.

"Maybe she'll leave a voicemail," Desmond offered.

"My mother doesn't leave voicemails," Sarah said as her phone started ringing for a third time. Clearly her mother hadn't liked the idea of her and Parker remaining in Hatchet Lake.

Desmond stared from her to the phone in confusion.

"I applied for that ER job," Sarah said, trying to explain.

"The one James was telling you about?"

Sarah nodded. She was glad they'd moved past the James thing enough to openly talk about it now. James would probably get a kick out of unknowingly having come between them.

A text message came through: Sarah, answer your phone.

"Is staying here what you want?" Desmond asked, sounding genuinely curious.

Another text: I know you're ignoring me.

Sarah sighed. "I don't know. I think I did it mostly to annoy my mother."

Maybe it was selfish of her, but a small part of her

also knew that applying would give her a real excuse to stay in Hatchet Lake a little longer. To let Parker spend the holidays with the Cardiffs and to let her have a little more time with Desmond.

The final text: Why do you insist on making everything so difficult?

Sarah responded: Sorry, busy.

"Annoying your mother can't be the only reason you applied for the job."

Sarah stuffed her phone in her pocket. "Oh, I have done many things over the years in sheer defiance of that woman."

His smile drew her to him, and as Desmond reached for her, Sarah saw how dangerously easy it could be between them.

"Tell me," he whispered.

"The entirety of my teenage years. Moving across the country for school. Raising Parker on my own."

"And you're doing a fabulous job with that last one," he said, the words spilling across her cheek.

Her heart thumped hard at the sincerity of his words. "We shouldn't do this," she said, but they were like magnets and she could hardly stay away. She let her eyelids close.

"Why not?"

She knew immediately that he was talking about more. Asking for more. "It's not real," she said, tasting his lips.

"It has to mean something."

"Why?"

"Because it's too good not to." He frowned, taking her face in his hands. He pressed his lips to hers until she was dizzy with the feeling. "It can't mean nothing."

"Desmond," she warned, unable to focus on anything but his fingers ghosting down her neck.

"Tell me you don't feel this...connection. Tell me I'm wrong."

"You're not wrong," she breathed against him. "I just can't."

"Couldn't we just say it's complicated?"

She chuckled into the next kiss. How did she know he wouldn't end up hurting her? How did she know he wouldn't leave her? She couldn't take that chance. That was why she made sure she was always the one leaving. "It'll be short lived, whatever this is. You'll finish the renovations. I'll get a job somewhere. Isn't it better to just leave it where it was?"

He looked at her and slowly shook his head. "What are you afraid of? That we won't be able to stop?"

"Yes," she breathed. But it was more than that. If they started this, she worried they might not be able to stop *ever*. Some small part of her brain, the only part left functioning at this moment, knew that she could really love a man like him. And that was a terrifying thought for a woman who had decided not to love anyone like that. So she cast it aside, hoping the thought would disappear among the weeds. "It'll be harder when it ends."

"It's hard now. Isn't it?" He brushed a strand of her hair behind her ear.

She could feel his breath, warm against her face. Feel the way his chest rose and fell against her. He was right about how difficult this would be while they were both still working and living here. She wanted him...all the time. Maybe she could have him. He could be hers right here, on the ranch. And when they left it would be over. "Maybe..." she said with a shaky breath. "Just for now."

Desmond's face broke with relief. "Yeah?"

"Just don't go falling in love with me," she warned. It was playful but serious. Sarah meant every word.

"I wouldn't dare," he said, surging down to kiss her. Footsteps sounded outside, and Desmond's fingers stilled against her hips. The stable door swung open, and Nathan hurried in.

"There you are!" he exclaimed as she and Desmond broke apart. "I wanted to show you something. Well, ask you something. Get your opinion on something."

Desmond's lips pursed, and Sarah had the distinct impression that he already knew what Nathan was going to say.

"Are you okay?" she asked. "You're out of breath."

Nathan nodded. "Your son was chasing me around the kitchen island. Doesn't he ever get tired?"

"Not a chance."

"Anyway, I slipped away from him and Kate for a moment." Nathan dug into his pocket and produced a ring box.

Sarah's jaw dropped. "That better not be for me," she joked.

Nathan popped it open, and Sarah marveled at the teardrop-shaped diamond. She took the box from him to admire it.

"Do you think she'll like it?" Nathan asked. For the first time since she'd met him, he seemed genuinely unsure of himself.

"She'll love it," Sarah promised.

"I know it's only been six months and that's hardly any time at all," he spluttered, "but sometimes you just know when it's right. And this is right. I can feel it in my bones."

Sarah did her best not to glance at Desmond. Though that thought was too much to entertain, she understood what Nathan was saying. "You're not going to get any protests from me," she said. "You make her so incredibly happy."

"Good." Nathan let out a breath. "I was hoping you'd say something like that because I sort of want Parker's help."

"With what? Proposing?" she said, the word popping out of her mouth in utter disbelief.

"Kate adores him. It'll be perfect."

"Sure, if you want him to drop the ring in a pile of horse manure."

Nathan and Desmond both laughed at that.

"At least it'd be memorable," Nathan said.

Sarah rolled her eyes. "When are you going to do it?"

"I was thinking about next month. Maybe during the holidays. Or just after. Might be a spur-of-the-moment thing."

Sarah handed back the ring box. "I'm sure Parker will grow out of his terrible twos by then."

"Excellent," Nathan said. He eyed Desmond. "I wasn't interrupting anything, was I?"

"No," Sarah said, pulling her jacket closer and heading for the door. "Nothing at all."

She turned around and shot them both a smile, but realizing that she now had to keep this secret from her best friend, Sarah was sort of glad to have Desmond as a distraction.

Chapter Sixteen

"I've figured it out," Kate said, walking into the kitchen while Sarah was folding a load of laundry on the couch. For one tiny human, Parker went through more socks than the entire Cardiff household combined.

"What did you figure out?" Sarah asked, sticking two mismatched socks together because she just didn't care anymore.

"You're in a *situationship*," Kate told her. She flopped down onto the couch, upsetting the piles of socks.

"What?"

"It's what the kids are calling it."

"Oh God," Sarah muttered.

"Not a full relationship. But a step above friends with benefits. A situationship."

"Please stop saying that. Sounds like breaking news on CNN."

Kate grinned. "It has a ring to it, doesn't it?"

"I regret telling you anything."

"You didn't have to tell me," Kate said. "I could read it on your face."

"And what exactly are you reading?"

"The utter bliss."

Sarah snorted and threw a sock at her. Kate was sort of right; the past few days had been nothing but perfection between her and Desmond. She was preparing to roll right into December breaking all of her own rules. Though technically, she'd simply decided that her rules didn't exist here. The ranch was a bubble—it was like Vegas. So what happened here, stayed here. And with those new working rules, Sarah had stopped trying to fight her attraction. They were playing pretend; she knew that. And sometimes she reminded Desmond of that too. But he would just hum and kiss her until she forgot what she was saying.

"Come to the cabin," he would whisper into her ear. And she would go because—besides being with her son—it was where she wanted to be most in the world.

Sarah gathered the piles of clothes back into the laundry basket.

"Aren't you supposed to be leaving soon?" Kate asked.

"About ten minutes," Sarah said. She swung the basket onto her hip and hurried upstairs to change.

When Sarah peeked in on him, Parker was still sleeping, his candy cane-striped pajamas bunched up around his legs. The festive spirit had hit the Cardiff house hard, and a pile of brand-new Parker-sized holiday-themed pajamas had arrived courtesy of Anne. Decorations appeared in every nook and cranny of the house, much to Parker's amusement, though it was the constant stream of Christmas cookies emerging from the oven that really held his attention.

Sarah tiptoed back to her room, exchanging her pajamas for a pair of comfortable but more interview-appropriate slacks. To no one's surprise, Sarah had secured an interview with the nursing manager of the ER. She'd been informed that their immediate need had been filled, but they had another position opening at the end of February that they were starting to interview for now. Kate had agreed to look after Parker while Sarah drove up to the hospital. She still didn't know how invested she really was in this job, but she figured she owed it to herself to keep her options open and to James, who'd obviously talked her up. When Sarah had spoken to the hiring manager on the phone to arrange a date, she'd been very excited by Sarah's resume.

Sarah finished changing and ran her fingers through her curls, letting them bounce easily on her shoulders. Trying to tame them back into anything else would take time and products she didn't have right now. Mascara was a must though. And to make her feel extra confident, she rubbed some blush into both her cheeks and wiped a subtle shade of gloss across her lips.

When she came back downstairs, she could hear voices coming from Dale's office. Desmond emerged a moment later. He caught her in the hall, a smile immediately breaking across his face.

"Good morning," he said.

"You're here early." In recent days he'd been showing up earlier and leaving the ranch later. Sarah pretended not to notice.

"I had an idea for the addition that I wanted to run by Kate." He tried to kiss her, but Sarah ducked out of the way.

"I have to go." She laughed at the look on his face. "I'll be late."

"Don't you want a kiss for luck?"

"If we start that, you and I both know I'm not going to leave on time. Plus Parker's upstairs."

The corner of Desmond's mouth twitched. "You don't need luck anyway."

"I *am* pretty good at interviews." The bonus of travel nursing and taking random jobs around the country was that Sarah had become quite good at talking about herself and her experience. She'd never had trouble with those awkward situational questions, and after her time with Team Rebuild, she had a whole new genre of experience to pull from.

Desmond followed her to the kitchen where she made a quick cup of to-go coffee. The nice thing about Kate and Nathan getting up before dawn to tend to the horses was that someone always brewed coffee in the main house. It wasn't the same as her Starbucks in the city, but she'd grown to appreciate it.

Kate and Nathan appeared a moment later, and Sarah pulled more mugs from the cupboard. Just as she was topping off Nathan's mug, Anne kicked the front door open. There was a giant box in her arms, and bags dangled from each of her hands.

"Mom?" Kate said, almost slopping the coffee from her mouth.

Desmond jumped to help Anne, sweeping the box from her arms and setting it on the island.

"What's all this?" Kate asked.

Anne heaved the rest of the bags onto the island and released a great sigh as she thanked Desmond.

Nathan started plucking decorations from the box that were distinctly non-holiday themed.

"Party favors. Can you believe Diane had all of this at the diner? She found it when she had to clear things out so Team Rebuild could finish the repairs."

"Actually, I can believe it," Kate said. "Diane's probably been hoarding things since my eighth birthday party. But *why* do you have party favors?"

"For Doc's party, of course."

Sarah had to stop and figure out which Doc they were talking about. A lot of Kate's clients called her Doc, but there was also Doc McGinn, the town veterinarian Kate would be taking over for shortly. It could also be a Doc that Sarah had never heard of before.

"Party?" Kate said.

"Yes, Doc's retirement party. Just after New Year's. We talked about this."

Kate blinked at her mother in disbelief. Finally she said, "You mean when you asked me if we should do something to celebrate me taking over as resident livestock vet and I said *no*?"

Anne waved her off.

"Mom, I don't want a party."

"It's not for you, it's for Doc."

"Well, knowing him, he doesn't want a party either."

"Doc's taken care of this town and its animals for a long time," Anne said. "Besides, it's too late. Diane and I already put a deposit down on a space at the resort. We're going to see it in person later this morning."

"The resort? How many people are you inviting?"

Anne hurried off down the hall with her bags of party favors without answering.

"Mother!" Kate followed her.

When Sarah turned around, Nathan was smirking into his mug. "Well, on that note, I'm off," she said.

Desmond nodded. "I think I'll get to work too."

"And I will help you," Nathan announced.

The three of them fled the house. Winter in Hatchet Lake had been mild thus far according to Kate, and though it was bitterly cold most days, the grass was still green and the sky was clear. Desmond stood outside the ranch truck Sarah was borrowing while she climbed in and rolled down the window.

"New Year's is going to be wild here," he whispered.

Sarah hummed. Between Nathan and Kate's proposal, which she was expecting to happen soon, and Doc's retirement party, the Cardiff household was in for a busy holiday season.

She let Desmond press a chaste kiss to her cheek. "See you when you get back."

And with that, Sarah drove off, the dry country roads escorting her all the way to the city.

When Sarah reached the hospital, she parked and studied it. She hadn't noticed the last time she was here, but it was smaller than any hospital she'd ever worked in. That meant nothing, really, in the grand scheme of things—emergency medicine was the same. Sarah had been directed to an office on the first floor, so she asked the clerk for directions once inside and made her way down a busy hallway.

Every hospital felt vaguely familiar to her. Maybe it was just that she'd worked in too many of them now, but Sarah stood by the fact that all hospitals smelled the same, and when stripped back of their fineries and finishes, they even looked the same.

She found the door open when she reached the office and knocked.

A whirlwind of a woman greeted her. Her name was Darlene. She had curly hair that was even more untamable than Sarah's and so many papers on her desk that it was hard to tell if there was actually furniture there holding everything up or if it was just more paperwork. She had the energy of every ER nurse manager Sarah had ever met or worked with—controlled chaos in human form. Sarah liked her immediately.

She sat down in a chair as Darlene shuffled things around on her desk, making enough space to take notes.

"James says you've been staying in Hatchet Lake?"

Sarah nodded.

"What brought you there?"

"I came to spend some time with my best friend and ended up volunteering with Team Rebuild until recently. I guess I just haven't gotten around to leaving yet."

Darlene laughed. "Hatchet Lake is like that. There's something about it that sucks you in. We spend time there at the lake with our kids every summer."

Sarah nodded. "It is pretty special."

"So, let's cut to the chase. Your resume is impressive. I could sit here and ask you a dozen situational questions, but I suspect you've probably seen them all and James has personally vouched for you, so I feel like that might be a waste of your time and mine."

Sarah laughed. "I have my answers down to a fine science."

"That's what I thought. Though there is a practical portion of the interview. We have a simulation lab."

Sarah nodded. A lot of the hospitals she'd worked at had simulation labs for training and exercises.

"We're gonna throw a scenario at you. Nothing major. Just basic run-of-the-mill stuff. Sound good?"

"Let's do it," Sarah said.

She followed Darlene down the hall to the simulation lab. Inside, the room was sterile and white, with a fresh set of supplies laid out on a crash cart and a robotic mannequin lying on a hospital bed.

"This is Alfred," Darlene said fondly of the mannequin. "He's old but still puttering away. Hang out for a second, and I'll get the technician to key up the scenario."

Darlene disappeared through a door.

The mannequin came to life, and a speaker crackled. "Good to go," Darlene announced.

Sarah jumped into nursing mode and started her assessment by introducing herself. She talked to Alfred, her fake patient, took his history and assessed his symptoms.

Sarah had done these simulations before.

She knew immediately that the symptoms were probably pointing to a diagnosis of pneumonia, but her job wasn't to diagnose the patient, it was to assess him and tell them what she would expect next. Breathing treatments. Chest X-ray. Antibiotics. Sarah rhymed off her report and her suspected nursing interventions.

"That felt too easy," Darlene said. Sarah could hear her murmuring with the tech. "Oh no! I think Alfred's having some chest pain."

Sarah smirked. This was a little more in-depth than an interview scenario usually went, but she'd always enjoyed these simulations. It was a great environment to learn in when no one could actually die. Sarah started her cardiac protocol, and when Darlene announced that Alfred had gone unconscious, Sarah shouted for help the way she would in a real emergency and began chest compressions.

To her surprise, the door to the lab swung open and James walked in.

She laughed when he rolled up his sleeves. "Just hanging around, were you?"

"Darlene texted me, so I took my break." His friendly grin faded, and he was suddenly in doctor mode. "What do we have here?"

Sarah rhymed off the history as James got a bag valve mask over the mannequin's mouth to simulate respirations. In reality, there would be an entire team of people if someone coded in the ER, but Sarah and James went through the motions the best they could. They got the fake AED hooked up and sent off one shock.

Darlene didn't let the simulation run much longer. "Oh, look, the patient's all better. Good job, team."

James and Sarah both grinned.

"Easiest code I've ever done," Sarah said.

Darlene entered from the other room. "Well, that about wraps us up—unless you have any questions for me?"

Sarah shook her head.

"Okay, as you know, I'm looking to fill the position that's going to be empty at the end of February. But I'd like to have the ideal candidate start toward the end of January to do training and hand-over and all that good stuff. Hypothetically, I think I've just found my ideal candidate."

Sarah smiled as Darlene attempted to unofficially tell her that she had the job.

"I've got some more interviews scheduled in December. You know, so I can check the boxes, dot the i's, all that great bureaucratic stuff. That being said, you likely won't hear from me for an official offer until after the holidays."

Even though Sarah had known that getting the job was a possibility going into this interview, her head swam at the thought.

"That okay?" Darlene asked.

"Sounds good," Sarah managed to say. At least she would have until January to figure out if she really wanted to stay. She reached out and shook Darlene's hand.

"C'mon," James said as the interview concluded. "Let me give you a proper tour before you go."

He directed Sarah through the ER, and though she'd been here a few months ago with Greg, she was looking at the space through different eyes now. The ER was a circular space with twelve beds, a resuscitation room, a back bubble that could accommodate some less urgent patients and a massive nursing station.

The other staff nodded and smiled when James introduced her, which Sarah took as a good sign. Though they were busy, there was a general camaraderie among them that she'd learned only existed in certain units. When she'd found one like that in the past, she'd always made a point of extending her contract for as long as she could. Nursing was a hard job on a good day, so it was nice to know that your coworkers were truly in your corner. If James was trying to convince her to stay, he was sure pulling out all the right stops. They finally said goodbye at the entrance. Sarah thanked him for all his help, and James waved her off with a hopeful, "See you in January."

Sarah hurried back to her truck feeling good about the whole experience, which was possibly the most surprising thing of all. She'd not really intended to let this job become a contender in her decision of where to settle down next with Parker. The fact that she was now considering it added an extra layer of stress to her decision. Sarah knew she wouldn't get the official offer for several weeks, so as she climbed into the truck, she decided that big decisions could wait a while. She would simply enjoy her perfect bubble of happiness for the holidays and burst it in the new year. New year, new her. That was what everyone always said. No use in changing everything up right now.

Settled, Sarah drove off, a flickering of newness and hope still whispering in her gut. Snow had started to fall while Sarah had been inside, and though it wasn't quite sticking to the pavement yet, a light layer clung to the grass that lined the sidewalks. The radio was drowning the truck in soft rock, which would soon switch to Christmas music, and as she made her way out of the city and back toward the ranch, the lazy flurries batting against the windshield grew heavy and thick.

By the time she reached the ranch, there was almost an inch of snow on the ground.

Desmond waved as she got out of the truck. He was heading back from the stables with Nathan.

Kate came out the door with Parker. He was dressed in boots and a coat, and she was trying to wrangle a pair of gloves onto his fingers.

"Snow!" he cried.

This was the first year he was really old enough to enjoy the snow, and every time a small flurry had started or the sky had looked particularly gray in the past couple weeks, he would get excited. Now that the snow was actually collecting on the ground, he would not be still.

Kate gave up and let him go. Parker hurried down the stairs as fast as his toddler legs would take him and hurled himself onto the ground, getting a face full of powder. He lifted his head up, blinking, and instead of the tears Sarah expected, he started to laugh.

"How'd it go?" Kate asked, coming down the stairs to meet her.

"Really well, actually. Pretty sure I have the job if I want it." Wouldn't her mother be thrilled when Sarah told her that? She already thought that Sarah had spent long enough intruding on the Cardiffs.

Kate tried to hide her smile. She knew Sarah better

than anyone and wouldn't want to get her hopes up about them staying.

Parker got up and ran to her, holding up his hand to show her the snow he'd collected. He immediately shoved his hand into his mouth.

"Oh, yummy," Sarah muttered, grabbing him long enough to force the gloves onto his hands. "Let's not eat it, okay?"

"'Kay!" Parker screamed, running away. He dove at Desmond, who'd gotten wise to his tactics. Desmond caught him mid-headbutt and carefully but animatedly laid him down in the snow. Parker exploded with laughter.

Sarah smiled at the scene.

If the glances and lingering touches and evenings spent at the cabin weren't obvious enough signs that something more was developing, then the shift in Desmond's relationship with Parker was a giant waving flag. She'd never heard him giggle as much as she had these past weeks. And though it was breaking more of her own rules, she'd just blamed it on the ranch and let them have fun together.

A flurry of snow exploded beside her suddenly, and Sarah realized that Nathan had hit Kate with a giant snowball.

Kate gaped, dusting off the front of her coat. When her shock wore off, she immediately bent down to gather snow into her hands. Desmond scooped Parker up and took off running behind the truck as battle lines were drawn. Sarah saw Parker's head pop up over the bed of the truck long enough to throw a snowball that soared exactly a foot before crashing down.

Sarah laughed, but then a flurry of snow hit her. She shouted and covered her head, realizing that Kate and Nathan had teamed up.

"Oh no!" Desmond told Parker. "They got your mom!"

"Mom!" Parker yelled. He came running around the end of the truck, and Sarah pretended to dramatically hit the ground.

She laid there, bracing herself for the moment Parker flung himself at her. Even though she was expecting it, she still grunted as he landed on her chest.

"Mom," Parker said, patting her face with his snowy gloves.

She couldn't help but snicker.

"Mom, you 'kay?"

She kissed his rosy cheek. "You saved me. Thank you, baby."

Just as she said it, another snowball landed next to her, drenching them with snow. "Look what Auntie Kate did. Go get her!"

"No hit!" Parker yelled, tearing across the field. He picked up a pile of snow on the way, throwing it with all the strength a two-year-old could muster.

"Heard someone over here might need some rescuing," Desmond said suddenly. He crouched beside her as she wiped snow from her face.

"Oh, I'm already dead. My son has gone to avenge me."

Desmond glanced across the field to where Nathan had just taken a mortal wound from Parker and was flopping on the ground.

"I don't know," Desmond said. "Sounds like you might have a little life left in you. And I have a pretty good track record as far as saving people goes."

Sarah lifted her arms up, expecting Desmond to pull her to her feet.

But when she was on her feet, he swept her off them and into his arms.

She laughed. "What are we doing?"

"This was a full-service save. Didn't you know? It comes with a bridal-style carry and the kiss of life."

He placed her softly onto her feet once they were safely behind the truck. Then he bent down and pressed his lips to hers. The chill in her bones faded and the frost at the tips of her fingers melted away as she pressed her cold hands beneath his coat.

Her foot hit something, and she broke the kiss to look down. A pile of snowballs. "You've been busy over here."

"I don't lose snowball fights." He bent down and retrieved a snowball. "You ready?"

Sarah's heart pattered for ridiculous reasons. *God, this man.*

When she was done staring at him, she helped Desmond unleash his snow pile. Her aim wasn't the greatest, but she was fast, sending Nathan and Kate diving all over the field with Parker.

"We give up. You win!" Nathan shouted, holding up Parker and waving him back and forth like a flag of surrender. Parker squealed and waved.

When Desmond dropped his last snowball and tugged her close for another kiss, Sarah truly felt like the victor.

As wheels puttered down the drive, munching over gravel and snow, Sarah turned to see Anne, probably returning from her trip into town to see the resort for the retirement party.

But as she pulled up, Sarah realized there was another woman sitting beside her. She went slack in Desmond's arms as the woman stepped out of the vehicle. It was such a shock that Sarah had to do a double take.

"Mom?" she said.

"Look who I found at the resort," Anne exclaimed.

There was something tentative and apologetic about her smile.

"Wasn't it fate?" said Bonnie Schaffer in the flesh.

She marched through the snow, and Sarah took a giant step away from Desmond, putting as much distance as she could between them in the millisecond of time she had to react.

"There I was, in the lobby, about to inquire with the front desk about the easiest way to get over to the ranch, and there Anne was."

Sarah hadn't stopped gaping. Her mother pulled her into a quick hug, darting down to kiss both her cheeks in a way that had always reminded Sarah of a bird of prey pecking at its next meal.

"What...what are you doing here?" Sarah sputtered, still wondering if she was hallucinating. Part of her thought she'd taken a snowball to the head and was suffering from a concussion.

"What? A grandmother can't fly in and surprise her daughter and grandson for the weekend?"

Sarah felt like a fish drawn onto a bank. She was just lying there, flopping and gasping, wondering when the earth had tilted off its axis. Kate walked over. Sarah looked blankly at her, noting the similar expression of confused shock.

"Uh... Of course you can," Sarah sputtered. "I just meant a heads-up might have been nice."

"Where would be the surprise in that?" Her mother patted her shoulder. "And it's not exactly like you're running out the door to work. I figured dropping by while you're still unemployed was the best time to catch you."

Every cell in her body ever programmed for anger

caught light at once. Sarah hunched over, shoulders to her ears, like she was preparing to explode.

"Now, where is that grandson of mine?" her mother said.

Parker, still standing with Nathan, made no movement in the direction of his grandmother. In fact, he seemed to shift behind the safety of Nathan's legs. As Sarah was contemplating hitting her own mother with a snowball, Anne came to her rescue.

"Oh, come inside, Bonnie," Anne said without missing a beat. "I imagine you're tired after your flight. Warm up with some coffee. Or I have tea if you'd prefer. And you'll have to stay for dinner, of course."

Anne linked her arm with Bonnie's, giving her very little opportunity to refuse, and promptly strode off with her inside the house.

"Did you know she was coming?" Kate asked.

"I had no idea," Sarah said, gritting her teeth. This was about to be the longest weekend of her life.

Chapter Seventeen

Bonnie Schaffer had blown into Hatchet Lake like a winter storm, and Sarah was ill prepared to deal with her. Even Team Rebuild, an actual disaster-relief organization, wasn't equipped to handle her mother. Honestly, Sarah probably would have preferred a storm. She'd take blowing flurries and four-foot drifts against the door and snow so high they had to use a snowblower on the driveway over one weekend with her mother.

Sarah led Parker inside, taking off his coat and boots, setting him free. He clung to her, unsure of his grandmother. They'd met before, of course, multiple times, but he was so young and it was so infrequent that he didn't recognize his grandmother the same way he did Kate or even Anne.

"Are you going to give Grandma a hug?" her mother asked.

Sarah sighed. "He's being shy."

"Oh, well, none of that." Her mother snatched Parker into her arms.

For a moment Sarah wasn't sure what he would do. He stuck his lip out and wrinkled his nose, more perturbed by being contained than anything. When her mother pressed her lips to his cheek, so similar to the way Sarah often did, he finally relented with a smile.

Sarah breathed a sigh of relief.

But like most toddlers, his patience didn't last long, and soon he began to fidget and fuss. When he was released, Sarah occupied him with *CoComelon* on their tablet, the one that had kept him occupied on the plane, and sat him on the couch next to Dale.

"You're growing your hair out," her mother said the moment Sarah joined the others in the kitchen.

Sarah made a noncommittal noise. She'd learned that the less she said, the better. Making comments of her own only gave her mother more ammo with which to fire. Sarah had always known her mother to be a trying and impatient woman. Their personalities were vastly different, almost as different as their looks, which Sarah had inherited from her father. Where Sarah was average, her mother was tall; where she was curvy, her mother was willowy; and where Sarah's hair could be unruly, her mother preferred hers neatly trimmed and styled. Sarah remembered being a child, forced into salon chairs while women with combs and brushes tried to manage her curls. It had irked her mother to no end that Sarah had refused to use the endless products or styling wands she'd bought her.

"It's lovely," Anne said, cutting into the conversation.

"Lovely," her mother repeated with a tight smile.

Sarah wanted to roll her eyes and throw herself down onto the couch out of exhaustion, and it had only been five minutes. In an instant, without even trying, her mother had destroyed the perfectly peaceful bubble Sarah had been existing in for almost a week. Days of playing pretend with Desmond had just poofed from existence.

It felt like waking up from a bad dream.

Sarah resurfaced from the nightmare as Anne introduced everyone. Nathan she introduced as Kate's boyfriend, and Desmond she introduced as a friend of the family. It didn't feel like the right introduction for Desmond, but Sarah didn't know what else she would have said.

This is the man I'm sleeping with? Who hangs out with your grandson and stays for family dinner? But we're not serious. We're not anything. We're just having a good time for now.

It all felt too messy to explain, and Sarah didn't want to give the wrong impression, so she let Anne carry on. When her mother was whisked away on a tour of the house, Sarah leaned against the island, holding her head in her hands.

"So," Nathan said, breaking the awkward silence. "This is an interesting development to the day."

Sarah scoffed loudly. "That's the understatement of the century."

"Right," he said. "Well, we'll be in the stables if anyone needs us."

Wishing she could join them, Sarah gave Desmond a close-lipped smile, catching his eye only briefly. Obviously she hadn't intended for him to meet her mother this way.

Maybe this would send Desmond running for the hills. Truth be told, it would probably make breaking off this situationship easier than either of them expected.

"Can I get you a drink?" Anne asked as the two women returned to the kitchen.

"Oh, anything," her mother replied airily. "Coffee would be great."

"But she'll have white wine later," Sarah whispered under her breath to Kate, knowing very well what her mother's expectations of dinner would be.

Kate nodded and disappeared into the cellar.

Sarah watched her mother glance around the house. She took everything in, passing silent judgment as she always did. Sarah could read a thousand things in her expression. She'd always been a quietly dismissive person, so much so that Sarah often thought her mother should have come with a warning label.

When Kate returned with the wine, Sarah contemplated pouring herself a glass, but she figured she needed to be able to bite her tongue more than she needed liquid courage to prepare for the afternoon they were about to have.

Thankfully, Kate, like Anne, kept up a running string of commentary as the afternoon wore on and they started to prepare dinner. *How was your flight? And how is California? Your husband? Life on the other side of the country? Oh, yes, Parker seems to be growing like a weed. He's a brilliant little boy.*

Sarah had never been very good at normal conversation where her mother was concerned. It was either surface-level pleasantries or cutting commentary. They dug like knives at each other, picking at loose threads and ripping off scabs. It was how they'd always been.

"He looks just like Sarah did at that age. I almost couldn't believe how much hair she'd been born with. And it just got curlier and curlier."

Sarah gave her mother a wry smile, surprised that

she cared to remember back that far. Her mother had complained profusely throughout Sarah's teenage years that she'd done nothing but give her wrinkles and gray hair. But she supposed somewhere in her parents' house was a photo album filled with pictures where Sarah looked just like her son. Maybe one day she'd be able to show him.

"Of course, his eyes are exactly like his father's."

Sarah suddenly wanted to gouge out her own eyes. "Yes, thank you, Mother. Let's not rehash Parker's genetics," she muttered, very aware of the fact that Parker was getting old enough to start picking up on some of this conversation. Old enough to start asking about a dad. About *his* dad.

Sarah didn't relish having that conversation yet.

Anne put a salad on the counter. "Girls, you want to set the table?"

Kate and Sarah scooped up the salad and a bread basket and scooted out to the dining room.

"This is like something out of my nightmares," Sarah said quietly as they set out plates and cutlery. "A weekend visit? What the hell is that about?"

Kate shrugged. "Spontaneity?"

"I've never known my mother to do anything spontaneously in her life. She's here for a reason. I just haven't figured out what yet."

"Maybe she really did just want to see you both."

Sarah leveled Kate with a look.

Kate held up her hands, a fork in either one. "People change. Maybe Bonnie's mellowed out."

"It's been thirty years—I think I know my mother."

By the time they'd finished setting the table, Anne had plated the rest of the food. Desmond and Nathan returned from the stables, and with everyone's help, they managed to get the food on the table and everyone in a seat. Anne and Kate continued with more of their running commentary, the two of them hardly touching their dinners, and Sarah felt horrible. She chewed every bite like it was sand, waiting for each moment her mother threw out another scathing remark. The only thing that kept her somewhat sane was doting on Parker. She cut his food into tiny pieces and answered every one of his questions as he held up chunks of food and asked, "What's this?"

When he was finished, he started sliding from his chair. Sarah caught his arm. "Hang on, let Mommy wipe your hands."

Parker agreed, though it very clearly interfered with his after-dinner schedule of rolling toy cars across the floor.

"Children in our household had to sit at the dinner table until everyone was finished," her mother commented. She didn't look at Sarah, but she might as well have been glaring at her from the corner of her eye.

Sarah sighed. "I don't make him sit at the table, Mom. If he's finished with his plate, then he can go play."

"You want to start developing good habits early."

"He's two."

"That's not how you were at two."

"Pretty sure I had a nanny at the table to keep me occupied."

The rest of the table was quiet, and Sarah clenched her fork so tight she thought it might snap in half. Her mother met her eye then, and it was as if they were at opposite ends of the ocean, not just opposite sides of the table.

Saturday morning was spent walking through town. Bonnie had decided to stay at the resort overnight despite Anne offering up a room, so they met on Main Street. Sarah wasn't surprised in the least. In fact, for once she was grateful that her mother was so particular because it allowed her to drink her coffee in blissful silence at the ranch before having to meet up. Sarah had opted to leave Parker with Anne, knowing he'd have more fun, but also because she was trying to weasel out the true purpose of her mother's visit. Having that conversation would be easier without a toddler underfoot.

Hatchet Lake's shops had been decorated with garlands and bows and lights for the holidays, and Sarah took her time pointing out all the work Team Rebuild had completed over the past few months.

Her mother was only vaguely interested in that, instead badgering Sarah about her plans for the new year. Honestly, she'd expected the inquisition last night, so she was surprised her mother had lasted this long.

"You said you interviewed for that local job?"

"I did," Sarah confirmed.

"How did it go?"

She shrugged. "Well, I think. I'll hear back after the holidays."

The interview had gone better than *well*, but Sarah was hesitant to give away too many details of her life here or of her plans for after. She'd always guarded them closely, even before coming to Hatchet Lake. Her parents had been a strange mixture of distant and controlling when she was growing up. They'd wanted to be involved in everything she did, just not necessarily present. It had been a strange dynamic to navigate as a child, and as soon as she could escape that environment, she had.

"You're not seriously considering staying here?"

Sarah stopped outside the diner with its garland-trimmed windows. "What could you possibly find wrong with this place?"

Her mother wrinkled her nose in answer but kept walking, and Sarah filled in the blanks of her silence. *It's too small. Too neighborly. Everyone is always in your business. Heaven forbid you need a moment of privacy.*

All those things were true. Sarah had seen them for herself. But she'd also seen the very best of this town and its people. Sometimes living in a place where everyone knew your name had its perks.

"Parker is getting older," her mother said.

"Yes."

"It might be nice for him to be closer."

"To what?" Sarah said without thinking.

Her mother scoffed. "His grandparents, of course."

Sarah could only stare at her awkwardly. Her parents had never really struck her as the doting-grandparents type. They wouldn't be the first ones she called when Parker got sick. Nor would she ever call and ask them to grab him from day care. The thought of relying on them in that way was so foreign she almost laughed.

Her mother looked at her pointedly.

"You're not serious."

"Of course I am. I told you I would speak to some of my friends about securing you a job, and I have."

"I told you I'm not moving back to California."

"Why not?"

Sarah shook her head, expecting her mother to let it go, but apparently it was a genuine question and Sarah was going to have to come up with a genuine answer. Before she could, that familiar rental truck came trundling down the snow-lined street and pulled up beside them. Desmond rolled down the window, wearing an immaculate smile.

"Morning, ladies," he called.

Sarah smiled back. "Where are you headed?"

"The hardware store. I could actually use some help, if you can spare a second?"

Sarah glanced at her mother. "Do you mind?"

Her mother waved her off without protest. "I was actually going to pop into that store back there. Might pick up a trinket or two for the holidays."

"Okay. I'll be back to grab you in a bit." Her mother nodded, and Sarah climbed into the truck, the warmth of the cab like refuge from a storm.

"You looked like you could use a breather," Desmond commented as he drove off down the street.

"Oh, I need an entire oxygen tank."

Desmond laughed out loud, the sound filling the hollow space around them until Sarah had no choice but to laugh too. She settled back in her seat, feeling at ease, and for the first time since last night, she didn't have to force her smile.

Desmond pulled over by the hardware store. Through the windows Sarah could see Colm behind the counter. "Oh," she said. "You were actually serious about the hardware store? I thought it was a ruse."

"I never joke about hardware."

Sarah snorted. "And how is that working out for you?"

"I mean, it got you here, didn't it?" He leaned over to kiss her.

Sarah let the kiss linger, cupping the side of his face and holding him close when he tried to pull away. "You're right—it did."

"Ladies can't resist the allure of a good power tool."

Sarah grinned against his lips.

"Circular saw. Jigsaw. Sander. Grinder."

Sarah laughed and kissed him again just to get him to stop.

"See," he breathed against her neck. "It's working."

They never actually got around to going inside, but eventually Sarah glanced at her phone and sighed. "I should go before my mother blames me for abandoning her."

"You would never do such a thing," Desmond said.

"No," Sarah said. "But I would definitely think about it." She left Desmond and the warmth of the truck behind, hurrying back down the street to locate her mother. She found her in a tiny art gallery, the walls filled with paintings of a shimmering lake and burly evergreens with a sunset-dappled ridge looking out over it all. Hatchet Lake in the summer, Sarah guessed.

"I thought you might not come back," her mother said as Sarah scooted to her side.

"I considered it," Sarah said evenly.

"I can't tell if you're being serious or not."

"How about lunch?" Sarah said, changing the subject as they left the gallery and headed down Main Street.

"All right," her mother said. "Lunch would be lovely."

Sarah led them to the pub. Her mother paused outside the door, considering the establishment with that subtle wrinkle around her nose.

"Come on," Sarah said, yanking the door open and ushering her mother through.

"There's a perfectly good restaurant back at the resort."

"What's wrong with this place?"

"What isn't?" her mother complained, eyeballing the greasy tabletops, worn seating and dingy windows.

Sarah led her to a booth, and they sat down. Her mother picked up a napkin and tried wiping away the old water spots that were permanently stained into the wood. "You don't bring Parker here, do you?"

Sarah crossed her arms. "There's nothing wrong with here."

"I'm almost afraid to think what state the kitchen might be in."

"Just steer clear of the meat."

Her mother's eyes widened.

"I'm kidding."

"That's not funny."

Sarah bit her lip. It was a little funny, but at the look on her mother's face, she wisely chose not to rub it in. Instead, she laid both elbows on the table—something her mother had chastised her for doing since she'd been a child—and leveled her with a look. "What are you really doing in Hatchet Lake, Mom?"

"What, you thought that by purposely ignoring my phone calls I'd disappear from your life?"

"I wasn't ignoring your calls," Sarah muttered, thinking back to that day in the stables with Desmond. She'd absolutely been ignoring her mother. "I was busy."

"So busy with your nonexistent job?"

Sarah bit the inside of her cheek. At this rate, they were going to end up in a fight before Joe even arrived to take their order. She should probably just head Joe off and place the order to go. That way they could go their separate ways—her back to the ranch, and her mother back to the resort.

"You know," her mother continued, "if you worked half as hard at settling down as you do at cutting your father and me out, you'd be married with three kids by now."

Sarah's entire body tensed. "I'm not cutting you out."

"You're putting up walls."

"It's called a boundary," Sarah said. "Look it up. It's good for you."

Her mother rolled her eyes. "You know who really needs boundaries? Your son. Do you even know how much time he spends watching inane shows on that tablet of his?"

Sarah scoffed then. She could not believe her mother was trying to lecture her on screen time right now. "As if I wasn't parked in front of the TV growing up."

"Never," her mother said. "You had all sorts of lessons and sports."

"That I didn't attend half the time."

"That's not true."

"First of all," Sarah said, holding up a finger. "How would you know? You were never there. Second of all, Parker spends most of his day outside, playing or visiting the horses in the stables. The half hour of screen time I let him have once a day isn't going to detrimentally affect him."

"If you say so," her mother said, picking up a menu and scanning it.

Sarah was so angry she could've flipped the table. "I do."

Chapter Eighteen

By Sunday Sarah was considering jumping onto a plane and flying to the opposite side of the globe. The only thing stopping her was the knowledge that her mother had a flight this afternoon. Rusty happened to be flying home to his family for the holidays as well, and though his flight was tomorrow, he'd opted to spend a night in the city. So Nathan was dropping both Rusty and her mother off today, leaving the house hectic with good-byes and Anne trying to pawn off baked goods.

"All ready to go?" Sarah asked her mother. They'd picked her up from the resort that morning so she could spend a few more hours with Parker at the ranch.

She nodded, watching Desmond exit the house holding a carrot. "He's a nice young man."

"Desmond?"

"Yes, Desmond. Who else would I be talking about?"

"I'm not sure, Mom. You think every man is a nice young man. When I dated Seth Patterson in high school you thought he was a nice young man. When Danny Ochre took me to prom you thought he was a nice young man too."

"Well, weren't they?"

"Yeah, Mom, they were fine."

"I just thought perhaps there might be something there."

Sarah peeked out the window to where Desmond had stopped to help Nathan reconstruct the snowman they'd accidentally backed over with the truck. She bit her lip to stop a laugh from tumbling out.

"You two certainly looked cozy enough when I arrived," her mother added. "All cuddled up and kissing."

Sarah's laugh died in the back of her throat. She hadn't realized her mother had seen that, but hell if she was going to discuss her love life or Desmond with her. "He's just a friend," she insisted.

"You do that a lot," her mother noted.

"Do what?"

"Cut people from your life before you give things a chance."

Sarah scoffed.

"You're carrying on this fling around my grandson, which, knowing you, will be short-lived because you're so unwilling to commit to anything."

Her mother's words poked and prodded at some of Sarah's genuine fears about introducing Parker and Desmond. She'd had the same thoughts, the same concerns, but who was her mother to waltz in here with those comments? Bonnie Schaffer had no idea about the choices Sarah made concerning her son.

"But why am I surprised?" her mother carried on. "You've always done it. Ever since you were little. You've always been…unsettled."

"Unsettled?" Sarah couldn't keep the incredulous look off her face. "Me, unsettled. You and Dad were the ones who could never decide if you were together or apart. Your relationship shifted faster than the wind."

"Your father and I made peace with all that," her mother said. "A long time ago. When you left for school, I always imagined you'd come back. But you didn't. Then when you started working, I thought you'd settle down somewhere, build a life for yourself. But you didn't. And then Parker happened."

"He's not a thing that just happened, Mom. You're talking about him like he was on sale at the supermarket."

"That's not what I meant. You know that. But you and I both know he wasn't planned. When you had him, I thought you'd finally stop running all over the country. But look at you. Hatchet Lake today. Somewhere different tomorrow?"

"What are you getting at?"

"Parker needs a home."

"He has a home with me."

"Somewhere stable, Sarah. Somewhere he can have a proper childhood."

"This coming from the woman who picked nannies for me like she was picking outfits in the morning. You always do *this*—act like you're the good guy, swooping in to save me because I have no idea what I'm doing."

Her mother bristled. "I may not always have been there when you were small, but at least you had one place to call home. You knew where you were eating dinner every night. You knew where your friends were. Can you say the same for Parker?"

Sarah watched Parker belly flop onto the couch, occupied by his crackers and *CoComelon*. "I don't think Parker particularly cares about any of that right now."

"You need to get serious, Sarah. Stop running around from job to job. Get married. Settle down."

"There it is," Sarah said, turning away from her mother. They'd had this argument since the moment Sarah had decided to parent Parker alone. "Why do I have to be married for Parker to have a good life? It's the twenty-first century!"

"You don't," her mother said.

"Then why do we always end up here?"

"I'm just trying to make sure you do what's best for Parker."

Sarah lowered her voice. "He doesn't need a father in his life to know that I love him, so why do you keep pushing me?"

Her mother looked defeated in a sense, like she'd finally reached the end of her argument. "It's easier."

"On who?"

"You. Him. Everyone."

Sarah glared at her mother. The silence between them grew into an ugly, festering thing.

"Tell me I'm wrong," her mother whispered.

"You're wrong," Sarah said without hesitation. She stalked out of the kitchen and up the stairs.

"Sarah?" her mother called, footsteps following after her.

"No." Sarah twisted to face her, halfway up the stairs. "You don't get to do this. You don't get to show up and cause chaos."

"That's not what I—"

"And you don't get to be a grandmother only when it suits you."

The look on her mother's face hardened. "I just want you to have a happy life, Sarah."

"I am happy." Her mother looked at her pointedly, and Sarah threw her hands up. "I'm figuring it out."

"Then let me *help* you."

"I don't need your money."

"That's not what I was going to say. Let me take Parker back to California with me."

Sarah almost fell back down the stairs. "What?"

"Just…wait…before you start yelling again. Think about it. He'd be happy. Well cared for. He'd have stability. He'll start school in another year or so. Don't you want that for him?"

Sarah couldn't even formulate a response to that. She knew what that life would look like. Parker would have everything they thought he would need: tutors, private schools, the right sports teams, the right activities. And grandparents who never got too close. She didn't want that for her son.

"I could take him," her mother said. "Until you can figure out what you want."

Sarah held the handrail to keep herself steady, staring down at her mother. "Parker, come say goodbye to your grandmother! She's going home."

Sarah was still fuming as she watched Nathan's truck pull away. How could her mother even think she would consider letting Parker move to California without her?

"Long weekend, huh?" Kate said.

"I don't even have words right now."

"I don't think she meant for it to end this way."

"What? By insinuating that I'm unfit to raise my own child? Oh, I think that's exactly what she meant to say. We've been tiptoeing around this conversation for a while now."

"You're a good mom, Sarah."

Sarah heard the words, waited for them to land, but all they did was slough off the part of her that held on to her greatest fears. Because wasn't that every mother's fear? That they weren't good enough? That their children weren't happy or cared for or loved enough?

"And she knows that," Kate continued. "It just came out all wrong."

Had it been wrong though? Or had Sarah fought so hard against her mother's words because they'd cut too close to the truth? Her jaw trembled even as she clenched her teeth. "Can you watch Parker for a little while?" she asked. "I need to clear my head."

"Of course," Kate said. "You want the keys to the truck?"

"No, I think I'm just going to walk. Do a couple laps of the ranch or something."

Kate nodded. "Bundle up. It's cold."

Sarah took her coat and boots, stuffed her hands into her pockets and headed outside. The brisk air nipped at her skin, and she took a gasping breath, letting the chill infiltrate and freeze out her anger.

It truly was clearing in a way, and for a moment she just stayed on the porch and breathed.

Then she set out, mulling over the explosive fight and everything that had built up to that moment. She could tell her mother had been hinting at the conversation for months, pestering her about leaving her last job, about figuring out where she was going next, about moving around constantly.

In hindsight, she wasn't all that surprised that her mother wanted them to come back to California. What had truly shocked her was the offer to take Parker off her hands like he was some stray dog she needed to get rid of. Parker hardly knew his grandparents. How could she even think—

"You okay?"

Sarah slowed as Desmond walked over from the stables. She'd meant to stick to the fence line, but her feet apparently had a mind of their own.

"Yeah," she said. "Just walking."

"I heard what happened earlier with your mom."

Sarah raised a brow.

"Caught the tail end of it when I came back to the house for some buttons."

Sarah's brow jumped higher.

"For the snowman."

"Oh," she said flatly as he fell into step beside her.

"Look, I wasn't trying to eavesdrop."

"No, it's fine," she sighed. "That's what we get for arguing out loud for everyone to hear."

The worst part of it all was that she'd started to have some of these same thoughts herself lately. When she lay in bed at night, alone, she'd started to wonder what it would be like to have a partner to share the good bits with. And the hard bits. What it would be like to have someone to laugh with when Parker was an absolute goofball. Or what it would be like to have someone smile at her from across the room just because.

In her visions the person had started to look more and more like Desmond.

Sarah squeezed her eyes against the picture, but it was useless because when she opened them again, there he was, in the flesh.

"Look, I know we're not a *thing*," he said diplomatically. "We're…whatever we are. And it's not my business, so feel free to tell me where to shove my two cents, but if you want to talk, I have two perfectly good ears."

"There's nothing to talk about, really."

"You're sure? Is that why you're marching across this frigid field? Even the horses are inside."

"I just mean it's nothing new. My mom's always on my case about settling down and I can usually brush it off like it's nothing, but—" Her brow puckered in the middle.

"But?"

"This time was different."

"Okay," he said, leaving room for her to fill in the gaps if she wanted.

She thought about what her mom had said. The moment that had filled Sarah with so much fury. "She offered to take Parker to California this time. Said she would take him until I could sort myself out." A familiar heat filled her. "You know, I joke about it. That my mother thinks I'm a terrible mom. But then she goes and says something like that. How exactly am I meant to take that comment?"

Desmond opened his mouth to say something, but Sarah plowed on.

"And as if I'd actually let my son out of my sight. Send him off with two grandparents he barely knows. Two people who were barely around when *I* was growing up." She'd had a different childhood than Kate. Sarah would have been lucky to share three words around the dinner table with her parents or to see them after school before being carted off to bed by some babysitter or nanny. "And then she says she doesn't understand why I'm so angry? Meanwhile she's just planning to march off with my kid. What was *she* thinking?"

"Maybe she wasn't," he said.

Sarah's hands had curled into fists. "That much is obvious."

"I mean, maybe she wasn't looking at it the way you are now."

"Whose side are you on?"

"Yours," he said, smiling so gently at her that Sarah thought her insides might melt. "Always."

She hummed, turning away to hide the flush in her cheeks.

"I think she's trying to protect you."

"From what?" Sarah laughed. "Myself?"

He shook his head. "From making the same mistakes she made as a mom. Maybe she's worried that by doing this whole parenting-and-career thing on your own, you'll be too busy figuring things out to be there for Parker. But I think you've already proven her wrong. Since the moment I met you, I could tell how loved that little boy was. How every decision you made was for him."

"So you're saying in her backward way she really was trying to help?"

"It obviously wasn't exactly the help you needed from her, but…" He shrugged, and Sarah understood. Or, at least, she thought she did.

Sarah had always felt like her mother meant to be confrontational. But maybe Sarah had never really given her mother a chance to be anything but that. Sarah's guard went up the moment she saw her mother's name pop up on her phone, the moment she heard her voice, the moment she'd stepped out of that vehicle with Anne. She was always expecting to have to defend herself, so she'd never really stopped to consider that their relationship might be different now than when she'd been a teenager. Would things have changed in the years she spent away? Since becoming a mom herself?

Sarah wasn't going to make excuses for all her mother's behavior, but perhaps things didn't always have to be this way. They could be better.

"Maybe this is the best she knows how to do," Desmond said quietly.

Sarah had very few memories of her own grandparents besides frilly dinner parties and the occasional birthday card. So perhaps those things were all taught. The distance. The awkward family dinners. The offers to help that felt more like burdens.

Sarah wanted Parker to have everything she'd never had. Deep down, that included a relationship with his grandparents. It would take work, she knew that. But maybe they could build something stronger than what they had.

"You think I should start letting them in more?"

"Your mom did fly all the way here just to see you." Desmond shrugged. "Then again, it might only have been to kidnap your son."

Sarah chuckled, the air crystalizing with her breath. Suddenly the weight of the entire weekend dissipated, and the burden she'd been carrying around felt a little more manageable.

"Families are imperfect things," Desmond continued. "All you can do is give as much of yourself as you're willing to. If you're not ready, that's okay too."

"And what if I'm depriving Parker?"

Desmond glanced over at the porch, where Parker and Kate had emerged from inside the house. Parker looked like a tiny gingerbread man, stuffed into his snowsuit. "Does that look like the face of a boy who's deprived of anything? You're a good mom, Sarah. And one day, when you're ready, your parents will be good grandparents to your son."

Sarah nodded, more choked up than she'd expected to be walking around in the cold. But Desmond had that way about him. She smiled at him, a silent thank-you. He took his cue to head back to the stables, but Sarah caught his hand. The heat of his palm was like fire against hers. They'd kept a careful distance the entire time her mother had been here, and now Sarah wanted nothing more than to make up for lost time.

She wanted to kiss him.

But more than that, she wanted him to know how much his words had meant to her. She pulled his hand close, tucking it against her heart. "You told me once that you worried you weren't supportive enough in your last relationship. That your ex left because you weren't there for her."

Desmond tilted his head, his brows drawn together. "Sarah—"

"I just wanted to reassure you that it couldn't be true. You're a good man, Desmond Torres. She would have been lucky to call you hers." Sarah paused, then added, "Any woman would be."

Chapter Nineteen

Over the following days, everything in the house began to smell like gingerbread and Parker's face was perpetually covered in icing. Though Sarah and the Cardiffs both mutually agreed that the holidays were infinitely better with little kids who still saw magic in everything, the buildup to Christmas was proving to be one Parker-shaped disaster after another. He'd gotten into the wrapping paper, unspooling it around the house, found Anne's Christmas gift-hiding spot and even eaten the chimney off the gingerbread house.

"I don't understand it," Sarah said, wiping Parker's face down for the umpteenth time that afternoon. "Where is all the icing coming from?"

Though she'd snapped a few adorable pictures earlier when the cookie decorating had begun, Parker had been removed from the vicinity of the kitchen when he'd started to lick the faces off all the gingerbread men.

Kate couldn't stop laughing. "You have to admit it's hilarious."

Parker grinned mischievously, belly flopping onto the couch next to Dale.

"Stop encouraging him," Sarah said.

"He probably has a tube of icing stuffed down his pants," Dale said. "That's what Kate used to do."

"You let me run around with icing in my diaper?"

Sarah finally gave up and hauled Parker over her shoulder. He giggled all the way up the stairs, where she wrangled him into a brand-new icing-free outfit.

"Mom," he said.

"Yes?"

"Mom, Mom, Mom," he repeated, apparently just because he could, before throwing himself into her arms. He stayed there for a moment, and Sarah let herself enjoy the cuddle. She got up, walking them both to the window.

"Snow!" Parker said excitedly.

The recent snow had stuck around, and she could follow the tracks they'd made across the yard. She could see the straight line she'd made as she'd walked back and forth to the stables. The twisted circles where Desmond had chased Parker. The tracks to three crooked snow angels. And even the place where they'd mourned the melted snowman before a fresh layer of powder had fallen and they'd built a new one.

There were memories in those footprints.

Memories Sarah knew she might regret in a couple months, but right now she wanted to experience every moment, even if that meant entangling Desmond further into her life. She'd already kissed him under the mistletoe at every opportunity, and if he also happened to be her New Year's Eve kiss this year, then so be it.

The rules were nonexistent at this point. Sarah was

going to keep living this farce until it all came crashing down around her.

When they returned to the main floor, Kate and Anne were packing up boxes of cookies.

"If you wanted to give these away as gifts," Kate was saying, "you probably shouldn't have employed a two-year-old to decorate them." She added a mangled cookie to a pile that was clearly unfit for gift giving.

Anne laughed, dropping more sprinkle-covered sugar cookies into tins destined for their neighbors.

Sarah deposited Parker onto the couch, then joined the women in the kitchen.

"Here," Sarah said, collecting Kate's reject pile onto a plate. "I'll take some of these out to the guys. They don't seem to mind Chef Parker's concoctions."

As Sarah climbed into her boots and strung her arms through her coat sleeves, she glanced out the window. Desmond's rental truck was backed right up to the stable door. She could just make out the flurry of movement as he unloaded supplies.

With Rusty away visiting his family, Nathan had been spending more and more time helping Desmond with the renovation, and the two of them had managed to completely frame the addition. Large blue tarps had been stapled in place of drywall until they could build out the walls, and they snapped and popped with each gust of winter wind.

Sarah pulled the open ends of her coat together as she hurried across the field. She'd only shrugged into it, not planning on being out here long, but as the chill nipped at her skin, she immediately knew that had been a mistake. She shivered as she entered the stables. They were warmer, barely, and Sarah followed the sound of power tools out to the addition. With everything framed, she could physically step inside the space that would become Kate's office.

"This looks great," Sarah said, noting how much progress Desmond had made over the past couple of weeks. "Where's Nathan?"

Desmond flicked his head toward the paddock. "Out taking some photos of the horses." He came up and pressed a kiss to her lips.

"I brought you guys some cookies."

"These more of the Parker rejects?"

Sarah couldn't help but laugh.

Desmond put his tools down and slid his hands between the folds of her coat, curling his fingers around her waist. "Thanks, but I'd rather have you."

Sarah resisted the urge to sigh as his lips went straight for her throat. "Behave," she whispered, though she wanted him to do anything but.

"We're alone."

"There's a man with a high-quality zoom lens standing not fifty feet from us," Sarah noted. Desmond let his lips drag along the curve of her jaw. She was so dizzied by the motion that she clung to him.

"Nathan's distracted."

"By what?"

"His proposal speech. He's been rehearsing it for days. I think he's getting nervous."

Sarah hummed, grinning at the thought of Nathan out there running his speech by the horses.

"Will you come over tonight?" Desmond whispered.

Her heart fluttered in her chest whenever he asked her that question. She still never stayed the entire night, but sometimes it was pretty close to dawn by the time she made her way back to the ranch. Sarah never really knew which night they would declare it over, so each evening that they spent wrapped up in nothing but skin and sheets always dragged on a little longer than the last.

Even now, tucked against his chest, Sarah wondered about it. Would Desmond finish up with the work on the stables and get called back to North Carolina? Would Nathan propose to Kate, setting Sarah and Parker free? They never talked long term. Even things happening as early as next week felt unpredictable in a way, and Sarah and Desmond steered clear of any conversation that remotely pertained to the future.

Here at the ranch they were living for the moment, but as thrilling as that was, Sarah had to admit that a nagging feeling now festered in her gut. She knew their time was coming to an end. Soon she was going to have to decide on the ER job. Soon they would have to say goodbye.

"I'll come over tonight," she said softly, letting herself be comforted by the circle of his arms and hoping, just for a moment, that tonight wouldn't be their last.

Christmas unfolded much as Sarah had expected it would. She'd been blasted out of bed before dawn— by Kate, no less—and had spent the morning under a mountain of wrapping paper while Parker decided to unbox every one of the new toys the Cardiffs had put under the tree for him. It was all too much—Sarah knew that. But putting a stop to anything Anne or Kate had planned when it came to celebrating Christmas with a toddler was out of the question.

Desmond had arrived in time for an early lunch, after which Parker had fallen asleep on the couch surrounded by his presents.

"I think that boy got everything he could have ever wanted," Desmond said, looking over his shoulder.

They'd been left alone to clear the table. Lunch had been light, and Anne was already busy prepping a turkey for dinner.

"Oh, he was more than spoiled this year. The Cardiffs have set an impossibly high standard for me. Thankfully he's young and probably won't remember next year."

"What about last year?" Desmond asked. "How'd you celebrate?"

"I was actually working a double to cover for a co-worker, so this is a huge improvement."

"That's too bad," Desmond said.

Sarah shrugged. "Parker was still too small to understand what Christmas really was, so I knew he wouldn't miss it. Plus I figured there would be years when I actually wanted the day off to spend with my kid so I should probably start building up some good karma."

Desmond laughed, but Sarah could only manage half a smile.

"You look contemplative," he said. "Something else on your mind?"

She sighed, gathering up silver spoons. "I was just thinking about my parents. Regardless of what shift I was working, I usually managed to call them at some point on Christmas morning."

"And you haven't yet?"

Sarah shook her head, not quite meeting his eye. "I haven't even spoken to my mother. Not since…you know, the disaster that ended her visit."

"Go," he said. "I've got this."

Sarah shook her head, not just because she hadn't intended to leave him with a mountain of dishes, but also because she still had no clue what she was going to say to her mother if she even picked up the phone. "I'm not sure I'm ready."

Desmond reached out and caught her hand, taking the silverware from her. "Go," he said gently. "Make the call. It'll bug you for the rest of the day if you don't."

"And what if she doesn't answer?"

"What if she does?"

Sarah grimaced. "That might be worse."

"You won't know until you try."

"All right," she relented. She took the quiet moment, while Parker was napping, to slip upstairs. Kate and Nathan had decided to brave one of the toy sets Parker had been given. Their voices drifted up from the living room as they tackled the thirty-two-page instruction booklet. Sarah sat on the edge of her bed and listened to them, debating if this phone call was worth destroying what she already considered to be a perfect day.

But if it really was perfect, then why did her chest feel so heavy?

Sarah looked out the window, to the snow stamped fields and beyond. To the line of silent evergreens that patrolled one side of the property and the naked deciduous that shivered along the other. She watched the horses, like tiny figurines, wearing their plaid blankets for warmth. Eventually, Sarah realized she was procrastinating.

Refusing to give herself another moment to debate, she picked up her phone and called her mother. Downstairs, commotion sounded. Sarah heard the thudding of tiny feet on the hardwood floor and the whiny postnap demands for juice.

She had half a mind to hang up and do this later. To go down and enjoy the afternoon with her son and the Cardiffs and Desmond.

Then the phone connected.

"Hello?"

"Hi, Mom," Sarah answered reflexively. "Merry Christmas." There was a beat, and Sarah cringed, wanting to crawl out of her skin. Why had she wanted to do this again? This was a terrible idea. This was one of those ideas that should have remained buried at the bottom of a dusty filing cabinet.

"Merry Christmas," her mother finally replied.

Sarah sucked in a sharp breath. She hadn't really thought through the rest of this conversation. There were a lot of ways she could play it. They could pretend like nothing happened, wish each other well for the new year and be done with it. Or they could talk about what happened. About what had been said and *why* it had been said.

"I didn't think we'd hear from you," her mother remarked, interrupting Sarah's internal debate.

"I honestly wasn't sure I would call," she confessed before she could think better of it. Maybe that was half her problem. She was always trying to tiptoe around her mother, around difficult feelings and hard conversations. But all that did in the end was encourage the miscommunications that had been a hallmark of their relationship thus far. "I've been thinking a lot about the other weekend," she said. "About that fight we had right before you left for the airport, and… I wanted to apologize."

"Oh?"

"Not for what I said," Sarah clarified quickly. "Well, not everything I said. Mostly for getting so angry with you and for leaving the conversation where we did."

"I see."

Part of Sarah wished they could have had this conversation in person. Her mother could be a difficult person to read at the best of times, but on the other end of a phone Sarah could only imagine what her face looked like. Then again, she wasn't sure she would have had the nerve to say all this in person. For all the mountains Sarah had conquered in her lifetime, her relationship with her mother was the steepest of all.

"It wasn't my intention to fight with you." Her mother sighed. "You know, I didn't fly all the way to Hatchet Lake to argue with my only daughter right before the holidays."

"I know."

Her mother hummed on the other end of the line. "I actually thought the weekend had been quite nice up until that point."

Sarah laughed. She couldn't help herself. Her idea and her mother's idea of a nice weekend were clearly two very different things. "It was stressful," Sarah said. "I'm not going to lie. But it was nice to see you."

"Look, Sarah, I know things with us haven't always been easy. That they're *still* not easy, but—"

"You were just trying to help," Sarah finished for her.

There was a lengthy pause as they both let that fact settle.

"I appreciate you wanting to do that," Sarah continued. "I really do. And I know you don't always approve of how I'm living my life, which is your prerogative. But the point is that it's *my* life. And Parker is *my* son. We're doing fine, despite whatever else you might think." Her mother tried to interrupt, but Sarah plowed on. "And if we're ever not doing fine, if I ever *do* need your help, I'll ask for it."

"Does that mean you're not coming back to California?"

"Probably not for good. At least not right now. But

I've been thinking, regardless of where I go next, I'll bring Parker out to visit you and Dad next summer."

"I think that would be very nice," her mother answered after a moment.

Sarah exhaled heavily. The pressure in her chest eased at once, and for the first time in weeks it felt like she wasn't walking around holding her breath everywhere she went. One amicable conversation didn't magically fix everything. Sarah knew that. There were years' worth of a complicated relationship to untangle, but for the first time in her life, Sarah felt like the foundations of a bridge were being laid.

"And what about Hatchet Lake?" her mother asked.

Sarah listened quietly to the voices downstairs: Desmond's warm laughter and Parker's shrieks of delight, Kate and Nathan arguing over thirty-two pages' worth of instructions for a children's toy and Anne and Dale bickering over whether or not to stuff the turkey.

There was a job offer here. And her son. And a family that had embraced them with open arms. This was the most at home Sarah had felt in a long time.

"I think it's in the running," she admitted.

"Well, let me know when you decide."

"I will," Sarah promised.

When she hung up the phone, her relief turned into a flood of tears. Sarah sat on the bed and let herself cry. It was oddly freeing, like the emotion that had been building up inside her for weeks, or even months, now had a way to escape. Desmond had been right about her making this phone call today. Carrying around all that weight and stress would have continued to exhaust her without her even realizing. Now, as she rubbed tears from her eyes, she felt light enough to fly.

Chapter Twenty

Rusty returned to the ranch after New Year's, his suit-cases filled with presents. Parker was gifted his very first toy camera, and he followed Rusty around the ranch dutifully, taking pretend photos and asking everyone to pose.

Sarah watched Nathan grab Kate in the middle of the living room while they were dismantling the Christmas tree. He dipped her dramatically, then gave her a smacking kiss for Parker to "photograph." When Nathan tried to pull away, Kate wrapped her arms around his neck, holding him close, the two of them losing themselves in only each other.

Sarah had watched Kate fall in love with Nathan over and over again every day for the past few months, but it was at that exact moment that Sarah truly knew how very much in love her best friend was.

It was three days later when Nathan found Sarah in the kitchen, pouring her first coffee of the day.

"Today?" Sarah said as soon as she spotted the look on his face. It was caught somewhere between exhilaration and the pale, sweaty, shaking throes of nausea.

He nodded. "Today."

"Okay." Sarah clapped him on the shoulder, trying to pass on as much calm and serenity as she could manage. She also started praying to whoever would listen that Parker didn't drop the ring in anything that resembled horse poop. "And what does Kate think is happening?"

"She thinks we're taking more photos for the website," he said quietly. "The interior construction's almost done, so we've planned for her to come down this afternoon to pose in the stables. Desmond's going to clean up the space. Rusty's going to take the proposal photos since I will be otherwise engaged."

"Literally," Sarah said, smiling at him.

He grinned back. "And you're gonna coach Parker."

"It's going to be great," Sarah said. "Really. She's gonna love it."

"I sure hope so." He ran his hand through his hair, and Sarah could almost feel the nerves radiating off him.

She grabbed his hand. "I mean it."

The stables were where Nathan and Kate had first met. Sarah still remembered that phone call last summer when Kate had exploded, insisting she despised this man who was caring for their horses and living in her parents' guest house. The stables were where Kate had let herself love him moments before a tornado had whipped through town. It was all very romantic as far as Sarah was concerned.

"Does Anne know?" she asked.

Nathan shook his head. "I love her, but there's no way she could keep a secret like this. She'd be an absolute blubbering mess, and Kate would work out what was going on immediately."

"That's probably for the best," Sarah agreed, though she couldn't wait to see the look on Anne's face when she found out.

"Dale knows it's happening," Nathan said. "Just not *when* it's happening."

"Sounds like everything's in order." Sarah downed half her coffee in one gulp. "Also, as the best friend, looks like you're gonna be stuck with me for the rest of your life."

Nathan sighed dramatically. "Guess it's a burden I'll have to bear."

"The heaviest of burdens. I come with a lot of baggage. It's mostly Parker's stuff. Books. Toys."

"Good thing Kate's very partial to all those things."

Sarah smiled. She would never take for granted the way this family loved her son. "Well, on that note, I'm going to go be a great best friend and supervise Desmond cleaning up the stables."

"A very important job," Nathan said, hiding his smirk.

They both knew Desmond needed no supervision, but Sarah went anyway. To her surprise, he actually put her to work and she spent most of the morning tidying. She'd never been the home-improvement type, but she was invested in the success of this afternoon, so she sweated her mascara off lugging around sheets of plywood and hiding power tools behind strategically placed hay bales.

Nathan stopped by once to walk them through the setup, showing them approximately where he planned to get down on one knee. Being a photographer himself, he'd thought about the space and what he wanted it to look like for their big moment. He also handed Sarah a box of fairy lights and told her to go to town.

So that was exactly what she did.

Desmond held the ladder as Sarah strung lights up every post and across every support beam. She wanted it to look magical. The ladder wobbled a little, and she felt Desmond's hand on the back of her knee.

"Thanks," she whispered, smiling down at him.

"What are you looking at?" he asked.

"Just enjoying the view."

Desmond's brows lifted, his hand traveling from her knee to her thigh. "I was just thinking the same thing."

Sarah batted his hand away. "We have a very important job to do here."

"I think Parker has the hardest job out of all of us."

"Which is exactly why he's taking a nap. But I'll have a pocket full of candies to bribe him with just in case." Sarah finished wrapping the lights and made sure there were batteries in the tiny little control box that now dangled inconspicuously against the wall. When she was done, she turned around on the ladder and slid into Desmond's arms.

He didn't let go even as her feet hit the ground.

"Who's in charge of the lights?" he asked.

"I guess I am."

"No pressure."

Sarah snorted. "Oh, Kate's answer definitely hinges on whether or not I get these turned on before Nathan pops the question." She stared at his lips. "Is commandeering the stables for the proposal going to put you behind on your work?"

"I'll make up the time."

As he brushed the curls back from her face, she wondered for the umpteenth time that week just how much time they had left. She felt like they were standing on the precipice of something, and even if they jumped back, the cliff would collapse out from under them, sending them both tumbling in opposite directions.

January was that cliff. Once the proposal was out of the way and Doc McGinn's retirement party—which Sarah had now promised her toddler they would attend—was over, she would be free to go. Perhaps Desmond sensed the same thing. Maybe he felt the construction drawing to a close. Maybe that was why he held her a little tighter than he had in the days before. Or maybe Sarah was just imagining it all.

He kissed her then, standing under the unlit fairy lights. She parted her lips for him, letting his tongue dance with hers. It was messy and wet and a little desperate, but Sarah didn't care what they looked like or who might walk in. She let his hands roam because she wanted the roughened pads of his fingers on her skin. She liked the thrill of it all. The excitement of kissing him out in the open, taunting the universe with their feelings, daring it to try to take him away.

In this moment alone, she knew he was hers, and nothing the universe did would change that. The next moment was up for grabs, of course, but this one belonged to her. Desmond thumbed the underside of her breast, and she pressed her chest against his.

She wanted him. Here. Now. All the time. She kept thinking this desire between them might fade. That she might finally get him out of her system, but exposure therapy wasn't working. The more time they spent together, the more she wanted to be with him. And when she spotted him with Parker, the two of them wearing matching carefree smiles, she wanted him most of all. Not even just naked in bed with her, but sitting beside her at the dinner table or across from her in the living room surrounded by the Cardiffs' chaos or out in the fields with his hand tucked against hers. She wanted Desmond the way a shadow needed the light to survive.

Sarah liked who they were here. She liked the fantasy they'd built.

"God," he groaned against her skin. "I want you."

"I've noticed," she laughed, the sound like flint to a waiting spark. She pulled back, doing them both a favor, letting her heart settle. "I would take you up on the offer if we weren't about to stage the greatest proposal of all time."

The shutter of a camera sounded.

Sarah looked over to see Rusty.

"Sorry—wrong couple. I was just checking the lighting. Also, we're T-minus twenty minutes," he said before disappearing with a sneaky grin.

Sarah rolled her eyes. Rusty knew very well they weren't a couple. Then again, what did you call your situationship partner? Sarah didn't let her thoughts linger long. This equation was complicated enough without trying to make the variable that was Desmond fit. Because if she really did think about it, then she would have to admit to herself that she would chase this thing between them across the country. She would uproot Parker for it. Move to North Carolina. Get her heart broken again. And then she would recognize the mess she'd made of her life over a man.

Sarah knew how the story ended because Desmond was perfect and the world was cruel. Eventually something would break between them. And Parker would be caught in the crossfire.

"I should go get Parker up," she said. "Almost time for his big debut."

"I should go find a cold shower," Desmond joked.

Sarah smirked despite how wretched she felt on the inside. She was truly going to miss this when it was all over. She turned and hurried back to the house. Parker was already awake and sitting on the couch with a cup of juice courtesy of Anne. As soon as he saw her, he stood up and reached for her.

"Hi, baby." She scooped him into her arms. "You want to come help Mommy with something very important?"

"Party?" he asked.

As Christmas had wound down and Anne's preparations for Doc McGinn's retirement party had taken center stage again, Parker had become enthralled with the idea. Every time a decoration so much as showed up in the house, his excitement level skyrocketed and it took all evening to calm him down again.

"No party today," Sarah said.

Parker frowned, kicking his tiny legs.

"But soon," she promised. She wondered if he would be as excited when he realized the party was mainly going to be a bunch of adults shoved into a room together with finger foods and punch.

Probably.

What did toddlers really know about fun?

"You wanna come outside?" Sarah said as a distraction from Parker's obsession with party planning.

"Yah!" he said, abandoning his sippy cup on the couch.

Sarah picked it up and put it on the side table. They were off to a good start.

By the time she'd put his coat and boots on, Parker had fully woken himself up and was animatedly babbling in her ear.

Kate joined them at the door.

"You two gonna come out and watch me take some pictures?" she said, pretending to sweep her hair over her shoulder.

"Obviously," Sarah said. "Rusty was already scoping out the best place for your close-up."

"Oh, goody."

"Hey," Sarah said, catching Kate's hand. "I think you're going to be really happy with how they turn out. The stables look great, and Cardiff Ranch & Veterinary Practice is going to look even better with your face front and center."

"Great," Kate said, blushing a bit, "now I'm gonna overthink how I'm smiling."

Sarah snorted. "As if you'd look anything but amazing. We'll meet you out there."

Kate rolled her eyes, heading out the door and down the porch.

"Okay, little man," Sarah said, hauling Parker to his feet. "This is it. Your two years of existence have led to this moment."

"Okay," Parker said, unfazed.

Sarah led him outside. Nathan met them at the door of the stables.

"Is she inside already?"

"Yeah. Rusty's keeping her busy." He sort of looked like he might be sick.

"Hey," Sarah said, mustering some last-minute encouragement. "You've got this. There's only one thing she's going to say."

He handed her the ring box. "Okay."

Sarah bent down and handed it to Parker. Holding a box and handing it to Kate should've been a piece of cake, but toddlers were unpredictable, and now Sarah also wanted to be sick. "Hey, baby, can you give this to Auntie Kate for me?"

"Yah!" he said.

Sarah pointed him inside the door and slid in after him, ducking into a corner as Parker toddled off with a very expensive ring.

He got distracted by the horses, holding his free hand up for a pat.

"Parker," Sarah stage-whispered. "Give it to Auntie Kate."

He toddled farther into the stables, and Sarah followed along at a distance. From the corner of her eye, she spotted Desmond crouched down behind a pile of straw, and she joined him there.

"Auntie Kay!" Parker screeched when he saw her, holding the box up and running toward her. Before he reached Kate, he tripped, face-planting onto the ground.

Sarah watched the ring box bounce and land by Kate's feet. She stared down at it, and Sarah watched as the gears started to click.

"Ouch!" Parker declared at the top of his lungs, picking straw off his hands. "Yuck."

Sarah pressed her hand to her mouth to keep from giggling. Beside her Desmond shook with silent peals of laughter.

Parker stood up, picked up the box and held it up to Kate. "Here go." Then he turned and booked it in the other direction.

Desmond reached out and snagged Parker, pulling him behind the pile of straw. Parker giggled the entire time.

Kate just continued to stare at the box in her hand. While she did, Sarah snuck out and turned the fairy lights on, sending a sparkle of light across the stables.

Kate only had time to look up and gasp. Then suddenly, Nathan was there, plucking the box from her hand and getting down on one knee.

"That was supposed to go a little smoother," he said, popping open the box. "But we've rehearsed it now, so I think it'll go better next time. I might even remember some of the speech I thought I'd memorized."

"There's gonna be a next time?" Kate whispered, her face still sort of stunned.

Nathan tipped his head and grinned up at her. "Well, not if you say yes *this time*."

"Should I hold out for the speech?"

"It was a good speech," Nathan assured her. "I used the word *love* like twelve times."

Kate chuckled softly. "Save it for your vows."

"That's a yes, then?"

"That's a very emphatic *yes*," Kate said, and Nathan slid the ring onto her finger.

Sarah squeezed Parker to her before whooping and cheering for her best friend. A round of toddler applause erupted, and the shutter of Rusty's camera was endless.

If Sarah needed an excuse as to why she showed up at Desmond's cabin later that night, she would have blamed it on all the love and marriage and proposal talk. She didn't need an excuse, though, because the moment the door opened, Desmond snagged the front of her coat and hauled her close enough to kiss.

Her lips were chilled from the January night, her fingertips cold where she pressed them to his jaw.

"Your fingers are like ice," he complained. "How long have you been standing out here?"

"Not long," she said. Truth was she hadn't given the

truck even a moment to heat up and the steering wheel had been freezing on the drive over.

"Get in here," he growled, his warm hands running down her neck and across her shoulders, shoving her coat from her arms. It flopped to the floor, and neither of them bothered to pick it up, too busy trying to maneuver their way to the bedroom without separating their lips.

They made it across the front room and down the hall before Desmond's back hit the door frame that led to the bedroom. His breath left him in a soft oomph. Sarah took advantage of the moment and snaked her hands beneath his shirt. His skin was fiery warm, like he'd just stepped from a hot shower. She felt his muscles recoil against the temperature of her hands, but he didn't stop her as she pulled the shirt over his head.

He let her marvel at him for a moment, fingers stealing heat where they could, then he tugged her toward the bed. "It was a nice proposal, wasn't it?"

"Parker definitely set it over the top," she said, twisting out of her clothing.

"Not bad for his very first job."

"It's going straight on the resume," Sarah said.

"Never too early to start prepping for college."

"I agree." She slid against the bed sheets, Desmond's towering weight stretching alongside her, the planes of their muscles meeting with a delicious friction. She kissed him everywhere, along the strength of his jaw and down the sensitive flesh of his neck and across the expanse of his collarbones. And when she felt the now-familiar stretch of him, she let her lips speak while she couldn't, before pressing her head back into the pillow.

Sarah squirmed as a fire flamed to life inside her. The thought of ever being cold again became a distant impossibility as a demanding warmth spread, inch by inch, beneath her skin. It was a hunger and a comfort all at once.

"I would have done it differently," Desmond said out of the blue.

Sarah's eyes snapped open, her thoughts halfway over that precipice already, her body seconds away from losing control. "What?" she mumbled.

"A proposal," he whispered into her ear before pressing them together again.

Then she was gone, falling and flying, squeezing her eyes tight as she trembled from a place so deep that the aftershocks rippled right to the tips of her fingers. She tensed beneath him, that tingling heat filling her up until she could no longer see straight, no longer think straight.

But slowly the aftershocks faded and her breathing eased and the thoughts that had been cloudy moments ago started to clear.

What the hell was he talking about?

"This isn't really our life," she said, reminding him. Reminding herself.

"It could be," he said after a long bout of silence. He stroked the hair back from her face, but Sarah caught his hand.

He knew better than to do this. They didn't talk about the future for a reason. They didn't talk about them or what the parameters of this relationship meant, especially not here, in bed together, when there was nothing between them. Not a sheet or a scrap of clothing or a crumbling piece of pride for her to construct a wall out of. She was laid bare in all the ways that mattered and he knew that.

He knew she had nothing with which to protect herself from these questions.

Not like this.

"Say something," he said.

She searched for his eyes in the dark. The stars were dim tonight, and she could barely make out the shape of him beside her. "Why are you trying to ruin this?"

He knew it was dangerous territory, filled with traps and old scars. Why was he trying to wreck what was left of their time together?

"I'm not trying to ruin it. I'm trying to protect it. Trying to make you see that we could—"

Sarah pressed her fingers to his lips, hushing him.

"Sarah?"

"Stop," she begged. "Just let it be good the way it is." She sat up on the edge of the bed, her chest tight, feeling suddenly panicked. It was too much, being here in this room with him, alone. She needed fresh air. She reached down and snatched up her shirt, pulling it over her head.

Desmond reached out and caught her hand. "Stay?"

"You know I can't."

Not now.

Not ever.

That was what they'd agreed when they'd started this.

Chapter Twenty-One

The more they recounted the story of the proposal over the following days, the funnier it became. From Parker's shenanigans to his face-planting with the ring box to Kate's utter confusion and everyone hidden in different corners of the stables, it was certainly one for the books. Anne was ecstatic, though she couldn't stop tearing up at random intervals.

"Mom, you can stop crying now," Kate said as they walked through the parking lot of the resort. "People are going to think something's wrong."

"I'm just so happy," Anne said, clasping Kate's hand. "So happy."

They were all currently on their way to dinner. Dale had made a reservation at the resort's very expensive restaurant to celebrate the engagement. The entire family and the proposal crew had been invited, which meant that Sarah, Parker, Desmond and Rusty were all in tow. Sarah had been hesitant about bringing a toddler into a place like this, but she figured it would be a good trial run for the retirement party that Parker couldn't stop asking about.

They'd already spent most of the morning having conversations about using their inside voices and about not throwing fancy food onto the floor. But Sarah had no doubt that she was going to spend the entire meal trying to keep Parker's cutlery on the table.

The resort lobby was exactly what Sarah had expected: modern finishes, clean lines and muted brown tones. They were really leaning into that country-living thing. Mosaic Resort and Wellness Retreat was printed on a sign near the door in fancy calligraphy.

"There," Anne said, indicating a sign on the wall with arrows pointing off in different directions. Spa. Reception. Pool. Restaurant.

"This place is something else," Kate said, glancing up at the large light fixture that dangled above them.

Sarah hummed in agreement. "They're going to have to liven up the nightlife in town."

Kate laughed.

The restaurant was more accommodating than she'd anticipated. They sat them at a large round table and quickly cleared away all the glassware that was within Parker's reach. Sarah was glad to find that the chef could do chicken fingers and french fries, though it wasn't on the menu. She ordered that for Parker and a seafood linguine for herself.

Parker spent a good portion of the meal in his high chair but eventually started to fuss, so Sarah parked him in her lap. Once she did that, Parker spent the majority of his time dropping his fries and having to climb up and down to retrieve them. Sarah equated herself to a jungle gym.

Halfway through dinner he ended up on Desmond's lap, and he stayed there, mostly because he'd decided he wanted to eat Desmond's chicken Parmesan.

"I'm sorry," Sarah said as Desmond held his fork up to Parker again.

He chuckled. "It's fine. He's had, like, two bites."

Sarah smiled at the way Desmond's arm wrapped protectively across Parker's middle, partly to keep him contained and partly to keep him from falling off his lap. They hadn't yet talked about the conversation Desmond had started the other night in bed. Sarah didn't know if he'd taken her words to heart or if he was simply giving her time to cool off before bringing it up again, but it was clear nothing had shifted in his relationship with Parker. If anything, he was even more doting. He didn't grow embarrassed when Parker spoke too loudly or dropped cutlery onto the floor, just calmly reminded him of the rules they'd talked about earlier. A thick ball of emotion lodged itself in Sarah's throat for the rest of the meal, and she couldn't even finish her pasta.

For dessert, the restaurant brought out a half slab of cake in celebration of Kate and Nathan's engagement. There was even a sparkler on it, and Parker scrambled back into Sarah's lap, clapping and wide-eyed until it fizzled out.

Kate doled out pieces of cake to everyone.

"What kind?" Anne asked.

Kate licked her finger. "Chocolate and something else. Passion fruit, maybe. It's good."

"You want to try it?" Sarah asked as Parker made grabby hands for the plate. "Here, Mommy will help."

Sarah gave him a small bite off the end of her fork. "Is it good?"

Parker grinned and nodded, and everyone laughed.

"Who can say no to chocolate?" Anne said.

Sarah gave him another small bite, then another.

"Guess you don't get dessert when you have kids," Nathan joked.

Sarah laughed. "You usually get the slobbery leftovers."

Desmond leaned over, laying his hand along the back of her chair. "I'll share mine."

Judging by the look in his eyes, that wasn't the only thing he was considering sharing. Her eyes darted down to his lips until Parker started to cough in her lap.

"Is that enough?" Sarah asked, looking around at him. "Here." She handed him his sippy cup of water.

He took a long drink but kept coughing. His cheeks had gone bright red, the flush traveling down his neck in splotches. In an instant, Sarah's heart was in her throat.

"Parker?" she cried. "Parker!"

Sarah's pulse hammered between her rib cage like a charging bull—any moment it would burst from her chest, snorting and snarling.

The splotches on Parker's neck became hives. Sarah pulled back the collar of his shirt. They traveled right down his chest.

"What is it?" Kate asked, getting to her feet.

"Something he ate, probably," Sarah said, glancing at the cake. Her mind was racing. *Passion fruit.* Had he ever had that before? She couldn't remember.

Immediately, Parker started to whine, each breath growing wheezy. She forced his mouth open and spotted the first signs of swelling. She'd seen this before in the ER. She'd treated it.

Anaphylaxis.

For a moment Sarah couldn't breathe herself. Anything and everything she'd ever known about medicine seemed to seep from her mind like it was a sieve. Her entire body went limp. It was as if she'd climbed out of her own skin just to stand outside herself and watch.

The world moved in slow motion around her, and the only thing Sarah could do was stare. Stare down at her baby. This child whose airway was constricting. Desmond was on his feet suddenly, yelling and asking for help.

"An EpiPen! Does anyone have an EpiPen with them?"

His words were drowned out in the chaos, and all Sarah could do was hold on. She clutched Parker to her chest, those straggly breaths puffing in her ear.

She'd dealt with this a hundred times before. She'd been the measure of calm that stood next to hospital beds, helping people breathe after allergic reactions. She'd helped save their lives. But now that it was her own child, she felt helpless. She wouldn't even have known her own name if someone had asked her.

Next to her, Kate spoke a mile a minute into the phone. A sob lurched from Sarah's throat with enough force to split her open.

Then sirens wailed somewhere in the distance, and Desmond was scooping Parker from her arms.

"No," Sarah managed to say. "No!"

She was out of her chair in an instant, but Desmond was already racing out of the restaurant and through the lobby. When Sarah caught up with him, it was on the front steps of the resort.

Desmond had Parker laid out on the ground as a police cruiser slammed to a halt on the pavement. Ryan Mullens appeared a second later, racing up the steps with a first aid kit. He dropped to his knees beside Desmond, ripping the bag open.

"There's one for kids," Ryan was saying, rifling through the kit. "There's one…here. If they're under the weight limit…wait…this one?"

He finally got his hands on an EpiPen, and Desmond snatched it from him, administering the medication. Then they were moving again, scooping Parker up. Kate ushered Sarah down the stairs, and she felt like it was all a dream, a nightmare. Her face was tacky, smeared with tears and snot, but it couldn't be real. None of this was real.

Kate shoved Sarah into the back of the police cruiser with Parker and Desmond. Parker's tiny body was splayed in her lap, and all she could do was clutch him as Desmond buckled them all in.

"We're gonna meet the ambulance on the way," Ryan called out as Kate slammed the back door shut. Sirens whooped, drowning out the worst of Sarah's thoughts as she clutched her son. The ride was all tears and sirens, but then Ryan braked hard and they all lurched forward. Red-and-blue lights flashed across them as the ambulance approached. Ryan climbed out of the car and took Parker from Sarah before she could protest.

"What has he had?" the paramedic asked as Sarah and Desmond climbed out of the car.

"A dose of epi," Desmond answered, shoving Sarah into the ambulance after Parker. "Breathing is still labored."

She glanced back at Desmond through the tears and the chaos. She could hear Parker's gasping coughs coming from the stretcher, but he was still breathing. He wouldn't be if it weren't for Desmond. The ambulance doors slammed. Desmond hadn't followed her in, but she wished he had. Through the tiny window, she watched him climb back into the cruiser with Ryan.

They followed them all the way to the hospital. It felt like an eternity, but the moment they arrived, a team of doctors and nurses were there to greet them. Sarah spotted James in the fray. He immediately took charge of Parker's case while she stood there in the middle of everything, trying to form words that made sense. This was Sarah's domain. This was where she was most comfortable, and yet she couldn't stand it. The whirring machines were too loud. The hiss of the oxygen was too frenzied. She watched medication vials accumulate on a counter and heard the hastily shouted orders pile up. Her hands twitched. She was supposed to be doing something. Helping somehow. But all she really wanted to do was scream.

Desmond arrived shortly after, and someone pushed her into his arms. She still felt like crawling out of her skin, but at least she was certain that she wouldn't collapse with him holding her. It was all very routine after that. Medication was handed out. Breathing treatments were started. An IV. A drip. The nurses ran some vitals. James listened to Parker's lungs.

Parker was going to be okay.

But the wretched fear in Sarah's chest refused to budge, leaving her gasping for air. Desmond got her into a chair, holding her face, trying to get her to focus while the nurses around them muttered "It's going to be okay, Momma," and "Breathe."

Chapter Twenty-Two

When it was all over and Parker had been moved from the resuscitation room to a private exam room, Sarah was calmer.

She and Parker spent the rest of the night in the ER. She didn't sleep—couldn't sleep—but clutched his tiny hand in hers as he slept, running her thumb across his skin, carefully avoiding the spot where his IV had been placed.

The motion seemed to ease her as much as it did him. As Sarah sat there, the events of the previous day came back to her in fits and starts. Most of it had been a blur as it had occurred, but now she could see it all with some degree of clarity. And in every frame, there was Desmond.

A knock sounded, and a moment later James slipped inside the room. "How's my favorite patient?"

"You're still here?"

"We're about to do a shift change. I just wanted to

check in once more before I do handover with the on-coming doctor."

Sarah lifted her hand and ghosted it through Parker's curls. "He's good."

"And how are you?"

"Good."

James hummed thoughtfully, adjusting his glasses. "That's a lot for any parent to handle. It's okay if it takes a bit to settle in."

Sarah smiled gratefully at him. Now that she knew her child apparently had an allergy to passion fruit, she was less anxious. It felt like there was an enemy she could defeat with the right precautions and preparation. "It's strange to be on this side of the medical equation."

"I imagine so."

Sarah had spent all night watching other nurses flit in and out of the room. Hanging medications. Taking his vital signs. She knew what every number meant, and now that her head was screwed on straight, it felt odd to be a bystander.

James took his stethoscope from his pocket and gingerly pressed it to Parker's chest. "His breathing sounds good," he said after a moment. "I'm sure they'll discharge you before lunch."

"Thanks, James."

"Of course." He headed for the door. "You've got a visitor out here. Want me to send them in?"

Sarah nodded, wondering who it was. After standing vigil at Parker's bedside, Desmond had gone off to find a quiet corner in the hospital to get a few hours of sleep. Kate had stayed most of the night as well. She never slept in hospitals, so she'd taken to pacing the halls, and Sarah had eventually convinced her to go home. Anne and Dale had called.

Rusty had texted her funny memes to take her mind off of everything.

Even Ryan had hung around the hospital for a bit to make sure everything was okay before his deputy duties had called him back to Hatchet Lake.

Sarah didn't take any of them for granted. She knew very well that she was lucky to have this circle of people. A soft knock echoed, and Desmond appeared, smoothing down his hair. Of anyone who might have been waiting, Sarah was glad it was him.

"I didn't want to disturb you if you were sleeping, but I saw the doc go in so I thought it might be a good time for a visit."

"James thinks we'll be discharged in a few hours."

"That's great."

Sarah swallowed hard. Part of her still felt wretched about this entire thing. About holding her son in her arms and not being able to do anything to help him.

"What's wrong?" Desmond asked quietly, coming to stand behind her chair. He reached for her, and Sarah felt his broad hands on her shoulders.

She leaned into the touch, turning at his gentle insistence. She couldn't quite look him in the eye. She didn't want him to see how ashamed she felt. "I just can't stop thinking about how lucky we were."

"I know," Desmond said. "Ryan said the station only recently started carrying EpiPens. It's part of some new policy they're implementing. He said they haven't even had a chance to train all the officers yet, though I think after yesterday that's going to change quickly."

Sarah nodded along to what he said. "That *was* lucky, but I was actually talking about you being there. If you weren't—"

Sarah cut herself off. Desmond had jumped into

action immediately. He'd helped Ryan administer the medication that had probably saved her son's life. At the very least it had bought Parker enough time to reach the hospital.

"Don't," Desmond said, pulling her out of the chair and into his arms. "Don't think like that. I *was* there. He's okay now."

"I just stood there," she said. "Staring. Utterly useless."

"You reacted the way any parent would. No one can blame you for that."

"But I'm not just a parent." She shook her head. "God, do you know how many times I've had people wheeled into the ER in the exact same condition as Parker? I've never hesitated even for a moment."

"But how many of those people were your son?" Desmond said. "You don't have to be a good nurse right now. No one is expecting you to. All you have to do is be his mom and do what all moms do best."

"What's that?"

"Freak out."

Sarah stepped back and chuckled, wiping the tears from the corners of her eyes. "I think I have that part covered." Desmond pulled her to him again, and this time she just breathed him in.

"I'm glad I was there," he said softly. He reached down, touching Parker's head gently, the fine brown curls sliding through Desmond's fingers.

The sight stirred something in Sarah's gut. It had been nice to have someone else to rely on. Someone to share her fear with.

"I'll always be here, Sarah. For Parker, for you. I know you said you don't do serious—"

Sarah pulled back suddenly. "Desmond—" She

shook her head, knowing this was more of the conversation that had almost happened the other night. "Please, don't."

"I know what you're going to say," Desmond whispered. The words hung between them like scalding coals, and Sarah flinched away like she might be burned. "You don't give anything away for free, Sarah Schaffer. I know that. But I don't care. I want to be with you. I want to spend my time with you. You can't just make someone fall in—"

"Stop. Stop it!" she hissed, holding up her hands. They trembled, almost too heavy to lift. "I told you not to."

"I know," he said like he was admitting to his greatest fault. He reached out, catching one of her hands and pulling her to him. "But we've been tiptoeing around something serious for weeks. Tell me it doesn't feel like that to you."

Sarah bit her tongue.

"You can't." His words were hot against her skin. "Don't you think we should give this a real shot?"

"It wasn't real, Desmond."

"Maybe when it started," he said. "But now it feels pretty real to me."

"We were just supposed to be having fun."

He took her face between his hands, cradling it. "What about this feels just fun to you? Doesn't it feel like ending this will cost us everything?"

"It wasn't supposed to," she said. "We were supposed to be careful. *You're* supposed to be going back to North Carolina."

They weren't supposed to fall this hard.

"But I lo—"

"You don't!" she almost shouted, still somehow

aware of Parker sleeping next to them. "You don't mean that, Desmond. You can't."

"Why can't I?"

"Because it'll only hurt more."

"Is that what you're worried about? That it's going to hurt?" He tore away like she'd slapped him. "God, Sarah, it hurts now. And I can't promise that I'm never going to hurt you. That we won't end up hurting each other. I'm sure both of us will do and say things we regret at some point. That's just how relationships go. But I can promise that I won't leave. I'm here, Sarah. If you'll let me be."

"Please," she said, tears clouding her vision, though only the heavens knew what she was pleading for. Understanding, maybe. This wasn't about her in the end. This wasn't even about him. This was about Parker. She couldn't afford to be rash when it came to her son. Feelings were fickle things. Fleeting things. She'd seen that before.

And hers wasn't the only heart at stake here.

She couldn't gamble with Parker's. His was too small, too delicate to bear it.

Because words were just words in the end. They filled up all the empty spaces with *promises, promises, promises*. So many promises that it was easy to forget the words that came before. Easy to pretend like they didn't really matter after all. Sarah couldn't trust words. She'd done that before.

Tears gathered on her lower lashes. Stubborn ones that refused to fall.

"It would be easy between us," Desmond said, some of the fight having gone out of him.

"Too easy," she said. That was the problem. After everything she'd been through, having Parker alone, raising him, loving him, being two parents when some-times she hardly had the capacity to be one, this couldn't be her story. She already felt weaker for what had hap-pened to Parker, for having had to rely on someone to be there for *her*. As nice and as comforting as it had been to have Desmond there, if she let herself get used to him, how would she manage when things didn't work out? She wouldn't. She would fall apart, and what kind of mother would she be then?

"I'm sorry," she said.

"Don't be sorry." He kissed her forehead gently. "You told me not to fall for you. I guess I should have tried harder."

Sarah swallowed the gasp that crawled up her throat, watching him disappear through the door. She knew this was the right thing to do. That didn't stop her heart from stuttering in her chest or the tears from falling as she listened to his footsteps fade away.

Kate came to visit a little later. By then Sarah had rubbed away the makeup that had smeared down her cheeks. Though that did nothing to stop her jaw from trembling.

"Are you okay?" Kate asked as soon as she walked into the room. Her first instinct was to flit to Parker's side.

"He's fine," Sarah said quickly. "He's going to be discharged soon."

"Yeah, Desmond was just telling me," Kate said. "He came by the ranch and got right to work. I thought he might have wanted to get some sleep, but he said he'd rather keep his hands busy."

Sarah swallowed hard, curled up in the hospital chair. She refused to look at Kate.

"Did something happen?" Kate asked.

Sarah brushed her off, climbing to her feet as she gestured to the chair. "Aren't these the most uncomfortable things?"

"Yeah," Kate agreed. "I spent a lot of time in one when my dad was sick."

"You don't think about it as a nurse. How terrible they are. Not until you're stuck sitting in one."

"Sarah?" Kate began.

"I'm fine."

"What happened?"

"Nothing."

"It was Desmond, wasn't it?"

Sarah crossed her arms, picking at the holes in her sweater.

"Is everything okay?" Kate continued. "Did you guys have a fight?"

"It wasn't a fight," she said, jaw trembling again. "There was no reason to fight. It was just a conversation."

All at once Kate seemed to understand. "Oh, *Sarah*."

"Words don't mean anything, Kate. Anyone can string pretty words and promises together." Sarah started pacing the length of the room. "I can't bring people in and out of Parker's life every time the word *love* is tossed around."

"He said he loved you?"

"I didn't give him the chance."

"Sarah—"

"It's okay."

"Sarah, *stop*!"

"Really. I'm fine."

Kate caught her by the shoulders and forced her to sit on the edge of the hospital bed. Parker stirred but didn't wake. Then Kate dragged up that terrible chair behind her. "Look, I'm not going to try to tell you how to feel. Goodness knows I'm barely qualified to figure out my own feelings. All I'm going to say is that Desmond could have finished up at the ranch weeks ago."

"What?"

"Sarah, I've lived in a small town most of my life. I know how long it takes to build something. That man purposely dragged out the work at his own expense. I'm not paying him to be here anymore. He even let Nathan and Rusty slow him down, just so he could spend the winter in Hatchet Lake, of all places." She squeezed Sarah's hand. "He stayed for you." Kate's eyes drifted down to Parker. "He stayed for both of you. And if you're looking for more than words…if you're waiting for actions or a sign or divine intervention, I think that's as plain as it'll ever get."

Sarah couldn't find her voice, but it was okay because Kate kept talking.

"Desmond has gone out of his way to do everything possible to stay, Sarah. And you might not see it this way, but so have you."

As she said it, Sarah realized that Kate was right. What was supposed to be a couple weeks at her friend's ranch had turned into months. First she'd used the volunteering as an excuse, and then the job interview. Then she'd hung around for Kate and Nathan's proposal, and now they were here so Parker could go to a retirement party for a man neither of them had met. Sarah could have left at any time. She could have taken any number of the travel nursing jobs in her inbox, but she hadn't even bothered to look at the contracts.

She didn't really want to leave; she'd just been too stubborn to say it out loud. To let herself want something and someone. She felt safe with Desmond, and that had scared her. After having only herself to rely on, giving up that control and trusting someone else with it, knowing they could hurt her, was terrifying. But she wanted him, and she loved the community that she'd found here. Hatchet Lake could be good for her, could be good for Parker.

And if Desmond still wanted to be a part of that, maybe they could find a way to make it work.

Kate slipped away, and Sarah sat there, thinking. She put herself back in the chair beside Parker and took his little hand once more.

This time his eyes fluttered open as she rubbed her thumb over his knuckles.

"Hi, baby," she whispered, choking back tears as she ran her hand through his curls.

Parker blinked sleepily at her. "Party?"

Sarah laughed out loud. The resilience of kids never ceased to amaze her. "Yeah, buddy," she said. "You're still going to the party."

Chapter Twenty-Three

"What are you wearing?" Kate asked as Sarah stood in front of the bathroom mirror a day later, trying to slick back Parker's hair. No one would be able to tell that they'd just had a big medical scare twenty-four hours earlier. Not the way Parker was shoveling raisins into his mouth.

"Um," Sarah said, frowning down at her son's stubborn hair. "I hadn't really thought about it."

Obviously, she had thought about it. She'd intended to get a beautiful dress and zip herself into it for the evening, but between the holidays and the proposal and the hospital visit, securing a dress for this retirement party had slipped her mind.

"I didn't really pack anything appropriate," she finished weakly.

"We'll figure something out," Kate said. She disappeared into her closet.

Besides all that, Sarah's mind had been occupied by

one thing. She still needed to talk to Desmond. He'd been gone by the time they'd returned to the ranch yesterday, and Sarah had been too busy with Parker to go looking for him at the cabin. Her plan was to go tonight, after the party finished and Parker went to bed.

They needed time to talk, uninterrupted, where they could untangle these complicated feelings. Most of them were hers, and Sarah wasn't exactly sure how she was going to tell him to disregard everything she had said at the hospital. Desmond was the one she wanted something real with, but in figuring that out herself, she'd rejected him, and she wasn't sure if she could win him back.

But regardless of what happened tonight, Sarah had made her decision. She was staying in Hatchet Lake with Parker. She'd accepted the ER job this morning and already had some promising leads on a couple of apartments on the outskirts of the city. She knew the Cardiffs would tell her to stay on the property, and Sarah loved that idea, but she figured they'd already more than worn out their welcome.

They could be neighbors though, and she would bring Parker to visit all the time.

"Here!" Kate announced, holding up two dress options in the mirror.

Sarah's eyes went wide. "There's no way I'm getting my boobs into that green one."

Kate tossed it aside, shaking a sparkly black dress at her. "Black it is. Black is sexy. Black is good for winning back romantic partners."

Sarah rolled her eyes. "I just want to get Parker there and back without him ruining any of your mom's hard work."

"Party!" Parker cried, wiggling away from her.

Sarah gave up trying to tame his hair and snatched him around the middle, lifting him off the floor. "We've got to figure out what you're going to wear, mister."

Kate appeared in the doorway again, her hands behind her back. "I might have an idea." She produced a tiny shirt with a bow tie and matching suspenders. "I hope you don't mind," she said. "But it's so cute. I couldn't pass it up."

Sarah smirked. One of the endless joys of having a toddler was getting to dress them in adorable outfits. "If we're quick we might even get a photo of him in it before he slops juice down his front."

"Oh, Nathan's already on standby with the camera," Kate said.

Sarah gladly passed Parker over.

"Are we going to put our party clothes on?"

"Yah!" Parker cheered as the two of them disappeared.

Getting a toddler ready for a normal day, never mind an event, was a chore, so Sarah was glad to have the help. She let Kate get him sorted in his tiny bow tie while she slipped into the black dress. It wasn't anything too formal, but it also looked like she'd put a little effort in, which, after the week she'd had, was a feat in itself.

Sarah had just enough time to brush out her curls a bit and swipe some mascara onto her eyelashes before Parker marched back into the room with an adorably embarrassed smile.

"What do we think?" Kate asked, clapping her hands.

Sarah thought he was too cute for words, but she tried not to gush too much because Parker just buried his head in her dress. Downstairs, the cuteness lasted approximately ten minutes before Parker was fed up

with taking photos and managed to get himself onto
the kitchen counter to play in the dishwater in the sink.

"I don't think so," Nathan said, rescuing Parker from
certain disaster.

Parker kicked and cried all the way to the car until
Sarah reminded him that they were going to the party.
On the way there, she had to give him a few crackers
to win back his affections, but it worked.

The resort parking lot was busier than Sarah had ever
seen it. Granted, she'd only been here a couple times,
but it was clear that all of Hatchet Lake had turned out
for the event.

"Mom," Kate said, "how many people are here?"

Anne muttered something unintelligible as she hurried out of the truck and toward the building, saying
hellos and shaking hands. Dale hurried off after her
when she hissed his name.

Sarah got out of the truck, her dress not nearly warm
enough beneath her winter coat. Goose bumps prick-
led on her skin, and she hurriedly got Parker out of his
car seat.

"Doc's gonna hate this," Kate said with certainty.

"The real question is how much do *you* hate this?"
Sarah said, snagging Parker as he attempted to run off
between the cars. "Because this is just a taste of what
it's going to be like planning your wedding."

Kate paled at the thought, and Nathan had to practically drag her inside.

Parker needed no coaxing, however, and took off
running across the lobby as soon as they were in the
building. Sarah managed to direct him to the reception
room, and his eyes went wide. There was a buffet-style
table set up with all sorts of finger foods and desserts.
The bar was serving drinks. A smattering of tables

filled up with the faces Sarah had come to know over the past few months. And a large space had been left open in the middle of the room, which Sarah suspected was for anyone brave enough to dance. Anne and her friend had really outdone themselves.

To no one's surprise, Parker immediately found a bouquet of helium balloons and started dragging them across the dance floor.

"Oh, my God," Kate said as she came up behind Sarah. "It feels like prom."

Sarah snorted. "I definitely don't need those memories back."

"At least I have a date this time," Kate said as she eyeballed Nathan.

"Mine's a lot shorter this time around," Sarah said, keeping an eye on Parker. She could tell he was trying to decide what kind of trouble he wanted to get into first. While he was still slightly overwhelmed, Sarah managed to get a couple of finger foods and half a sip of punch into him. As soon as he'd warmed up to his surroundings, he was gone, and instead of chasing him all over the room, Sarah parked it at a table in the middle where she could see him.

Thankfully, the light projections that lit up the dance floor acted like a toddler beacon and Parker spent most of his time trying to step on them. Eventually Kate and Nathan snatched him up for a dance. Sarah grinned at the delirious smile on his face, though her own smile faltered when she spotted a familiar figure cutting his way through the crowd.

It was Desmond, clad in a well-fitted suit. He wore no tie, leaving the top couple buttons of his shirt undone. He was so handsome Sarah's next breath was a gasp.

He stopped to chat with Nathan and Kate on the

dance floor for a moment, ruffling Parker's hair, then his eyes lifted, picking her out of the crowd instantly. Sarah couldn't take her own eyes off him. They shared a heated look for longer than was probably appropriate.

She smiled at him uncertainly, and when he walked toward her, she took it as a good sign. They'd left the hospital in an awkward place, one that Sarah desperately wanted to fix—she just needed a chance.

He stopped in front of her, holding out his hand. "Do you want to dance?"

Sarah nodded and took it, easily fitting into the space between his arms. One of his hands fell to her waist, squeezing just enough to make Sarah hopeful.

"You look stunning," he said, his chin resting against the side of her head.

Sarah leaned back to look at him. He was even more dashing up close. "I'm glad you're here."

"I honestly wasn't certain you'd still come."

Sarah chuckled. "Parker wouldn't have let me miss it."

Upon saying his name, they both glanced out to the floor where Parker was spinning circles around Nathan and Kate, much to the amusement of the other guests. Desmond spun her, which pulled her attention away from Parker and back to him.

"I heard you finally decided on the job."

"Who told you?" Sarah asked.

"Would you like me to write the names down or simply point?"

Sarah eyed the potential culprits. All of the Cardiffs made the list. "There's a good community here. I know Parker will be happy and cared for."

"Of course he will," Desmond said. The tone of his voice gave away nothing, and Sarah double stepped, forcing them to come to a staggering halt.

"There's only one thing that could make it better," she said.

Desmond's forehead creased. Confusion. Worry. Anticipation. Sarah saw it all ripple across his features.

"You," she said quietly. "I know what I said in the hospital. And I know that I've gone out of my way to tell you that this didn't mean anything. But what if it was real? What if it was serious this whole time?"

It took Desmond a beat to respond, but when he did, it was with a smile. "So what you're saying is that you're *seriously* in love with me?"

Sarah surged forward and kissed him, letting him know just how serious she was. It was a declaration she was making in front of all of Hatchet Lake. In front of her son. "Something like that," she whispered against his lips as she pulled away.

Desmond didn't let her go though. He caught her face between his hands, pressing kisses everywhere he could reach. "Do you know the moment I fell in love with you?"

Sarah shook her head. "Tell me."

"It was that night of the bonfire at the ranch."

"You hardly knew me then."

"It didn't matter. I looked across the fire and there you were, lit by the glow of the flames, Parker asleep in your lap. And I just remember thinking how beautiful the moment was. How much unyielding love you had for him. I fell *so* hard in that instant. And I thought to myself, this is a woman and her son that I could love forever."

Sarah remembered having a similar thought that same night. Then she remembered dismissing it, frightened of the implications. Of what it all meant. A bubble of emotion clogged her throat, and all she could do was give him a watery smile. "You don't care that Parker head-butts you in the knees?"

"I'm already dreading the day he stops."

Sarah didn't want to cry here, in front of everyone, but she couldn't help it. Desmond wiped the tears from her cheeks. "But how do we do this?"

"The same way we have been."

"Couch surfing at the Cardiffs'?" she teased.

He wrapped his arms around her waist. "If that's what works."

"Seriously though." Even if they did want to make a go of this, she wasn't exactly sure how they melded their two lives together. Hers here, and his in North Carolina.

He snorted. "Look who's so serious all of a sudden."

"*Desmond*," she said.

He shrugged. "We find a way to blend our lives. I want to get old with you, Sarah. Old and gray and wrinkly."

"You can get wrinkly," she said. "I'm getting plastic surgery."

"Fine—guess I'll have to start building some houses around here to pay for all that."

"Really?" she asked, her thoughts immediately jumping to Jordan and their construction business in North Carolina. "You'd keep working here?"

Desmond shrugged. "I've sort of run a move by Jordan already."

"And what does he think?"

"He's considering it. It's not Florida by any means, but after all the work we put in here, I think the place has grown on him. Plus I've even had a couple job offers. Apparently Anne's been talking me up in town."

"I don't doubt it," Sarah said. Anne was a meddler in the best possible way.

"Also, there's this couple that needs a house."

"Yeah?"

"A nice one. In the country. Halfway between town and the hospital. With a big kitchen for all their friends to visit and a bedroom for a little boy to grow up in."

Sarah was so in awe, she didn't know what to say. But as he'd been doing his whole life, Parker came to her rescue, running up and wedging himself between them. Desmond scooped him up, and they continued to sway. Just the three of them. This new little family.

There would still be big decisions for them to make in the future, Sarah was certain, but if this trip had taught her anything, it was that the right place to settle wasn't necessarily the one you were born into. Sometimes the place you needed to be was with the weird horse girl you met in college, in her endearingly small town, making plans for the future with a man who refused to change his own bandages just for a chance to see you again. And as Sarah wrapped her arms around Parker and Desmond, she knew this was as serious as it would ever get. So she pulled them close, vowing to hold on to them tighter than she'd ever held on to anything in her life.

* * * * *

#3039 TAKING THE LONG WAY HOME
Bravo Family Ties • by Christine Rimmer

After one perfect night with younger rancher Jason Bravo, widowed librarian Piper Wallace is pregnant with his child. Co-parenting is a given. But Jason will do anything—even accompany her on a road trip to meet her newly discovered biological father—to prove he's playing for keeps!

#3040 SNOWED IN WITH A STRANGER
Match Made in Haven • by Brenda Harlen

Party planner Finley Gilmore loves an adventure, but being snowbound with Professor Lachlan Kellett takes *tempted by a handsome stranger* to a whole new level! Their chemistry could melt a glacier. But when Lachlan's past resurfaces, will Finlay be the one iced out?

#3041 A FATHER'S REDEMPTION
The Tuttle Sisters of Coho Cove • by Sabrina York

Working with developer Ben Sherrod should have turned Celeste Tuttle's dream project into a nightmare. Except the single father is witty and brilliant and so much more attractive than she remembered from high school. Could her childhood nemesis be Prince Charming in disguise?

#3042 MATZAH BALL BLUES
Holidays, Heart and Chutzpah • by Jennifer Wilck

Entertainment attorney Jared Leiman will do anything to be the guardian his orphaned niece needs. Even reunite with Caroline Weiss, his high school ex, to organize his hometown's Passover ball with the Jewish Community Center. Sparks fly...but he'll need a little matzah magic to win her over.

Get 3 FREE REWARDS!

We'll send you 2 FREE Books **plus** a FREE Mystery Gift.

FREE
Value Over
$20

Both the **Harlequin® Special Edition** and **Harlequin® Heartwarming™** series feature compelling novels filled with stories of love and strength where the bonds of friendship, family and community unite.

YES! Please send me 2 FREE novels from the Harlequin Special Edition or Harlequin Heartwarming series and my FREE Gift (gift is worth about $10 retail). After receiving them, if I don't wish to receive any more books, I can return the shipping statement marked "cancel." If I don't cancel, I will receive 6 brand-new Harlequin Special Edition books every month and be billed just $5.49 each in the U.S. or $6.24 each in Canada, a savings of at least 12% off the cover price, or 4 brand-new Harlequin Heartwarming Larger-Print books every month and be billed just $6.24 each in the U.S. or $6.74 each in Canada, a savings of at least 19% off the cover price. It's quite a bargain! Shipping and handling is just 50¢ per book in the U.S. and $1.25 per book in Canada.* I understand that accepting the 2 free books and gift places me under no obligation to buy anything. I can always return a shipment and cancel at any time by calling the number below. The free books and gift are mine to keep no matter what I decide.

Choose one: ☐ **Harlequin Special Edition** (235/335 BPA GRMK) ☐ **Harlequin Heartwarming Larger-Print** (161/361 BPA GRMK) ☐ **Or Try Both!** (235/335 & 161/361 BPA GRPZ)

Name (please print)

Address   Apt. #

City   State/Province   Zip/Postal Code

Email: Please check this box ☐ if you would like to receive newsletters and promotional emails from Harlequin Enterprises ULC and its affiliates. You can unsubscribe anytime.

Mail to the Harlequin Reader Service:
IN U.S.A.: P.O. Box 1341, Buffalo, NY 14240-8531
IN CANADA: P.O. Box 603, Fort Erie, Ontario L2A 5X3

Want to try 2 free books from another series? Call **1-800-873-8635** or visit www.ReaderService.com.

HSEHW23